CHASING
A
CHANCE

CONTEMPORARY ROMANCE
BOOK 4 - THE QUEENSBAY SERIES

DREA STEIN

Book layout by www.ebooklaunch.com

V 10

The Queensbay Series
by Drea Stein

BOOK 1
DINNER FOR TWO - DARBY & SEAN

BOOK 2
ROUGH HARBOR - CAITLYN & NOAH

BOOK 3
THE IVY HOUSE - PHOEBE & CHASE

Chapter 1

Lynn Masters stood with sore feet and the beginnings of a knot in her back, looking over the patient board and saw with more than a bit of satisfaction that it was just about clear. If the clinic managed to avoid an outbreak of the flu, the common cold, or even a minor trauma, it could mean an early night for her. Sighing at the thought, she debated whether she wanted a cup of the gunk they called coffee or if she could make it through to closing time without another shot of caffeine.

After this shift, she was off duty for three days and her thoughts were excited as the prospect of a break stretched in front of her: empty days with nothing to do, the first real break she'd had in weeks. As far as pediatric residents went, she was senior enough to be at the top of the food chain, in terms of schedule but still, someone else had always called in sick or they'd been short-handed and she'd kept saying yes to working overtime. So now she was well and truly due for some time off and she planned on enjoying every last minute of it.

Skipping the coffee, she made her way down the hallway toward the front desk to start updating her charts. The Queensbay Sailors' Clinic, which had started life in the nineteenth century as a home for destitute sailors, had entered the twenty-first as a facility to provide cost-effective medical services, mostly to women and children. It tried hard, it really did, to be bright and cheerful, despite the dilapidated air about the place. Over the years, it had been housed in a small house, an old church, and other various spots around town, but now was in a building which someone had told her had once been a sail maker's loft. It was a big and spacious, but it hadn't been well-taken care of over the years.

The clinic took up the entire first floor. The second floor was mostly empty, except for a resident psychic who kept sporadic office hours. Her clients climbed up a set of rickety iron steps attached to the outside of the building to have their fortune told. Many of them headed straight down to the clinic, right after their psychic readings, where invariably Lynn would find something wrong with them.

Curious, Lynn had stopped by to see Madame Robireux once, to ask her how she knew there was something physical ailing her clients, but Madame, in true soothsayer's fashion had only waved her heavily ringed hands over a crystal ball and given an enigmatic shrug and started talking about auras. The psychic had offered to read Lynn's own aura, but she had declined, deciding that if was something wrong, she preferred to discover it the old-fashioned way.

In truth, the whole building had the air of an aging woman of the night, with great bones, the last vestiges of beauty not quite gone, but with a general sagginess, as if the whole thing was ready to slide in on itself.

The chairs in the waiting room were hard and uncomfortable and the tables in the exam room were old and the vinyl covers were cracking.

To counteract this, the staff and volunteers had made the inside of the clinic cheery enough, with murals painted on the walls, depicting scenes of oceans and jungles and even a more fanciful one, showing unicorns and fairies in a forest. The kids loved all of them, always stopping to search for their favorite fish or animal each time they came.

And Lynn loved it too. She had poured her heart and soul into her time here at the clinic, helping to raise money for it, donating her own time, and taking pride in watching her patients—kids—grow. She had even started a special program for some of her higher risk ones. Called Healthy Kids Now, she focused on getting her youngest patients exercising and eating better. Sure, everyone knew the basics—eat better, move more—but putting it into practice was harder, even if the parents were on board. Everyone was busy so Lynn had worked to make the program as simple and as easy to use as possible. The successful results were starting to roll in and she'd even received some attention from the medical community. She'd had half a dozen requests to write or speak about it to other clinics and doctors and was trying to field them all.

Lynn strolled the halls, well-being and contentment flowing through her. Sure she might have a bad case of sore feet, but there was nowhere else she would rather be. As she approached the front desk, she saw that the main receptionist, Lori, and her friend Sue, one of the nurses, were there, head bent down, deep in discussion.

"Can you believe it?" Lynn listened with only half an ear, finding the screen on the computer where she needed to sign in; she began inputting information. The two women had worked in the clinic together for years and were best friends. They were always gossiping about something or the other, whether it was what some celebrity had been wearing or who was beating whom on some reality show. Seldom was it of any true concern to Lynn. There had been a time when she might have been interested in all of that, but the last years of medical school and her residency had left little time to keep up on current events, of any kind. Besides she was more of a classic film kind of girl.

"We have a month," Lori hissed to Sue.

"And where are we going to go?" Sue sounded angry. "I've been here for eight years, and just like that they're going to…"

The two of them hushed when they noticed Lynn and in the silence she plainly read guilt.

"What? Is there something wrong with me?" Lynn did a quick scan. She was wearing scrubs and her white doctor's coat. She'd only had one vomiter today, and she had managed to sidestep the projectile launch. Lunch had been turkey on rye, no mustard or mayonnaise, so she knew she hadn't been messy there.

"Is it my hair?" she asked, touching the long ponytail she kept her wavy, dark locks in.

The two women just shook their heads. "You look fine, girlfriend. So fine you better go find a boyfriend."

Lynn shook her head. The two women were always razzing her about her love life, or lack thereof. Being a med student didn't leave a lot of time for dating. Of course, now that she was just about the real deal, a full doctor, the women had told she was a catch. They had even threatened to start setting her up on blind dates, just like her mother, if she didn't start going out on her own. It was just that she knew herself. Her relationships had always ended badly and she was in a good place right now, so why mess with it?

"Nice try, ladies. Fess up. What were you really talking about?" Lynn leaned in and dropped her voice. She knew that Sue and Lori loved to gossip not just about showbiz but what was happening in real life. They were a true treasure trove of information and couldn't keep anything to themselves if they had something really juicy to share.

"Well..." Sue matched Lynn's low tone and threw a glance over her shoulder, "you didn't hear it from us, but word on the street is that the clinic is closing at the end of the month."

"Closing." Lynn's mouth dropped open and her it felt like the bottom of her stomach dropped out.

"Shhh!" Lori and Sue said at the same time, and Lynn muttered a sorry.

"Aren't they always saying that?" Lynn kept her voice down. The Queensbay Sailors' Clinic was a town institution, but it generally ran on a shoestring budget and for as long as Lynn had worked there, there were always threats in that it was one month away from closing its doors forever. Still, she had planned on it being around and had even accepted a permanent position once her residency was done. She had never thought she'd be out of a job so soon.

"But this time it's for real. Mr. Petersen's finally selling and the new landlord wants to turn this place into a day spa. We need to find new space within the month or it's lights out."

"A day spa!" Lynn was too incensed to keep her voice down and Sue gave her another angry look as she shushed her.

"You heard us, girl. This place is going bye-bye to make way for a day spa."

"What do you mean bye-bye? Can't we just move to another location?"

Lori shrugged. "Mr. Petersen hasn't raised the rent on us in years. It would be difficult to find another location like this. And even so, that would take time. The lease is up at the end of the month. That doesn't leave long for the Director to find us another place and get it up and running."

"But that's not right!" Lynn said, feeling her anger rising. The clinic served an important need here in town. It couldn't just go away. And then there was the question of her paycheck. And the new apartment she had just signed a lease on. And her Healthy Kids Now program she was planning on expanding. She felt her head began to throb and her heart beat a little faster. This was so not good. It couldn't be that everything she had worked for the past ten years was going to evaporate in a matter of weeks.

"You tell us! Oh, look. Now she's getting angry; but I don't know what's that going to do," Sue said, shaking her short, fluffy red hair.

Lori laughed bitterly. "Don't go thinking this is like some patient of yours you can go and fix, Lynn. You'd be better off spending your time looking for another job."

Lynn pulled herself out of her own sense of injustice and looked at the two of them. "What are you going to do?"

Lori shrugged and looked at them over her half-moon glasses. "I've got a standing job offer to run my cousin's dental practice. Offered me a thirty percent raise."

Sue nodded. "I've got a lead in on a job at the hospital. Night shift, at least at first, but still it pays better."

"But..." Lynn looked at them. The two ladies didn't appear too concerned, only resigned. "The clinic is an institution, right? It's been here since the town was first founded. Are you going to let over hundred years of history go down the tubes without a protest?"

The two other women looked at her, then at each other, and Sue said, "When you put it that way...I guess so."

Lynn fisted her hands and said, "I'm not going down without a fight."

Sue and Lori exchanged looks as Lynn gathered her stuff and propelled herself out the door.

Lori pulled down her reading glasses and her eyes followed Lynn's exit. It was her best look, the one she used when she was going to pronounce something she felt was important. "Lordy. Think that Mr. Petersen knows enough to get out of the way when she's a coming?"

Sue shook her head as she watched Lynn's retreating back, "No way, she's tiny..."

"But mighty," Lori finished for her.

Chapter 2

Jackson Sanders dressed carefully, his mind going over the upcoming meeting. It was something he had learned playing baseball. Visualizing the play, imagining the outcome to virtually will it to happen. Petersen was playing hardball, blustering; but that was only to save face. Jackson was fairly certain the deal would go in his favor.

Jackson smoothed his tie, ran a hand over his hair, and looked out the window. The water, as always, had a calming effect on him, which was part of the reason why he had decided to return to Queensbay. Europe had been nice, Hong Kong bustling, Qatar sandy, New York alive, but now with this opportunity, he knew he was meant to be here. Finally, again.

He glanced away from the sparkling waters of Queensbay Harbor and scanned the screen of his laptop. As usual, his email inbox was overflowing. There were emails from Chase, his brother, who was on a sourcing trip in the Far East, with his fiancée Phoebe, concerning the prep for planned renovations to the Osprey Arms marina and hotel.

Then there was the email from the board of the local university confirming his meeting with them next week. Plus, emails from the project manager who had replaced him on the job in London, asking for his advice on how to handle some upcoming cost overruns.

Then there was the missive from Petersen, telling him to meet him today with his balls on, ready to deal. Jackson was paraphrasing of course, Petersen wasn't happy about selling the building and it was showing. And who could blame him? It had been in his family for years, but Petersen was on the ropes and needed the cash.

There was a ding, and Jackson looked at the new email. He winced when he saw the sender. Helen. He'd been careful, over the years, to only get involved with women who understood the deal. He was a serial monogamist, true while in a relationship, but he had no intention of falling in love or settling down. He had once, but he had almost suffocated, almost lost himself; and he didn't want that to happen again.

Most of the ladies in his life had understood it and taken what he could give them. It had led to several satisfactory liaisons throughout the world. He had thought that Helen, the latest on the list, had understood his position before they began their affair, but as he read the email, he saw that she wasn't quite as accepting about the way things had ended as she had led him to believe.

Jackson kept reading, blinked, and was slightly shocked when he got to the sign off. The coolly proper Helen Sellers had told him to go to hell. He smothered down a wave of guilt. She had known the score when she had gotten involved. Jackson Sanders wasn't the marrying type, no matter how eligible the lady.

He hit delete, since there was no use brooding on it, but he ran a hand through his blonde hair, then smoothed it back. He had always kept it short, as a true executive would. He'd been young to get so promoted so fast, and he had realized that dressing in expensive suits when everyone else his age was embracing corporate casual made him look more mature. The grizzled old veterans, who recognized a power suit when they saw one, had automatically given him more respect since he had showed them some.

He had never made any promises to Helen he hadn't intended to keep. In fact, he had promised her little, beyond some enjoyable time together. Dinners, companionship, an escort for the host of social functions she had enjoyed attending, and the checkbook to support it. Of course, he had shared her bed and she had been an enthusiastic, eager partner, but at the end of the day, he had realized that she fully intended to become Mrs. Jackson Sanders, convinced that she would be the one to change his mind about marriage and settling down. Just like all the rest of them, she'd been bound for disappointment.

Grabbing a bottle of mineral water, he opened the sliding door and stepped out onto the balcony of the apartment. It was a perfect fall day, mid-September, with a sunny, bright blue sky, unmarked by even a single cloud. A few boats skimmed about on the harbor and he could see a bustle of people in and out of the Osprey Arms Hotel's main entrance below.

He was in an annex to the main building of the hotel he owned in partnership with his brother Chase. They had bought it over a year ago and were slowly putting their plans for upgrades into action. The first had been the restaurant, which had been known for baskets of fried shrimp and limp French fries. Chase had brought in a world-class chef, Sean Callahan, and he had transformed it into an upscale steak and seafood destination that had half the coast clamoring for a reservation on the weekend.

Next up had been this building, at least the top floor, which had been chopped up into apartments. Seeing the potential for some steady income, to offset the seasonality of the hotel—summer was the high season, the cold, damp New England winter, not so much—they had decided to keep them as rental units. All it had taken were some simple renovations, like new paint and kitchen appliances, to leave them with a block of one and two bedrooms to rent.

In a few weeks, they would start the full-scale work to the guestrooms and the public spaces of the hotel itself, plus a freshening up of the first floor of the annex, which they intended to turn into retail space. The Osprey Arms was the anchor of downtown Queensbay and before he and Chase had purchased it, it had fallen on hard times. But now they had a plan in place to restore it to its former glory, to make it a centerpiece of the town and hopefully a true destination for people all over the region.

For now, Jackson was enjoying the fruits of his brother's plans, staying in one of those renovated top-floor apartments. Since Jackson only needed a temporary space, he had selected a one bedroom. It had a compact layout but still had everything he needed, from a decent-sized galley kitchen, to a well-equipped living space, complete with flat screen TV and, of course, the view.

He breathed in. The salty tang of Queensbay Harbor rose up, brought up by the light autumn breeze that danced around. He closed his eyes and the memories came flooding back. The first time he had taken Ashley to the beach. The moon-filled night he had convinced her to go skinny-dipping. The clambake the evening they'd announced their engagement. His hand gripped the iron railing and he opened the eyes. Sunlight flooded his vision and almost immediately, she was gone—the fleeting vision of Ashley carried away by the same breeze that tossed a seagull around.

He knew it would be hard, but he also knew that running no longer helped. If it had, he would have stayed away, and been ready to discuss tuxedo choices and wedding venues with a woman like Helen, instead of standing here, looking over the town he called home but had rarely seen in the past five years.

No, he'd finally realized that the only way to let Ashley go was to come back. To make peace with her memory, so he could get back the life he had wanted before that night. In truth, he had never meant to leave Queensbay, certainly never meant to stay away so long. But in the aftermath of the accident he couldn't stay, couldn't face the whispers, the looks—curious, pitying, but most of all accusing—that had followed him. It was even harder when he knew that it was based on a lie. But the lie was the secret he had sworn to keep. He just hoped enough time had passed to take the edge off the townspeople's curiosity. Curiosity he could survive. He just hoped with the passage of time and the absence of Ashley's parents that all he would get would be the curiosity.

The alarm on his phone beeped, signaling that the meeting with Petersen was near. Time to get his game face on.

Chapter 3

"What do you mean you're not going to do anything about it?" Lynn was balanced on the edge of her chair, which took up almost the entire space in front of Sadie Walker's desk. Lynn had rushed out of the clinic, filled with righteous passion and had then taken a deep breath, thought about her options and decided talking to Sadie first was the best course of action.

"Don't you think if I could, I would?" There was a weariness in Sadie's voice that Lynn had heard before but there was also a sharp edge to it, as if she wanted the conversation to be done.

Lynn took a deep breath. She knew that Sadie, as the director of the clinic did her best in a hopeless job. The clinic was essentially non-profit, providing affordable medical care to those who really needed it—and some who didn't. It was run on a shoestring, a budget that was met by a paltry endowment left over from its original benefactors, constant fundraising efforts, and whatever other money Sadie could scrounge together. It was under the official auspices of the local hospital but was more often than not treated like the forgotten child in the attic. Certainly they devoted little money to it, which Lynn thought was a deliberate move, probably hoping that the clinic would run into a crisis like this so they could swoop in and officially take it over.

But that would mean ousting the current board of directors, a tough crew of old biddies who took their jobs quite seriously, and probably moving the clinic to the hospital itself, which wasn't as close to the town, or on a bus line, making it difficult for patients to who didn't drive to get to them. Now, being right here was the best option for the clinic.

When Lynn had accepted the job here, she hadn't taken it for the money. There would be plenty of time to go out and make that later, and thanks to a small inheritance from her grandmother, who had a passion for buying and holding blue-chip stocks, she'd been able to pay for medical school, with a bit left over. No, the clinic had become her personal *raison d'etre* and even more so now that she'd been working on her Healthy Kids Now campaign. She just couldn't watch all of that slip away, not without doing something.

"The Petersen family has been in Queensbay a long time, and the space has been leased to us at below market rates for years. But he has to sell, and the new owner isn't interested in keeping us on. Apparently, kicking us out is a condition of the deal."

"But without the clinic, all these patients will have over an hour's ride to the next one. Or they'll have to go the emergency room at the hospital—and that's unnecessary and expensive."

"I know, Lynn, you're right. But unless you can come up with some alternative plan, then I really don't see what we can do. It's been a good fight, but it's been a battle, almost each and every day. I know how committed you are, but you don't have any idea of the day-to-day realities of running an operation like this. Look, don't worry, about your residency. I know the hospital will find a way for you to finish it out."

Sadie didn't say anything about the job Lynn had accepted at the clinic once her residency was done. That, Lynn knew, was surely in doubt. Right now, though, that was the least of her concerns. It was the clinic itself she was determined to save.

Sadie was a rumpled-looking middle-aged woman with frizzy hair that had once been red, but now, thanks to out-of-the-box hair dye, was closer to orange. She wore glasses that were attached to her by a long chain strung with beads. Her clothing style could only be described as eclectic, usually leggings, chunky heeled boots, with drapey tops thrown over that camouflaged her true shape.

Sadie's heart was in the right place, Lynn knew, but with her trained eye she could see the Sadie was tired. Dark circles pouched under her eyes, and she had put on her eyeliner crooked. Her hands moved restlessly, squeezing and releasing a rubber band ball as if that would help mitigate the stress.

"Lynn, I've worked here for fifteen years, and trust me, if there was a way to change this decision I would find it."

"But hasn't Mr. Petersen threatened to close us down in the past?"

"About every six months, but he can never get a new tenant in." Sadie shrugged her shoulders.

"That's because this place is a dump," Lynn said. As if to punctuate the observation there was the sound of a slamming door somewhere out in the hallway, and the building shook from the reverberation while a small piece of plaster, dislodged from the flaky ceiling, tumbled down, leaving a vapor trail of dust.

The carpet was an indeterminate mix of gray and beige, with suspicious stains dotting across it like polka dots. The walls in the office were a dirty white, scuffed and grimed by handprints and other bodily fluids. Sadie's door sat unsteadily on its hinges and the framed prints of garden scenes, set in cheap frames, did nothing to alleviate the gloom.

"Well, apparently this time, he's selling the place and the new owner has the money to fix it up."

"Why wouldn't Petersen do that himself?" Lynn asked. She wasn't an experienced real estate investor, but it seemed that if the building had belonged to the Petersen family for decades, it was probably already paid for and keeping it as a rental property was a better way of managing the investment.

Sadie shrugged, looked around and said, "Word is Petersen is about to go through a very nasty divorce and he's going to need the money."

"Why?" She'd met Duane Petersen once and he was middle-aged with thinning hair, the beginnings of a belly and a droopy air. His wife, on the other hand, was aerobics class-thin, pretty in that way, and had a highhanded way about her.

"Supposedly," Sadie dropped her voice as if about to impart a state secret, and Lynn wondered if Lori or Sue had been her source, "Duane's mixing it up with his secretary and he wants to get all the liquid cash he can stashed away before Mrs. Petersen comes after it."

"Oh." Lynn sank back in her chair, suddenly feeling overcome. It did not sound like a promising situation. "And it's the new owner who wants to put in the spa client?"

Sadie nodded as she too slumped back into her chair, the air of defeat clearly visible around her.

"That's the story."

"And you're sure it's true?" Lynn asked.

Sadie laughed, but without any humor. "Of course not. That information about Petersen and his secretary came straight from the two little birdies at the front desk, if you know what I mean."

"That doesn't necessarily mean a thing then." Lynn straightened up, rallying.

"Since Petersen sent a letter effectively terminating the lease, I would say it does."

"Doesn't he have to give us any warning?"

Sadie shook her head. "When Petersen stopped making repairs about two years ago, I refused to sign a long-term lease, instead going month to month. I even made like I was visiting other spaces, to see if I could bluff him into thinking we were leaving."

"And did you find any place?" Lynn asked hopefully. It would be a pain to move the clinic, but she considered that a minor obstacle that could be overcome with a couple of strong backs, boxes, and lots of packing tapes.

Sadie sighed, the corners of her mouth turning down. "Not for what we're willing to pay. But I think the hospital might be willing to give us some space, incorporate us into their facility."

"But they're not on the bus line and are thirty minutes away, at least. It's going to be hard for a lot of regulars to make it there."

"I know, I know. But like I said, it might be our only option."

Lynn nodded. At least Sadie had tried, she thought, glancing around. The problem was that even though the building wasn't on the water, it wasn't far from the center of town. You could still walk into the restaurants and pubs, and it might make a nice location for apartments or even a small office building. Or a fancy medical spa, Lynn supposed.

Lynn wasn't quite sure what to say next, only knowing that she wasn't quite ready to sink into the gloom along with Sadie. It just wasn't in her nature. There had to be a way. She loved working at the clinic, much more so than if she had been in a private practice. The patients here were grateful, relieved to know for the most part, that their problems were fixable, whether it was with a prescription, a bandage, or even some common sense. Of course, it didn't always work out that way, but that was the nature of medicine. Lynn wasn't a god. She was a human with a vast amount of knowledge and skills—growing every day—that she could apply to solve many problems. But not all of them.

This, however, wasn't one of those medical cases where the odds were not good. This was a real world, human being, financial, fixable problem.

There was a commotion and then the receptionist was yelling, "Doctor! We need a doctor...!" There was a scrum of voices and she heard a child crying, then the soothing voice of someone saying, "It will be ok, it's ok..."

Lynn launched herself out of her chair, adrenaline pumping. It might just be a kid with a sore throat, or a broken arm, but still she was a doctor and this was her job. Petersen would just have to wait a bit longer.

Chapter 4

Jackson looked at his watch and stopped pacing, and took a seat. He had made it to Petersen's real estate management company with plenty of time to spare for his four o'clock meeting. All the paperwork was in his attaché case, the terms reviewed and reworked meticulously. Petersen thought he was going to pull one over on him, but Jackson's intel was solid. Petersen was in the midst of a sticky situation between the current Mrs. Petersen and a future one, and he needed cash.

That Petersen needed some was evident in the shabby appearance of the waiting room. It might have been nice once, but the carpet was an indistinct gray, highlighted here and there by a darker patch, obviously some sort of stain. The wall had been papered in a pale cream, but there were scuff marks where chairs had rested against them, and the edges were starting to peel. A water stain decorated the corner of the ceiling and the furniture was vinyl and plastic and patched with pieces of plastic tape.

Yup, Petersen needed some cash—which Jackson happened to have, and plenty of it. Unlike many other buyers, he could offer an all-cash deal, without any bank financing needed. The deal could close within a few days and Petersen could do hell all with the money.

Petersen was late and it was irritating Jackson. Actually, it was infuriating him, but he told himself he was merely annoyed, because once you let emotions get hold of you during a business negotiation, you were done for. Besides, he knew he wanted this piece of property a little too badly. In fact, Petersen had offered him the pick of his portfolio, but Jackson had narrowed in on this one. Not for sentimental reasons, but he was pretty sure that since Petersen hadn't wanted to part with it, it was the best one to have.

There was a banging on the door and he saw the blur of a face pressed against the glass doors and the sight of long, dark curly hair. The door swung open and Jackson watched as a slim brunette walked over to the girl at the desk and asked to see Mr. Petersen. Her voice was clear, crisp, and authoritative.

Annabel, who had said she was the 'fill-in' receptionist, gave the same weary, disinterested reply that she had given Jackson, that Petersen was out and she didn't know when he'd be back.

The girl huffed and stamped her foot. She looked around and he saw she was attractive, pretty even, except that her face was twisted up in a frown and her brown eyes snapped with irritation and annoyance. Jackson smothered a smile. Apparently, Petersen being out was really cooking her goose too and she wasn't afraid to show it. She was older than he had first thought, late twenties, but with a youthful, energetic look to her.

Her hair was pulled back in a ponytail leaving a curly mass that swayed down her back and few stray tendrils had escaped, framing her face. She crossed her arms, chewed her lip, and tapped her foot. Expensive sneakers were on her feet, a riot of neon colors. She wore no makeup but she didn't need it. Liquid brown eyes were snapping with impatience.

And, Jackson thought, swallowing, there was something that looked suspiciously like blood splotched across the right side of her light blue scrubs.

"You're not Petersen, are you?" She had all but thrown herself into the worn plastic and metal chair next to him, since in the small waiting room, there weren't many options.

"No, I'm waiting for him too," Jackson said as he shifted slightly in his chair, feeling as if he needed to put some space between him and this bundle of energy. The woman gave him a quick once over and he braced himself.

"Do I know you? You look kind of familiar, you know?" Her eyes squinted as she took a long, careful look at him. He dreaded what she was going to say next, but then she snapped her fingers in triumph.

"I know you. You're Chase's brother, aren't you?" Her voice was firm and she spoke with a slightly flat accent, almost as if she were from the mid-west.

Jackson straightened, relieved and annoyed at the same time. He loved his brother, but it was tiresome to always be known because of that.

"Jax, right? The one who roams all over the place and barely comes home?"

"Jackson," he corrected her. Her mouth twitched up at the formality, and he wondered if she was laughing at him.

"I'm Lynn. Phoebe's friend?"

He gave a nod, his mind still working. Phoebe was his brother's new fiancée. He had met her exactly once on a quick London layover. She had seemed lovely, the perfect fit for his brother, but they hadn't had time to chat much before everyone had gone their separate ways.

"Of course," Jackson said, hoping that was vague enough. He was surprised. Phoebe was a California golden girl and he had trouble seeing what his elegant, fabric-designing future sister in law would have in common with this bundle of scrubs and stains.

"We used to live next to each other," Lynn offered. "I mean Phoebe and I. Before I moved to my own place. She still lives next to my parents."

Jackson gave another quick smile and then hoped that Lynn would be quiet. And still. Her fingers were tapping a beat on the arm of her chair and her leg; one sneakered foot crossed over the other was bouncing up and down.

He shifted in his chair again, wondering if he could ask her to stop moving. He was trying to rehearse the strategy he was going to use with Petersen one more time and she was definitely a distraction.

"Do you know when Petersen will be back?" Lynn twisted in the small chair and fixed him with chocolate brown eyes.

It took a moment to gather his thoughts before he could respond. Her eyes seemed to draw him in and he noticed that there was the slightest smattering of freckles across the bridge of her nose.

"I had an appointment scheduled to start twenty minutes ago," Jackson found himself saying, though he didn't know why. Any longer, and he would have to get up and go, force Petersen to call him. Waiting on the other man would leave him in a position of weakness. Right now, for some reason, he couldn't quite force himself to get out of the chair.

"Oh, I only need a moment of his time," Lynn said and there was a grimness in her tone.

"Then I am sure you won't mind waiting."

"Hmm," she said and fell silent, but only for a moment until both hands started to tap a steady tattoo on the side of the chair.

Jackson picked up one of the magazines. It was something glossy about people he didn't recognize and didn't care about, and he flipped through the pages mindlessly, trying to distract himself from the ball of nervous energy on his right.

"Do you mind?" he finally said.

"Do I mind? What?"

He gestured toward her tapping fingers.

"Oh, sorry," she said and her hands stilled. But it seemed that only made her brain more active, because she said, "Do you know what I do mind? I mind that when a little kid falls out of a tree and breaks his arm because the babysitter was texting on her phone. She doesn't hear the kid screaming for an hour, and then waits even longer to bring him in. And that's not to mention the bloody nose. That thing was a bleeder…Was too afraid to go to the ER at the hospital, and besides it was too far; she doesn't drive, they had to take the bus. What are people like that going to do when the clinic gets closed down…?"

She kept going, cataloging a list of injuries and other disasters. She hadn't drawn a breath once, Jackson thought, fascinated, watching her lips move. He had long since stopped listening to the actual words, too enthralled by her passion to pay attention to the subject of her tirade.

The glass door opened and looking like he had all the time in the world, in strolled Duane Petersen. He stopped short when he saw Jackson, who rose as the older man entered. Beside him, Lynn had fallen silent, but he could feel her vibrating with energy and intent next to him.

Chapter 5

Finally. Lynn thought, her mouth shutting and her eyes narrowing. She could barely remember why she had been wound up, but Jax, no Jackson, he wanted to be called, hadn't said one word, had just watched her with his icy blue eyes, his face impenetrable. Not once had he agreed with her, or shown any sign about what he thought of the injustice. Perhaps he thought cracking a smile would ruin the perfection of the blond hair, straight nose, and strong jaw.

Get a grip, she thought. She shouldn't be thinking about his beautiful white teeth, or his strong jaw, or his nicely sculpted cheekbones. It was only because it had been, what, like forever, since she had a date. Or even given a thought to a guy. Probably because she rarely came into contact with them. Nope, specializing in pediatrics meant she met a lot of cute kids and their moms. Just because she was in the middle of a dry spell, didn't mean she needed to lose her focus just because of a pretty face. It was Petersen she was here to deal with, and he had just walked in. And luckily his appearance didn't set her pulse racing.

"Just a moment, Mr. Petersen. I need to talk to you. It's about the Sailors' Clinic. I heard you're kicking us out of our space at the end of the month."

She jumped to her feet and spoke before Jackson was even fully standing. It was rude to interrupt, but she was on a mission.

Petersen, who looked as if he had just finished up a two-martini lunch, and if Lynn's nose was working right, smelled like it too, held up a hand.

"Well now, little lady, that's not my problem anymore. This here is the man you want to talk to, your new landlord. He told me it was a condition of the sale." He said it affably but there was a gleam in his eye that had Lynn thinking the joke was on her.

Lynn turned on her heel. Jackson looked at her and gave a thin smile which showed off his perfectly straight teeth.

"What?"

"Yup, I am just about to sell that property to Jax Sanders over here. Told me he'd only take it if it were an empty building." Next to her, she all but felt Jackson flinch at being called his nickname. Duane Petersen gave a sly little smile and Lynn suspected that he knew exactly which of Jackson's buttons to push.

Lynn swallowed, feeling her heart sink. "You're the new owner," she said turning to Jackson.

Jackson Sanders looked at his watch again. "If Mr. Petersen will be so good as to sign those papers, then yes, I guess I will be."

Lynn's heart sank. She remembered what Chase had said about his brother, that he was all business. Why,

Jackson hadn't even come home for Phoebe's engagement party, or if Lynn remembered correctly, been seen in Queensbay in years—too busy chasing his career all across the world.

Compassion and doing the right thing would be a hard sell with him, Lynn realized as she looked him over, in his tailored business suit, his face carefully neutral as if not one bit of what Lynn had told him about the importance of the clinic to the community had made it through that wall of armor. Well, she had always enjoyed a challenge.

Mr. Petersen gave a laugh, one that wasn't all that hearty. "Who would have believed it? Chase's baby brother, all grown up and trying to wheel and deal with the big boys? Can't believe you're back in town, but I guess time heals all wounds."

Lynn heard the edge in Petersen's voice and she saw Jackson bristle as Petersen gave him a slap on the back. It was designed to look like a friendly gesture, but the sound of it was too loud, as if Petersen had intended for it to hurt.

"Mr. Petersen, I have other business to attend to, so if we're done," Jackson turned back to Lynn and gave another of his tight smiles, clearly telling her to get out of the way.

"Oh, we're hardly done here, Jax," she said, making sure she put all of the emphasis on his name. She saw his mouth twist in a grimace, and strangely satisfied, she turned to go. With as much grace as she could muster, she walked herself out of the office. Unfortunately, she missed the fact that the wall was not all door. She just about smacked her face into the gold-colored 'N' in Petersen before she caught herself, stopped, and found the door.

There was the sound of heavy silence behind her and then she was almost certain that she heard the beginning of Duane Petersen's slightly tipsy giggle.

Chapter 6

She had decided to work off her anger and humiliation of how the meeting with Petersen and Jackson had ended by doing a hill run. Getting hot and sweaty had a way of taking her mind off things, and if this was the only kind of release available to her, then so be it. Wearing a fleece, running pants and a reflective vest, since dusk was already falling, she set off from the boardwalk in front of the harbor and headed up the streets to the hilly bluffs that encircled the water.

She jogged past the byways of the village proper, a mix of stores and houses close into the center of town that gradually gave way to single-family residences as she got further out. She passed by Darby Callahan's house, the owner of her favorite deli, The Golden Pear, and then she was pushing herself up higher and higher, taking a zig-zagging way up to the Heights, the neighborhood that sat on the east side of Queensbay.

For the most part, homes were a mix of styles, mostly colonials and Victorians, harking back to the days when Queensbay had been a true maritime town, its main industries shipbuilding, fishing, and whaling, with a few more contemporary homes thrown in. The jumble of styles was strangely harmonious, rather than jarring. She'd grown up in Colorado, where everything was open, new, and big. Queensbay was quaint and charming with none of the ruggedness of the western landscape. Everything here was snug and cozy. Sure there were a few sorry-looking worn-down buildings, but those were the exception. Queensbay had the air, ha—with the exception of the clinic—of a lady of a certain age getting a subtle facelift and undergoing a makeover.

She made it up into the Heights, where her parents lived in a sturdy Craftsman style home that was all solid and snug, with fireplaces and solid wood details and a spectacular kitchen, since her mother prided herself on being a gourmet cook. She passed their house, saw most of the lights were off, and figured that they were still out, maybe working late at the hospital or lab; or perhaps they had stopped and had dinner out. Next to that was her friend Phoebe's house, a beautiful, rambling white cottage, where she lived and ran her business.

Phoebe lived with Chase, her fiancé, who was Jackson's brother. Lynn discretely kept her eye peeled as she jogged past it. Maybe Jackson was staying there while Phoebe and Chase were out of town. If she just happened to run into him, then she just might have the chance to talk to him again about the clinic. And this time she would be prepared: cool, calm, and collected.

She sucked in a deep breath of air. Too bad she wasn't known for being calm and collected unless there was a medical emergency. Well, she would just have to channel her favorite movie star of all time, the late, great Savannah Ryan. The woman had known how to play every type, except for scattered and disheveled. That was just how Lynn must have appeared to Jackson in her dirty scrubs and passionate attitude this afternoon.

The Ivy House was dark as she ran by. Her second chance to talk with Jackson would have to wait, she thought, as she headed down the hill and home.

Lights were glowing in the houses and buildings as she passed them and the fall day was turning rapidly into a cool, crisp evening. Already she could smell the scent of wood smoke in the air, as the people of Queensbay lit their fireplaces, welcoming the change of seasons.

She came down finally to the relatively flat stretch of road in front of the harbor and slowed to a walk, allowing her body to cool down. She was breathing heavily, trying to fill her lungs with oxygen, and her thighs burned as she climbed the steps to her top-floor apartment.

Her back was slicked with sweat underneath her running shirt and she was thankful to enter the cool air of her home. She went into her bedroom, stripped off her sweaty workout clothes, dropped them in a pile with her dirty scrubs, and hopped into the shower.

The hot water came in a torrent over her as she scrubbed herself with the soap. She thought about shaving her legs, but decided against it, figuring that she had the next few days off and since she had nothing more planned than to crash on the couch with a glass of wine and some home decorating magazines, it probably wasn't necessary.

She wrapped herself in a warm, plush towel and threw herself down on the bed. The duvet cover was a housewarming gift from Phoebe, a celebration of the fact that Lynn had finally gotten her own place. Of course, she'd lived on her own—in dorms, student apartments— but when she had accepted the residency in Queensbay, where her parents had moved to, it seemed smart to save some money by living with them.

But now that she had—or about to be *did have*, she corrected herself—a real job, she had decided it was time to move out on her own. Her parents had wanted her to stay, of course. Her mom was a great cook and doing laundry didn't require hoarding quarters. Still, it was time for her to move on, to live like a grownup.

Here she was in her first real place, a neat little one bedroom on the third floor of the Osprey Arms annex. It was newly renovated and smelled of fresh wood and paint. So far, Lynn had the whole floor to herself. Chase had said he would be getting other tenants in eventually but he was happy to have her in here first.

Lynn suspected she'd gotten a friend and family discount on the rent, since it was fairly affordable for someone working at a non-profit, but when she had asked about it, Chase had laughed and told her just not to throw any crazy parties. And there, she thought, was the difference between the two brothers. Chase was thoughtful and generous and Jackson was a hard-ass, with his cold blue eyes, too blond hair and chiseled cheekbones. There was something about the way he stood; his fancy business suits that told her Jackson took himself way too seriously.

Stick up his ass, she thought and was about to think of a few other apt descriptors when her phone vibrated. Sighing, she roused herself, hoping it wasn't work calling her in for an emergency, and reached for it. With a groan, she pulled the phone towards her and saw it was a text from her mother.

Don't forget about your date with Nate…it's all arranged for you to meet him at Salsa Salsa.

Lynn groaned again. She had forgotten about being set up on a blind date by her mother. Why had she agreed to this? Oh right, so that it could be a disaster and she could prove her mother wrong and hopefully get her off her back about her love life. She just didn't understand why it was so important to everyone else that she date. Her mother said she was too picky, but Lynn preferred to think of it as being patient. Besides, she'd never felt that urgent need to couple up just for the sake of it. Her life had been so filled, so full of pressure that inevitably anyone she did date either complained of how busy she was; or if he was a doctor too was just as consumed and distracted by his career as she was by hers.

Lynn texted back *long shift today, feeling tired, may need to cancel…*

It was about half a second before the phone ring. She didn't need to look at the caller ID to know who it was.

"Oh no, you don't," Regina Masters said without preamble.

"Don't what? I'm tired," Lynn said. And she was. She was tired from her run, tired of thinking about the clinic closing, and worst of all, she was tired of seeing the smug look on Jackson Sanders' face as she had almost smashed through a glass door pop into her mind. She'd had enough humiliation for one day and a blind date at a mediocre Mexican restaurant could only be the icing on the cake.

"So, you're a doctor: you're always tired. You said you had a few days off. Why not spend a few hours of it going out with a nice young man?" Her mother's tone was reasonable, just like the dependable, methodical clinical researcher Regina was.

"Mom." Lynn knew her voice contained the beginnings of a teenaged-like whine. Her mother was meddling, which she seldom did, which made it all the more worrisome.

"Don't 'Mom' me. Look, you've barely had a date since college. And even those didn't sound very romantic. Hand holding a boy while his high school sweetheart dumps him and takes him back is not my idea of a relationship. Or how about the one who had the mother issues? I mean you keep going out with all these guys with so much baggage. It's no wonder they exhaust you."

Lynn frowned. She had confessed the sorry state of her love life to her mom in a fit of self-pity.

"I know, Mom. That's why I stopped dating. You know, so I could focus on finishing school, my residency, becoming a doctor. You're the one who told me I had a 'fixer up' mentality."

Her mother sighed. "You do tend to see the best in people, and that's just one of the things that's so wonderful about you. But you do keep picking boys that seem to need a lot of attention. But this one isn't like that. He's good looking, has a great job."

"And why did his last relationship end?" Lynn shot back.

"His mother said that the girl had to move back home to take care of her sick father, reconnected with her ex-boyfriend, and got knocked up."

"So he's probably still into her," Lynn pointed out.

"The point is not to get into a relationship, Lynn."

"It's not? Are you sure you're a mother?"

Regina Masters laughed. "You need to practice going on a date. I do not think Nate is the one, but he can afford to pay for dinner."

"At a taco place."

"Accountants are frugal. It's not a bad thing. Talk, have a drink, listen to what he says, pretend to be interested or don't; and at the end of the night you can walk away, but at least you'll have had some practice."

"So you want me to intentionally lead him on?"

"You know, Lynn, your father and I are very happy, but it wasn't like he swept me off my feet. Or that we looked across a crowded room and saw each other. I had to kiss a lot of frogs before I met your father, but that also meant I knew exactly what I was looking for."

"Mom, that's just it. I am finally settled, with a somewhat predictable schedule. For the past ten years I've been busting my ass to become a doctor, and now I am one. Why can't I just enjoy it, instead of getting all carried away with finding a guy?"

"Practice, dear. Besides, you deserve to be treated special, and that's what dates are. Everyone is nice and on their best behavior."

Lynn sighed. She loved her mother, but they were two different people. Her mom's idea of a good time was a four-course gourmet dinner and a game of Scrabble. Lynn's not so much.

"Sounds boring. How do you know this guy is so great?"

It was her mother's turn to sigh. "Look, you're right. I don't know if Nate is great or not, but he sounds normal. And for you, I think that's a step in the right direction. Besides, you haven't met anyone else here, have you?"

The hopeful question hung in the air. Lynn didn't answer immediately, wondering why her mind suddenly flitted to Jackson Sanders and the way he had looked in a suit that must have cost as much as a minor surgical operation. Lynn ran a hand over her face. What was she thinking? And she had barged in there in dirty scrubs. He probably hadn't given her a second thought, unless it was as part of a story he told over a glass of expensive wine to his cronies in the boardroom.

She took a deep breath. Maybe her mother was right. Perhaps she should go out and have some fun. Not that she needed someone to pay for her dinner, but the thought was sort of charming in an old-fashioned way. No one had bought her dinner since Joe, the one with the mother issues, and that had been on his meal plan in the campus dining hall. A nice dinner, a glass of wine, and maybe some conversation that wouldn't resolve around medical specialties all of a sudden didn't sound like such a bad idea. And how bad could this Nate be?

"He's not a doctor?" she asked, checking.

"No, he does something with computers," her mother assured her.

"Fine, I'll go on my date with Nate."

There was as audible sigh of relief from her mother. "Oh thank goodness. I think you'll have fun. And I promise you won't be embarrassed to be seen with him."

"That's the best you can promise?" Lynn asked, wondering if she really needed to go back into the shower and shave her legs.

"Just, don't wear your scrubs, ok? Something besides running shoes? And no fleece. One hundred percent natural fibers, ok?" her mother said before she hung up.

Lynn flopped back on the bed, staring up at her perfectly white ceiling, giving herself a moment to breathe through the panic that was coursing through her. A date. She hadn't been on one of those for years. Sure, guys had tried, but she'd always been able to say that she was too busy. The few times she had decided to give it a whirl, they had been predictable. Dinner at some budget-friendly place, the inevitable talk about work, a tangle over the bill, ultimately deciding to split it, then an awkward kiss with the predictable expectation of "we're students, we don't have much time, why not just get on with it?"

She hadn't succumbed—ok, maybe once, to a particularly charming and buff surgical intern, but he had an ego the size of the Rockies and she hadn't been too disappointed when their relationship lost its fizzle.

But Nate was not a doctor. He was a full-fledged grownup with a job. According to her mother. And Nate's mother. Mothers who had met while getting their hair done and decided that their children just had to meet. Too bad mothers were such lousy judges of characters.

She sighed. At least her mom's heart was in the right place. Her parents were madly in love and thought everyone around them should be as well. And if that was taking too damn long, well then, her mother wasn't above stepping in and helping out. If her older brother, Kyle, had been around, instead of halfway across the country, Lynn knew her mother would be giving him the same treatment. But it was a lot harder to fix someone up on a blind date remotely. So Lynn was the de facto winner of the maternal dating game.

Back to the shower, Lynn decided, knowing it was hopeless. If she actually shaved her legs it would practically guarantee no one besides herself would get anywhere near them tonight. But she was a doctor—being prepared was second nature.

Chapter 7

Jackson sat down at the polished oak bar of the Osprey Arms and had the bartender pour him a celebratory Scotch.

"Cheers," Jackson said as he raised his glass, toasting himself in the long mirror that ran the length of the wall behind the bar. Paulie, the bartender, was placidly wiping down glasses and only nodded. He was a much better listener than talker, which was why he as good at his job.

"Good day?" A questioning voice came from behind him.

"Jake!" Jackson swiveled in the barstool and took in his old friend. Jake Owen had been a star athlete at Queensbay Harbor High and now owned a thriving construction business. He had close-cropped brown hair, a summer tan, and a slightly wary expression on his face as if he couldn't quite believe what he was saying.

"It's been a long time. What, three years?" Jackson offered, by way of apology as Jake stood there, hands thrust in the pockets of his barn coat. Not a hint of a smile lightened his face. Jackson took a breath. He had known no part of this would be easy but he had thought that Jake, of all people, might be inclined to cut him some slack.

"Five years, Mr. Jet Setter," Jake corrected him, his hands still stuck in the pockets of his jacket. He rocked back on his feet, as if assessing the situation.

"Can I buy you a drink to make up for it?" Jackson offered, hoping Jake would say yes instead of turning around and walking out. He probably deserved that, but still he needed to make some amends, and Jake was one of the first on his list.

"Only a fool would say no to a free drink," Jake said, hiking himself up on a barstool. "I'll have the Macallan twenty-year-old, neat," he told Paulie.

Jackson raised an eyebrow. That would set him back a pretty penny. "I see your tastes have matured a bit."

"Only when someone else is buying," Jake said with just a hint of acrimony.

Jackson knew he should flat out apologize, get all of the gooey emotional stuff out of the way, but he was a guy and Jake was his oldest friend, and he just couldn't bring himself to say the words.

Paulie poured the drink and slid it over to Jake, who took, raised it and said, "It's good to see you."

"And you," Jackson acknowledged, and the two of them drank. There was silence and Jake stared straight ahead at the row of liquor bottles lining the wall behind the bar. Behind them was a quiet swell of conversation as the diners at the table ate their meals. Jackson waited, knowing Jake was making a decision.

"I hear you've been busy," Jake said, finally, as if no time had passed, and Jackson relaxed a bit. He'd been forgiven, at least enough so they could have a conversation.

"Yes, I've kept myself busy. I got placed in jobs all over the world, so I've been living in hotels or rental apartments. Couple of months here, a couple there, once a whole year almost in Dubai. I was in New York recently, except for the past couple of weeks when I had to go back to the desert."

Jake nodded, but his question was pointed. "You back for good now?"

"Yes," Jackson said. "I'm back. I hear you're going to be starting the renovations on the hotel soon."

"Didn't know you were going to be helping out," Jake said and there was an edge to his voice.

"Only if you need me, which I'm sure you won't," Jackson said. Jake and Chase had been working together for a while and Jackson hadn't really thought how his showing up would look to Jake.

"I see," Jake said unenthusiastically.

Jackson knew he should say more, tell Jake the real reason he was back in town, but he was afraid his friend would think he was crazy. It was a bit of a hare-brained idea, but then again he was tired of playing it safe.

Jake took another sip of his drink but kept quiet. Ok, so Jackson hadn't expected it to be just like old times. Or maybe he had. But here was Jake, playing it close to the vest.

"I hear you did a great job fixing up my grandmother's house."

"It will be done in another week, or so, then you can have a real estate agent come in and take a look, get a value on it. Should go for a lot, waterfront and all that. A little modern for most people, but I'm sure you'll still find a buyer," Jake said, giving him a sideways glance.

Jackson nodded. He had worked with closely with the architect on the house plans; to make sure it came out just the way he wanted it to. He'd had Chase handle the constructions details with Jake, because he figured that Jake wouldn't have taken the job if he'd known it was for him.

"Chase said you cut a deal on the work, but really that's not necessary."

Jake held up a hand. "I did it for Chase, not you. We do a lot of business together."

"Well, thanks. I actually might have a new project for you if you're interested," Jackson said casually.

"I'm not flying off to Hong Kong, or Dubai, or wherever you're shipping off to next." Jake's voice had a trace of bitterness.

"Nope, this one is local," Jackson assured him and waited.

"I might be interested," Jake said slowly, and Jackson could see the telltale gleam of curiosity in his friend's eye.

"It's the old Sail Makers' building."

"You mean Duane Petersen's property, the one with the clinic in it?" Jake's forehead creased in a frown. He twisted so he was facing Jackson, one booted knee propped up on the rung of the barstool. Jackson felt a wash of relief. Jake was a sucker for the old buildings around Queensbay, devoted to bringing them back to life. Jackson knew his real dream was to restore the old Queensbay Show House, a derelict hulk of a building that had once housed a theater.

"That's the one. I think the building will be perfect for what I have in mind, I'd love to turn it into an open concept office space, something high end." Jackson nodded, his fingers drumming on the table in excitement. A

DREA STEIN

new project always got him going and since he intended
this one to be personal, it was doubly so.

"Are you going to keep the clinic there?"

Jackson frowned, surprised that it had come up a
second time that day. "I wasn't planning on it. Doesn't
exactly fit in with the vision I had for the place. I was
thinking retail on the first floor, maybe a restaurant, offices
above, or possibly even apartments."

Jake gave a laugh and then took another sip of his
single malt. "Then that could be an issue."

Jackson shifted in his seat uneasily. He thought about
the little spitfire who had been in Petersen's office today.
Lynn had been her name. She had a fire in her eye and an
intense energy, especially on the subject of the clinic.
Memories of their encounter had kept popping up all
afternoon, even as he went about sealing the deal with
Petersen and handling the paperwork.

"How so?"

"Did you look over the building before you bought it?
Word is the town council has wanted to condemn the
property for a while, since Petersen hasn't dropped a dime
into it for years. But they don't, just so the clinic will stay
open."

"I would think the clinic would welcome the chance to
get out of there and find some more modern space."

Jake gave a quick laugh and shook his head. "I don't
think they can afford to find anything better."

"I thought the clinic had an endowment, funding, that
all the whole biddies in town were behind it," Jackson said.

"Tough economy, plus the old biddies are like that -
old. Sure, they've gotten some money from a few of the

local big donors, but it's really just a bandage over the open wound. Talk is the hospital wants to take it over, in which case they would probably have the money they need to stay, even if you raised the rent."

"Well, times change, don't they," Jackson said, finishing most of his drink. He didn't like to think that his plans wouldn't work out. He'd just assumed that the clinic would be willing to move, but now, based on what Jake was telling him, that wasn't necessarily the case. If they wouldn't go quietly, he'd just have to make them.

"Not everyone in Queensbay likes to forget the past," Jake said, and Jackson knew it was a deliberate jab at him.

"I didn't forget you. I just..."

"We were supposed to go into business together, Jackson. You were going to be the brains of the operation and I was going to be the brawn."

"You've done just fine for yourself," Jackson pointed out.

"No thanks to you." Jake's voice rose and Jackson was aware that Paulie, at the far end of the bar, had paused what he was doing and was standing at the ready, poised to intervene if things got heated.

"Look, I had a plan, everything mapped out. And then she...and then she's dead." Jackson found himself stumbling over the words, but kept going. "And you know what, I couldn't handle it. I couldn't be here anymore. No one wanted me here anymore."

Jackson was aware that he had stood up, pushed off his barstool and was in a tensed, ready position as if for a fight.

But Jake's quarterback bulk stayed right on the barstool while he eyed him. "That's not true. I was there for you."

Jackson ran a hand over his face. He couldn't explain it to anyone, couldn't quite explain just how much Ashley's death had cost him.

"But I get it."

"You do?" Jackson asked, not trusting the hope that was creeping in.

"Yeah. You said it. You admitted that you went off the rails after Ashley died. I get it, I would have too. But dude, you just picked up and ran—didn't talk to us, any of us, for years. We knew her too, you know. We were all friends. Not all of us blamed you for what happened, you know. Or we didn't care. We wanted to stand by you."

"Thanks," Jackson said, quietly, taking a deep breath. Yup, this was going to be harder than he thought, but better to get the subject of Ashley over with sooner than later. "I just couldn't, the memories…" He stopped. He was done lying, he had to tell himself. Ashley would always be a part of the past, but she couldn't take away his future anymore.

"I understand. And I'm glad you're back, whatever the reason." Jake clapped him awkwardly on the shoulder and Jackson decided he didn't need to say anymore, and that if it wasn't quite the truth, at least it wasn't a lie.

Jackson nodded. "Thanks." And then to change the subject, "So you think I'm going to have problems with the clinic? The director, Sadie, seemed very understanding about the whole thing." Or, if not understanding at least she didn't seem too upset. Perhaps she was imagining a nice retirement.

Jake laughed. "It's not Sadie you have to worry about. It's Lynn."

"You mean a brunette ball of energy about this big?" Jackson held his hand out about chest high.

"That would be her. Lynn Masters. She works there, has for a while, and it's become her pet project. I don't think she's going to take the closing lying down."

Jackson thought back to the woman he had met. Her brown, intense eyes, the way she had stared him down, even though she was half his size. Even her clumsy exit had been saved by the fluid way her body moved, dodging the glass wall and finding the door at the last minute. Jackson had never given much thought to how a woman would look in scrubs, but he had to admit Lynn had worn them well.

He shook his head. Maybe she would calm down, accept the news gracefully. If she was worried about losing her job, perhaps he could find a way to help her with that, call on some connections. She'd said she was friends with Chase and Phoebe, so there had to be a way to make this turn out right for her. Yes, he thought, all he needed was to make sure Lynn was taken care of and she would be no problem. Most women were fine like that.

Jake was gazing at him, a speculative look on her face. "She's a nice girl, you know…"

Jackson shook his head. "Don't even go there."

"It's been five years, my friend."

Jackson looked deep into the amber liquid in his glass. "That's what my mom says, as if it matters. I didn't come back here to get into a relationship. I managed to dodge them over seven continents so I think I'm safe in

Queensbay. After all, nobody in this town would touch me with a ten-foot pole."

Jake shook his head. "Maybe. Of course, some people do have long memories. But you have a thick skin, right?"

Jackson felt his stomach sink. He had wanted to think that time would have made it easier, maybe even had people forgetting about it, but now Jake was warning him that might not be the case.

"Thanks for the notice. I'll be sure to put on my elephant hide when I go out there."

Jake nodded and pursed his lips. "There will be talk, you know. Some people have long memories, but I think if you just try to be nice, you know."

"I can.be nice," Jackson said, surprised.

"Sure you can be, but most people remember you as an arrogant prick with a fast car, a baseball scholarship, and *fuck you* attitude."

"And as a murderer." Jackson pushed his drink away.

"Police said it was an accident," Jake said.

Jackson nodded. It had been one giant accident—his relationship with Ashley and the car crash had only been the icing on the cake.

"Try telling that to the Morans," Jackson said.

"Doesn't matter; just keep your head up high," Jake said.

"And that's the best bit of advice you can give me?"

Jake shrugged. "Yup. I don't have much else. I'm a single guy, working construction who still uses my old bedroom as an office."

Jackson laughed, knowing that Jake's humble act was mostly that. Queensbay Construction was doing a fine business since Jake had officially taken over the family business.

"Single? You mean Darby Reese turned you down again?" Jackson said, referring to Jake's old prom date.

"Turned me down? She went and married another man. She and Sean Callahan are going to have a baby any day now." Jake shook his head but Jackson could tell he was genuinely happy for the couple.

"Who knows, maybe there's a fish in the sea for you? We are, after all, on a harbor." Jackson raised his own glass in a toast.

Jake gave him a lopsided smile and they tapped glasses. "What about you? Ever thought of, you know…?"

"What, girls? Dating?"

Jake nodded.

Jackson gave a bitter laugh, thinking of Helen's last email to him. "I have dated. Even had as you might call them, relationships; but I'm just not the marrying type."

Jake laughed. "Funny, and I always thought you'd be the first to settle down."

Jackson shook his head, "Let's just say I don't believe in happy endings anymore."

Jake nodded, took a sip of his drink, and Jackson did the same, wondering why all of sudden an image of Lynn Masters flashed through his head. He gave a shake, as if to clear the thought from him. Getting involved, caring, was the last thing he needed right now.

Chapter 8

Lynn was nursing her disappointment over a glass of red wine at Quent's Pub, absorbing the cocoon-like feeling of the very British atmosphere. Quent had an accent that could only be described as vaguely British but was an avowed anglophile when it came to décor. His pub looked like it could have stepped out of a small town on the rugged Scottish coast, with its burnished wood bar, cozy red leather booths, dark green walls and dartboards. He kept the theme going with a menu of pub food, songs from the British invasion on the playlist and a full range of beers from across the pond.

As cozy as it was in here, with a small fire going and the low hum of conversation, Lynn was just about ready to go when she saw Tory Somers walk into the pub with what looked like the entire North Coast Outfitters softball team. They were loud and boisterous, but she managed to catch the other girl's eye and Tory came over.

"Did you win?" Lynn asked. She and Tory had met when she's agreed to donate her time to redo the clinic's website and they had managed to squeeze in a few social outings like coffee and a few runs together into their busy schedules. Tory was head of technology at North Coast

Outfitters, the local clothing and accessories business owned by Chase Sanders.

"Yup, beat Queensbay Construction two to one." Tory had light brown hair that was always a perfectly streaked blond, summer or winter, so Lynn had to guess most of it was artifice.

"Good for you." Lynn knew that the rivalry between North Coast Outfitters and Queensbay Construction was good natured but intense.

"Yup, it means that drinks are on them tonight," Tory said with a smile, and then she turned her attention to Lynn. "Killer boots, by the way. But aren't they a bit much for a drink at the pub? And if you're trying to pick up men, might I suggest online dating over hooking up with a barfly from the local dive?"

"This ain't no dive," Quentin, the owner of the afore-mentioned dive, stood before them, shaved head glistening, arms folded across his chest allowing the massive biceps in his arms to ripple. "It's a fine family establishment."

"Yeah, we've heard it all before," Tory waved Quent's objections away. "We'll have two pitchers, please."

Quent laughed. "And whose tab is this going on—yours on the other team's?"

Tory flashed a smile. "Not ours. Their star slugger didn't show up. Made it that much easier for us to bury them."

Quent let out a rumble, which for him, passed as a laugh.

"And get my friend here another glass of whatever she's having."

Lynn was about to protest, but decided that it didn't matter. After all, she was trying to drown her sorrows.

"Why the fancy duds?" Tory asked, leaning over the back of the barstool, taking in Lynn's dark jeans and v-neck silk blouse.

"I had a date," Lynn said before she realized it. She had vowed to keep her date with Nate to herself.

"What, you on a date? Do I get to meet him? Is he in the bathroom?"

"No, we said goodbye at the restaurant. I came home and decided that it was too nice a night to go home and drink by myself."

Tory shot a look around at the empty barstools surrounding Lynn. "I don't mean to bring my over precise computer developer brain to the situation, but you are, in reality, alone."

"No," Lynn corrected her, "not to bring my overly literal medical mind to the table, but there were twelve other people before two softball teams came in. Technically, I'm surrounded by people, and therefore I am not drinking alone."

"It was that bad, huh?" Tory said in sympathy, taking a seat on one of the barstools.

Lynn took another sip of her wine and looked over when she felt the pull of Tory's intense gaze on her.

"Oh no you don't. Look you can't drop a bomb like that and then go back to calmly drinking your wine like you were making small talk about the weather."

"It wasn't that bad," Lynn started to say, and then in spite of herself, she laughed. "Ok, so he took me to Salsa Salsa."

"You mean the newest version of Augie's?"

Lynn nodded and Tory laughed. "That place changes menus and cuisines every six months."

Lynn laughed too, since Tory was right. Augie's, located a bit off the main street and therefore out the way of the casual stroller by, struggled with an identity crisis. Greek, Italian, French cuisines, had all been tried—the one constant a killer margarita recipe. Finally, the owner, Augusta, had given in and gone for a Tex-Mex theme. Unfortunately, the margaritas were still the best thing on the menu.

"That's the one."

"I hope the margarita went down smoothly."

"It sure made listening to his stories about his Civil War figurines and his job a lot more interesting. He's an accountant. My mom thought he was in computers, but apparently that's his older brother."

"So?" Tory said. "My dad's an accountant and a cool guy. Too old for you but still, he's cool."

"His hobbies include memorizing vice presidential candidates. Did you know that John Quincy Adams used to swim naked every day in the river?"

"Ok, umm gross," Tory said as Quent slid two frothy pitchers of beer toward her, with a stack of glasses. "I guess there won't be a second date?"

Lynn shook her head. "Let's just say, the date with Nate was the icing on the cake of a very bad day." Nate didn't have anything wrong with him. He was good looking and he paid for dinner, calculating the tip in his head to exactly eighteen and a half percent. And most of his vice presidential trivia had been interesting. It was just that he didn't do anything for her. Lynn took a deep breath and twirled her wineglass in her fingers. She really didn't need it, had just wanted to be with some company in a familiar setting.

"How could it be any worse?" Tory asked as she gathered the pitchers and cups to her.

"Well, the clinic's closing," Lynn said.

"Closing? For real this time?" Tory's caramel-colored eyes were wide with concern.

"Yes, and it's all because your boss's brother has decided that a medical spa is more important than a clinic to the people of Queensbay."

"My boss's brother...Who? Oh, you mean Jackson Sanders? What does he have to do with it? Last I heard he was Dubai or New York, or something like that.

"Well, apparently he's here, all six foot two of him, and he's bought the building from Duane Petersen."

"Hmm," Tory said thoughtfully. "So the international playboy has gotten tired of the traveling lifestyle and come home to roost. I guess traveling the world worked out well for him. I wouldn't have thought he'd come here and buy a building. Especially that one. It looks like it's about to fall down. Wonder if he knew that."

"Well, he did buy it and apparently he's a rich enough jerk that he thinks he can do anything he wants, and that includes having a better class of tenants. Why does everything have to get gentrified? I mean a medical spa? Do they call it that just because the people who work there wear white coats? It's an oxymoron, that's what it is. I mean, Jackson Sanders can take his snooty attitude and five thousand dollar-suits and go jump in the harbor for all I care."

"You sound pretty worked up, but it sounds like Jackson. He's not exactly in touch with his soft side." Tory trailed off and Lynn looked at her sharply.

"Do you know Jackson?"

An awkward half smile flitted across Tory's face. "Not exactly. I mean, it's more like I know of him."

"Why, does his ice prince reputation precede him?" Lynn couldn't help asking, knowing that she was dipping into the gossip arena. She had been dwelling on her encounter with Jackson all afternoon and evening, even while eating dinner. Nate had brown eyes, while Jackson had blue ones. Nate's nose was slightly bulbous, while Jackson's had been sharp and perfectly straight. All she could think about was the way his light blue eyes had regarded her coolly, as if she were no more than an unwelcome distraction, distracting her from Nate and his facts about the vice presidents.

As a doctor, Lynn was used to being viewed in a variety of ways, from an angel of mercy to the harbinger of bad news. But never had she felt so inconsequential. It had gnawed away at her all day.

"No," Tory said. Lynn waited.

"No…so what happened? Did his puppy get run over when he was a little kid and that's his excuse for his bad behavior today?"

Tory shrugged, clearly not comfortable with the topic. "Something like that, but worse."

Slightly taken aback and shamed at her own flippancy, she stammered out a "Sorry...I didn't...What could be worse?

"No, it's cool. Look, it was a while ago but his fiancée died. Like right before the wedding and well, she was from around here and they were kind of the hometown couple, and after it happened, Jackson just kind of left town and that was it. I mean, don't get me wrong, Jackson's not like Chase at all. He was always pretty cocky, kind of a jerk, in fact. But I guess you know, his fiancée dying, that really hit him hard, so he left. He kept in touch with his family of course, but from what I gathered, he was working and traveling all over the world, trying to forget her and what happened."

"Wow, heavy stuff," Lynn said digesting it all, trying to put together the picture of Jackson and his business-like demeanor with that of a grief-stricken fiancé.

"Yup," Tory agreed.

There was a silence, and from behind them they heard a shout, then some laughter. The pub was beginning to liven up and she saw Tory glance back at the table of thirsty softball players she'd left behind.

"You should join us. Just one beer?"

"I do have tomorrow off," Lynn said. Suddenly, sitting at a table full of people her own age sounded like a very good idea. After learning about Jackson's past, she felt even more like she needed a distraction to put the thought of him, and his baggage train, out of her mind.

"And," Tory said, with a smile, "someone else is buying."

Chapter 9

The moon was up and almost full, casting a silvery trail along the calm surface of the harbor. It was getting late but Lynn still felt drawn to the water and decided a quick detour down to the boardwalk along the edge of Queensbay Harbor was in order. She'd grown up out west, among the plains and the mountains and had never thought she was a water girl until she came to Queensbay.

She'd left the bar and the softball players after another beer, ok, maybe two beers, but she felt fine, knowing the walk home along the quaint streets of Queensbay would help clear her head. She gazed down at the water into the ripples of silvered moonlight. She shivered, wishing she had thought to bring a coat. The heat of the day evaporated quickly now and the nights were markedly chillier, but the view was still breathtaking.

It had been fun to hang out with people near to her own age. Everyone had been friendly and the talk had been about normal things. No Civil War strategy rehashes or politics—historical or otherwise. She might even have agreed to join one of the teams, but of that she wasn't quite certain.

Cold now, she headed for her building and started the climb up the stairs, tottering a bit in her high heeled boots. She knew she should think about getting to bed, but in truth she wasn't tired. Her long nights as a resident, plus her own natural temperament had made sleep a luxury for so long she just didn't need as much as other people. Instead, she was restless, unsettled.

Maybe it was the full moon. After all, there was a known correlation between a full moon and a spike in emergency room visits. For whatever reason, people seemed just a little bit crazier when the moon was at full strength.

She didn't feel crazy exactly, maybe a bit morose. After all, she'd just had a lousy date and was about to lose her job. That was a blow, but she was more worried about what would happen with her Healthy Kids Now program. She had made so much progress with it in the past few months, really started to help a lot of kids, that she didn't want to see it all end.

She got to the top and was surprised to see the light was out on the landing, and because of the way the building was situated it was dark on the balcony that ran in front of the apartments. She wasn't afraid, but the light of the moon was a dim gray wash here and it was hard to see.

She fumbled in her purse for her keys and dropped them, of course. With a sigh, she bent down to retrieve them, her eyes trying to grow accustomed to the darkness. One of her high heels caught in the groove between the long deck boards and she wobbled, trying to catch herself when she crashed into something behind her. Her head hit something hard and before she could help herself, a curse slipped out, as if that could lessen the pain.

Fighting the impulse to just lay back and rest, she started to struggle to her feet when the world gave way behind her.

Chapter 10

"What are you doing?"

There was an angry voice and all of sudden she was blinded by a bright light. It took a moment for things to make sense, and when they did, she realized that Jackson Sanders was looming above her, and that the top half of her had somehow managed to find its way inside the door, while her legs, her boots, and keys were very much stuck outside in the cold dark moonlight.

In vain, she struggled to get up, using her arms and her thigh muscles in an attempt to propel herself forward. She almost had it when she felt, rather than saw, something swoop down. Within a moment she had been hauled upright, Jackson Sander's arm holding her steady. It was warm against her bare skin, a lick of fire in the cold night air.

His blond hair was slightly less combed than before, and his dress shirt was untucked and hanging out over his suit trousers. He was barefoot and she judged, after bringing her eyes back up to his face, seriously pissed.

"What am I doing? What are you doing?" Lynn managed to stammer, taking a step back. The high heel of her boot however, was still caught, and she would have stumbled but for his arm, which kept her standing. Drawing a deep breath, she put a hand up on the doorjamb and bent down, and pulled on her heel, releasing her foot. At least now she wasn't stuck, but even in her heels she was still much shorter than he was, and she was now at the disadvantage of looking up into Jackson's smug smile.

"I asked first," he said, his voice so dangerously low it sent a shiver up her back. She remembered what Tory had told her, about Jackson's past, and she wondered what if the icy façade really did hide a grieving man or if enough time had passed that this had become his true nature.

"I live here," she managed to stammer. She had a quick look around, making sure she really did recognize her door.

A not very nice smile came over Jackson's face as his eyes, full of insolence, traveling up and down her, taking in the black leather boots, her tight jeans and the filmy silk blouse that had slid proactively, and with unfortunate timing, off one of her shoulders, baring it to the cool night air. She saw his eyes drawn to the low cut V above her breasts just before they slid up to her face.

He stopped there, one eyebrow raised, a faintly amused expression playing on his lips. She felt her cheeks start to flame. The outfit had seemed like a good idea when she had gone out with Nate. In fact, he could hardly keep her eyes off of her, but his gaze was nothing like Jackson's cool appraisal and the effect it was having on her body.

"Live here? Is that really the best you can come up with?" He leaned against his doorjamb now, arms crossed over his chest. Dimly, behind her, Lynn was aware of some shouts and calls from the street below. It was probably some of the softball team on their way home after their final round of drinks at Quent's.

"What do you mean?" Lynn sputtered, anger rapidly taking over her embarrassment. His blue eyes were like ice chips in that face. A face with beautiful, well-chiseled cheekbones. A mouth with wide, somewhat, full lips. If she'd been feeling romantic and Jackson was being less surly, she might have called it generous. But then she remembered there was nothing generous about him.

"I mean, if you wanted to see me again, you could have called me, made an appointment. I would have been happy to fit you into my schedule during normal business hours. I assure you, you won't get very far trying out your tricks on me."

"My tricks?" Lynn felt as if her head was going to explode, not quite able to piece together what Jackson was saying to her. And then it all came together.

"You think I'm here to what…" Lynn fumbled for the words, "seduce you, proposition you? Because you want to close the clinic?"

Any sympathy she might have felt for him, because of what Tory had told her about his fiancée, evaporated.

The pompous look faded slightly from Jackson's face.

Lynn's anger launched her forward, so that the toe of her booted toe was touching Jackson's bare one.

"Well, I…" Jackson now seemed to be having trouble speaking.

"I've heard about you. Do you think that just because you're some sort of international playboy you can come into this town and throw your money and looks around and just have everyone bow down to you?"

Jackson's eyes widened in surprise and he held his hands up, as if only just now realizing his mistake.

But Lynn wasn't done, not by a long shot. "Listen, mister. I pay your brother good money to rent the apartment…" Lynn leaned back to check, "next to this one. I am sorry that I disturbed you, but the light is out on the porch and I dropped my keys. I had no idea you were staying here, and if I did I certainly wouldn't have bumped into your door."

"What? You're renting here? Chase said nothing was rented." Jackson seemed to have regained some of his composure and the smooth mask slid back onto his features as his arms closed, folded over themselves.

"You think I'm selling you a story? Seeing as how I'm friends with Phoebe, he let me in early. So there."

Lynn could have kicked herself. Seriously, she was spending way too much time with kids, if that was the best parting shot she could come with. She might as well have called him a booger nose and be done with it.

With as much dignity as she could muster, she turned on her heel and this time, it would have been a graceful exit, except she still didn't have her keys. She looked around and saw them, shining brightly in the light spilling from Jackson's door, resting in the soil of a potted plant. She scooped them up, remembering to bend from the knees so he wouldn't get the satisfaction of seeing her ass in the air.

She didn't, couldn't turn around to see if Jackson was still watching, but as there was still a puddle of light spilling from his doorway she had to assume he had watched every moment of her miserable performance. Trying to keep her hands from shaking, she managed to insert the key into the lock of her door, twisted it quickly and thrust herself into the safety of the dark space.

After a moment, she thought she heard the sound of a door closing shut and she saw, through the small crack at the bottom of the door, the puddle of light disappear.

Chapter 11

Jackson went back to the couch where he had his papers spread out, his laptop open, and a beer he didn't need growing warm. He had been running the numbers on his business plan one more time. He looked at the computer but everything merged together. He threw down his pencil and leaned back, running his hands through his hair.

He had officially made a mess of that, he thought. Looking back, he supposed that Chase had mentioned that one of the other apartments in the Annex was rented. The porch light was out, something he had noticed himself, had even made a note to tell the maintenance staff about it; and with it out, it might even be possible to mix the doors up, since no one had gotten around to putting numbers on them yet.

But, honestly, what was he supposed to have thought? There was the girl, the woman, he supposed, that he'd seen earlier in the day, dressed in dirty scrubs. And then all of a sudden she had shown up, with her rich, silky hair piled high on her head, with some stray locks falling down, framing those dark, chocolate brown eyes and the round, slightly freckled face. And then there had been those long, tall boots with heels so high that she maybe, almost might have reached his shoulder. And the jeans, which had molded to her body so that he nothing was left to his imagination. And then her shirt had slipped, giving him a glimpse of one, gorgeously tanned shoulder.

She didn't seem like the type who went for sexy lingerie, but at that moment he would have given quite a bit to find out, just one little peek. Despite his resolve, despite reminding himself that he had sworn off women, especially ones who seemed to want something from him, the thought of Lynn Masters in nothing but her bra and underwear, with her dark hair piled sexily around her shoulders, flashed through his head and had his heart pumping.

Just as abruptly, he shut the thought down and took a sip of his lukewarm beer. Jackson got up and wandered to the window. Chase had kept this apartment specifically for friends and family. It was decorated in a sleek, spare style that fitted a place that was meant to be for transients. The couch was comfortable but not too inviting. The kitchen counter boasted a toaster and a one-cup coffee maker. Throughout, everything was done in shades of neutral with an occasional nautical shade of blue as contrast.

It was efficient and effective, and Jackson didn't really need any more than that now. The work on his house was almost done, and he was eager to move in, to be in a real home. This apartment, as nice as it was, reminded him of all the temporary housing he'd lived in overseas and across the country. Just inviting enough to lull one into thinking it was homelike, but always lacking anything resembling warmth.

Jackson wandered over to the refrigerator, opened it, then closed it, knowing he wasn't really hungry, since he and Jake had sat together talking over steaks at the Osprey. He was just restless.

Was he crazy thinking maybe she'd come to talk to him? Pleading hadn't worked this afternoon, so maybe she thought that a more overt method of persuasion would tip the scales in her favor? What kind of man did she think he was?

But then, how could she have any idea where he lived? And she did finally let herself into her own apartment. With a key. But dressed like that, she looked like she was dressed for something...like a date. The thought bothered him, and then he remembered with a half-smile that if she'd come home alone, it couldn't have been much of a date.

He decided not to dwell on that, but instead look ahead. Tomorrow was the first day of the rest of his future, and he needed to be prepared for that. He didn't have time to worry about Lynn and the clinic. Besides, that decision was already made. If they didn't have the money for the new lease, that was their problem.

Chapter 12

"You mean to tell me you fell into his door?" Tory asked, putting a chunk of blueberry muffin into her mouth. Lynn watched fascinated. Tory seemed able to eat an ungodly amount of carbs and still stay in good shape. Must be genetics, Lynn thought, but her doctor's training knew that wasn't simply the case. Tory loved to run and had already finished two half-marathons this year.

They were sitting at The Golden Pear Café. Lynn had decided to come in for granola and coffee and had bumped into Tory. The café, with its clean nautical theme, punctuated by white bead board walls, topped by blue paint and black and white pictures of sailboats, was a popular destination for breakfast and lunch. It always smelled heavenly, like a mixture of chocolate, cinnamon, and vanilla; and right now, most of the small round tables were occupied as moms met for coffee, retirees complained about the local news, and Tory and Lynn chatted.

"Pretty much." Lynn shook her head. "It was another disaster."

"And he thought you were there to…"

"Use my feminine wiles to get him to not close the clinic."

"You were dressed to kill, so yeah I guess if I was the typical red-blooded guy and some girl like you knocked on my door in the middle of the night I might have thought just about every one of my fantasies had come true. Next time, try wearing your white doctor's coat with nothing on underneath—that might work better."

"Tory!" Lynn said shaking her head. "That's not what I had in mind."

"Sure, of course you didn't," Tory said, her voice brimming with false sincerity.

Darby Callahan, the owner of the café, came up to them, her pregnant stomach leading the way. She held up a carafe of coffee and asked, "Can I get you guys anything else?"

"She needs another shot," Tory said. "And I'll take a box of chocolate chip cookies for the office."

"Long night, making rounds?" Darby asked as she poured their coffee.

"Bad date," Tory answered for Lynn.

"Oh," Darby winced in sympathy. "I don't mind missing out on those." Darby was married to Sean Callahan, the chef at the Osprey Arms. Together they were working on expanding The Golden Pear into another location, and had opened another high-end restaurant. All while Darby was due with their first child.

Lynn waved her hand. "Yeah, yeah, all you happily married people just rub it in our faces."

Darby laughed and rubbed her stomach. Her face winced, and seeing it Lynn stopped and asked, "How are you feeling? Are you sure you should be on your feet?"

Darby laughed. "My doctor says I'm fine. Sure glad the heat of the summer is over. Only a few more weeks to go. Can't wait to meet the little bean." She touched her stomach again and waddled gracefully to the counter to box up the cookies Tory had ordered.

Lynn smiled. Darby and Sean hadn't wanted to know whether they were having a boy or girl, and now most of Queensbay was locked in a fierce betting pool over it. Odds were split evenly, but Lynn knew Darby was convinced she was having a boy.

"Is it me, or does it seem like everyone is coupling up?" Lynn leaned back and looked out the window with a sigh. She'd looked out the window, noting that the leaves on some of the trees were just starting to change from their summer green to their autumnal shades of dusky yellow and burnt orange.

She'd been in Queensbay for a while now, and with the passing of each season she found something more to love. In the summer it was all about being outside, hitting the water, grilling. Winter was about settling in, keeping the wild winter storms at bay. Spring of course, was about the promise of warmer days, watching the harbor come to life around you. Autumn meant festivals and snuggling in, decorating pumpkins, and asking kids what they wanted to be for Halloween. She loved it all.

"Nope, it's not your imagination." Tory said. "Half the guys on the softball team are all shacked up and head home to their honeys. I thought it would be a great way to find a boyfriend, but so far, no luck. Seems like it's harder and harder to find a good man around here."

Lynn's face twisted in a frown as her mind turned to Jackson Sanders. He was not a good man. First he'd been rude, then he'd been arrogant, and then, most likely, he'd been laughing at her. Her last encounter with him had been the icing on the cake. Or rather the straw that broke the camel's back. Not to mention that he was probably still mourning a dead fiancée. Maybe that was why he had come back to Queensbay, to be closer to her in spirit. The thought turned her melancholy.

"I guess we could swear off men forever?" Lynn suggested, hopeful. After all, it wouldn't be so hard; it would almost be like making it official, her current state of aloneness.

Tory looked at her as if she had another head growing out of her shoulders.

"Uh-uh and no way…I am still on the hunt, even if you seem intent on staying out of the game. Man, you must have really been burned. I saw you dump the numbers those guys gave you last night. What about Nate? Are you going to give him a second chance? Maybe he'll grow on you?"

"I don't think so," Lynn had already had two texts from Nate, seeing if she was around anytime soon. She had claimed a busy work schedule and hoped that would be enough for him to get the picture, without having to actually tell him she wasn't interested.

Still, what Tory had said stung a little, and she felt the need to defend herself.

"It's not that I was burned," she said, but stopped herself. "I mean not that badly."

"What happened?"

"Well, it wasn't so much that it was anything in particular. It was sort of a series of events, and I just decided I might be better off, you know, taking a break."

"Who were they?"

"Well there was Ben, who was trying to get over his ex-girlfriend. And there was Joe, who had mother issues, and there was Ryan, I think was gay and trying to use me to persuade his grandmother otherwise. And there was Grant."

"What did he want?"

"To play doctor with me." Lynn shuddered at the memory. "You'd be surprised how many guys have wanted to do that."

"No, not really. But let me guess. Ben got back together with his girlfriend, Joe still lives with his mom, Ryan's grandmother died and he didn't have to pretend anymore, and Grant plays footsie with a hot nurse."

"How do you do that?" Lynn shook her head. "I have what my mom calls a 'fix-it' complex."

Tory nodded. "Oh, you mean the kind where you date guys who have something wrong with them and you think you can fix them, and then you're terribly surprised when they don't want to change."

"Yes. Why, do you have it?"

Tory shook her head. "Nah, I go in with low expectations."

"What?" Lynn said, shocked.

"Except, you know, in bed."

"You mean you go out with guys not expecting it to go anywhere?"

"Well, it doesn't mean I jump into bed on the first date, or with every guy I meet, but I figure the chance of, you know, any guy I meet being the one is statistically impossible, even if, you know, there is the one, which again is highly improbable. So I just look to enjoy myself."

"But to just give up on everything else?"

"I'm not giving up, if it happens, great; if not, well then everything is a lot less complicated. And I'm happier."

Lynn said nothing, thinking over this.

Tory's eyes narrowed as she pursed her lips. "Out of curiosity, just how long has it been since you've, you know, gotten some action?"

Lynn paled. "Grant was the first year of my residency."

"Whoa!" Tory slumped back in her chair and looked at Lynn with disbelief. "That would be like what, months? Years?"

"Years," Lynn admitted morosely.

Tory shook her head. "Well, there's your problem. Maybe instead of looking for romance under the full moon, or a guy with issues, you should just go for the great sex. After all, you have to start somewhere."

"I think after last night's disaster of a date, I'd be better off being alone," Lynn said, but her insides sank at the prospect. Unfortunately, now that her hormones at least entertained the idea of getting lucky, it would be pretty hard to shut them off.

Tory shook her head in disagreement. "Oh no, you don't get to give up that easy. I think there's hope for you. Besides, work is getting predictable. I need a new project."

"I am not a project," Lynn huffed.

"Nope. you're not. You're great the way you are. But getting you laid is one."

Lynn shook her head, and Tory laughed. "Don't worry. Next time we'll do a double date. This way when one of them starts reciting the kings of England or something like that we can figure out an escape plan."

"It's a deal," Lynn said after only a moment's hesitation. Tory insisted on shaking on it and Lynn wondered just what she had gotten herself into.

Chapter 13

Lynn flipped over the chart, and then stacked it at the nurse's station. It was almost lunchtime, she thought, checking her watch, though there was no need for that since her stomach growled as well, clearly telling her it was time for a sandwich. She usually brought her lunch but today she hadn't planned that far ahead. Luckily, it was a nice day out, the patient load was manageable, and there should be more than enough time for her to run out and grab something.

She pulled on her cozy fleece and was out the door, debating whether or not she should take her car in order to save time or walk into town for the fresh air and exercise. Fresh air and exercise were about to win out when out of the corner of her eye she saw the side door of the building swing open and a familiar figure step out.

"I need to speak you," she said, going right up to Jackson. He was dressed again in a suit, and Lynn wondered if he ever took it off. Everything about him screamed expensive, from the crisp white French cuffs that shot through the dark charcoal pinstripe jacket to the discrete yet elegant print on his tie. His blond hair was neatly combed in place and his blue eyes were their usual icy blue.

He carried a simple leather suitcase, and if he seemed embarrassed to see her, he hid it well. Remembering that he had been the one who'd made an ass of himself, and that she was clearly the wronged party, helped her maintain her sense of outrage.

"You?" It wasn't exactly a question, more an intonation of mild surprise.

"Yes, me. I work here, remember?"

"Of course." Jackson shifted from one foot to another and actually checked his watch.

"Am I keeping you from something?" she asked in what she hoped was a sardonic tone. How dare he try to blow her off?

"In fact, I do have an appointment."

"Of course," Lynn said, and Jackson started to walk. She decided to follow. Time was, after all, of the essence. "Then I'll be brief."

A sound which may have been a stifled laugh came from him. Determined, she ignored it. There was a lot more at stake here than her wounded pride. She just needed to remember that she was a grownup too, a smart, savvy career woman.

"Did you know that last year the clinic saw over two thousand patients and prevented about five hundred unnecessary trips to the emergency room? As you might imagine, a trip to the emergency room is quite costly, but a lot of people without access to a regular doctor head there first. However, a place like the clinic you're going to shut down offers affordable medical care for those without a regular doctor and also cuts down on those emergency room visits, thereby saving everyone time and money."

Lynn glanced back at Jackson. She had decided that turning her case into a numbers game would be the right way to go. After all, if he was all business then he might be persuaded more by hard facts and statistics than an impassioned plea. His face was set, unreadable, but she saw him working his jaw.

She was walking as quickly as she could but his long legs were eating up the distance to the small parking lot where his car must be parked. Still, she managed to throw in a few more selling points about the importance of the clinic to the town. Unfortunately, all too soon they were at a car. It was a sedan, not a sports car, like she had expected, but a luxury model nonetheless. Next to it, her well-worn Subaru with its roof racks looked like the vehicle of a modern-day hippie. She made a mental note, telling herself that it might be time to take off some of the bumper stickers on her car.

"Well then, Miss Masters…"

"Technically, it's Doctor," Lynn corrected him. Usually she didn't care about a thing like titles. Half the time her patients assumed she was a candy striper, since she had what most of them nicely called a baby face. But with Jackson, she had a feeling that titles mattered.

"Well then, Doctor. I am sorry to say that this is really a straightforward business deal. Mr. Petersen has to sell the building to handle some cash flow issues. I am sure you can find another location."

"Not for what we pay in rent! Not to mention the location is ideal," Lynn burst out as Jackson reached for the handle of his car door.

They were almost toe to toe, and Lynn realized that Jackson, despite the fact that she had never seen him with a real smile, was handsome, if you went for the perfect hair, the white teeth, straight nose, and sculpted cheekbones type of thing. Lynn usually didn't she told herself, but right now, standing this close to him, she was starting to forget the reasons why she liked her men a little rougher around the edges.

They both reached for the door at the same time, Lynn to stop him from going, he to open it. She realized what she was doing and pulled back, her hand brushing against his arm. No, it wasn't quite a spark, she thought. More like a chill. Yes. Definitely a chill, she thought, looking into his frosty eyes. It couldn't possibly be her hormones talking. Jackson Sanders was so definitely not her type. And shouldn't be her type. From what Tory had told her, he had some serious issues, the kind that probably couldn't be fixed easily. And she was not supposed to be in the doctor mode where her love—make that her *sex*—life was concerned.

"And that is exactly the problem. Petersen was too soft, never raising the rents. On most of his properties. And now he's paying the price. Look, I don't make the rules."

"You just break them," Lynn said, wondering how she had, even for a moment, thought that Jackson was the least bit attractive.

"No, actually I like to think I play by them. It's a game you see. And I play to win."

"Good luck with that, especially seeing as how when you win just about everyone else loses." Lynn knew she sounded like a kid in the midst of a temper tantrum.

"Always a pleasure," Jackson said, wrenching the door open, the expression on his face showing it was anything but.

Chapter 14

Jackson's appointment could wait. In truth, he was interviewing a graphic designer and she had suggested lunch. He wondered if she asked for a lunch meeting with all of her potential clients or if it was something she only did with unattached male ones.

He shook his head as he drove. He needed to stop being so cynical about people's motives. It was a business lunch, a chance to get out and meet people. Standard operating procedure in the professional world. When had he become so jaded? He almost laughed at that. The answer was right there. It had been Ashley's death that had made him realize there were no happy endings.

His car seemed to have a mind of its own as it took him to the spot. He could have turned around, deliberately gone the other way, but he didn't, letting the car drive almost automatically to the faintly marked turnoff.

He turned the car into the small clearing and stopped. Ahead of him lay a rough path, almost too narrow to be called a road. If he had a 4x4 or a truck, he would have plowed through, but it wasn't worth the risk of getting stuck in his sedan.

He got out, shut the door, and was amazed by the quiet. Or as quiet as it could be with the sound of birdsong, the wind whispering in the trees, and the distant but steady beat of the breakers against the rocks.

It was overgrown, but you could clearly see the imprint of the path that wound its way under the canopy of trees and bushes. There was an empty beer bottle tossed to the side, along with a shoe, just one. Evidence that some people still knew about it.

He took a deep breath, wondering why he had come. To say goodbye? Or to say hello. He supposed most people would have gone to her grave to do that, but here he was, at Deadman's Bend—his and Ashley's own private version of Lover's Lane.

Carefully, he pushed aside a prickly bramble and continued along. The tall grass was matted down, but not worn bare. The trail was lightly used, he supposed, which was just as it should be. Who knew what stories the kids of Queensbay had spun about this place after Ashley had died?

Sunlight dappled through the branches and lit the way. Already he could see a round circle of blue ahead of him. He walked straight on until the tunnel of woods opened up and he stood on a bluff, high above the Sound. He could see far to the east from here, almost out to the ocean and across all the way to Long Island. It was a clear, brilliant fall day, the sun warm on his face.

Much like the last time he had been here. Ashley had asked him to meet her. It was the weekend, and he was home from his job in the city, staying with his brother. She was home too, of course, since she had gotten a position coaching at the junior high. He should have been suspicious, wondering why she was free on a fall weekend afternoon when she should have been at a game.

He had met her, again not thinking there was anything odd in the fact that she hadn't wanted to drive together. All the signs had been there, but he had been blind, hadn't he? He had grabbed a bottle of wine, some glasses, and a blanket, thinking that perhaps they might spend a lazy afternoon together. Because both of their schedules were so busy, time together had been hard to come by and he had been hungry for her.

She had already said yes to his marriage proposal, and though he had been nervous, determined to make sure everything about the event went perfectly, he hadn't doubted her ultimate answer. They were meant to be. And they had a plan. He would work in the city for a year, maybe two at the most, getting the experience he wanted, and then he would come back to Queensbay and go into business with Jake.

He and Ash would get married and they'd have kids. Not too soon, of course, since he wanted to enjoy being just with her, but he definitely wanted a family. Evenings on the boat, fishing, swimming, barbequing. Everything had been mapped out. He couldn't have been happier. But then she had talked about different things, wanting to travel, to have adventures. And he had changed his dreams; they had started to make different plans, her plans. And he thought she was happy again.

Then he had seen her, waiting there, in jeans and shirt, standing on the edge of the bluff, too close, like she always did, risking everything. Her long blond hair danced in the wind and he wanted to call her to him; but he enjoyed her beauty, savoring every line of her tall, powerful body, just watching her, wondering how such a wild and untamable creature could be his.

Because Ash had been that. She had turned down every boy in Queensbay High when they asked her for a date, until he had finally screwed up the courage and asked her, the day after the baseball team had won the state championships. He had been riding high on his MVP status and thought the world owed him. So he had tested his luck that day and asked her out.

It seemed too good to be true; and it was. He'd been too blind to see that Ashley was using him to make another guy jealous. Maybe that's because he had fallen for her, hard. But she had finally succumbed to his unwavering love. They became inseparable. Ashley became his world, and she needed him because, while she might have appeared like she had it all together on the outside, on the inside she needed him. Needed him to take care of her, to assure her he loved her, to keep her from doing wild things. It had become his mission to keep her safe, to talk her out of her wild, unpredictable moods.

Now, of course, he realized what Ashley had been doing. Creating dramatic situations so that she was the center of them and then demanding attention, energy from everyone, just to fuel her own ego. He'd just been the only one stupid enough to buy into it for as long as he had.

He had known it deep down, recognized it, even as he enabled it because in spite of it all, she was still his Ashley. He hoped that once they were married she would feel safe and secure, that she wouldn't need to be so wild. But even when she turned to him, he still didn't know, didn't understand the expression on her face.

She told him the engagement was off and that she had no intention of living in a small town for the rest of her life, to be saddled with kids, to be stuck with him. She told him she wanted to see places, travel, have adventures.

At first he had begged, told her they could hold off on getting married, that they didn't need to live in Queensbay, that they could do whatever she wanted. Even as he said those words to her, he hated himself for it. And then she delivered the deathblow: she threw Tucker Wolff in his face. Tucker had been the reason she'd said yes to Jackson all the years ago. She had wanted to make him jealous. Jackson had long ago stopped counting Tucker as a threat. As he and Ashley had moved on and upward, through school and college, making plans, Tucker had stayed behind in Queensbay, gaining a reputation as the town bad boy.

Apparently, while Jackson hadn't thought about Tucker in years, Ashley had. More than thought about him apparently. And that was all it had taken. He told her to keep the ring, and walked away, angry, pride hurt but with an overwhelming sense of relief. Ashley had set him free.

Jackson brought himself back to the present, found himself standing on the edge of the cliff, looking down to the rocky beach below. He swallowed and took a step back. He was used to heights—if you helped build skyscrapers you had to be—but there was no sense in tempting fate by standing on the crumbling edge of a sandy bluff.

The last time he had spoken to her in person had been here. A seagull wheeled and turned on the current above him. A light chop rippled the surface of the Sound. He swallowed. He was here and he felt what...nothing. Not her presence. She didn't haunt this place for him.

No, it was just the wind, the water, the ground. A beautiful place, one of his favorites. But she did not haunt him and he was glad. If he was going to stay in Queensbay, he needed it to be his town. Not theirs. He swallowed, taking a deep cleansing breath of the salt air.

"I forgive you Ashley," he said and the words came out aloud. He hadn't said it before. He'd been so angry with her. Because even after death, just when he thought he was free, she had reached back and pulled him into her drama. He'd done the right thing by Ashley and her family, let them take their grief and anger out on him. He hadn't thought that his decision, what had seemed so noble at the time, would turn the whole town against him. He thought if he kept the breakup quiet, kept what had really happened the night of the accident to himself, that the Morans would be spared embarrassment and pain. He would have to play the grieving fiancé for a while but then it would be over. He would be free. It just hadn't worked out that way.

He couldn't complain. Life had been good to him, professionally, financially, and he had learned an important life lesson early. Ashley had taught him one thing he wouldn't ever forget. Love was a trap. You got so consumed, lost in it, you were bound to lose yourself. So no, in some respects everyone was right. Jackson Sanders wouldn't fall in love again; but not because of Ashley, but because he was smart enough to know that love wasn't enough.

Chapter 15

Lynn took a sip of her coffee, letting the hot liquid slide down her throat. She had to be at work in just moments, but really there was nothing like a cup of Darby's coffee, even if she had to take it in a to-go cup. She decided she wanted it with just a touch more cream so she stopped at the milk and sugar station, took the lid off, and topped off her cup until the liquid turned into a frothy caramel color. She inhaled, the scent of fresh coffee and sweet, rich baked goods filling her nostrils. Darby should think about bottling it, the scent of The Golden Pear, and selling it.

She heard the door open, but didn't look up, but she felt the air in the room change as the general hum of conversation died down. Curious, she turned and looked. Jackson Sanders, in a business suit, polished shoes, and even more polished shoes, stood at the glass countertop carefully perusing the selection of pastries while just about every other person in the café stared at him, in utter silence.

As if sensing the attention directed at him, Jackson slowly turned around. His eyes were hooded and his expression grim. He stood though, with his feet spread wide apart, his arms at his side. All Lynn could think was that it was a fighting stance.

Jackson's eyes scanned the tables, looking at each and every person, nodding at some people, who stony-faced, didn't nod back. His eyes flicked up once to take in Lynn, and there was just the barest hint of recognition there and then he kept up his survey of the room.

The girl behind the counter, not Darby, was fresh-faced and young and stood in silence too, but hers was born out of uncertainty, just as Lynn's was. Just what in the hell was going on? Did everyone think Jackson was a cad for shutting down the clinic? Tory had said he'd had a reputation as a hard ass, an arrogant prick, but seriously, the public silent treatment—that was just weird.

Lynn swallowed, and she was moving before she had even thought about it, to stand next to Jackson, and pointing to something, anything in the case, "The croissants are delicious," she said, even though she hadn't had one. She was making an educated guess, everything was good here, but there was no way she could let Jackson stand in silence and not do anything.

He smiled, a half smile, rueful, and he gave her a curt nod. She could see his body was rigid with tension.

The door from the kitchen swung open and Darby herself appeared, the white apron straining across her belly. Her green eyes roved, quickly taking the measure of the situation.

"Jackson, how nice to see you. What can I get you?" Darby nudged the sales girl, who seemed to spring to life, blinking and holding up her tongs, ready to take the order.

Darby's eyes slid to Lynn and she gave a small, almost imperceptible nod. Behind them, the noise level slowly ratcheted up, though there were more than a few whispers and smothered exclamations. Beside her, Jackson's stiff demeanor relaxed fractionally and he inclined his head in Lynn's direction.

There was something in his eyes, something that made them look less icy and hard, and she accepted his silent thanks with a small nod of her own. She knew she should go now, that there was no reason to stay and that any longer and she was risking being late, very late to work.

"This doesn't change anything. I still think you shouldn't close the clinic down," she said as a parting shot. Jackson's eyes narrowed and seemed about to say something, but Lynn decided that it was as good a last word as she was going to get, and this time, as she spun on her heel to make an exit, nothing got in her way.

Outside, in the sun and the light breeze that was blowing off the harbor, she shrugged her shoulders; and sparing one more glance into the café, she headed off to work, while it was still there, wondering what in the hell that had been all about.

Chapter 16

"You're not so bad at this for a football player," Jackson told Jake.

Jake and Jackson were at the batting cages at Queensbay's newest sports complex. It was a huge, almost warehouse-like space that held almost every kind of sporting activity known to man, woman or child, including indoor soccer fields, batting cages, a rock-climbing wheel, a full gym, a yoga studio and even a laser tag arena for the kids.

Jackson had asked Jake if they could talk, and instead of suggesting coffee or lunch, Jake had said baseball. Jackson was happy to agree, and now he found himself facing balls being shot out at him at sixty miles an hour. It had taken a few rounds to get used to the feeling, but swinging the bat felt good, as good as it had felt in high school.

"Hey, I'm the star batter on the company softball team," Jake defended himself as he whacked another one.

"Aren't you the one who pays the team's salaries?" Jackson pointed out.

"They're still happy I'm playing."

It was Jackson's turn and he stepped up to the plate, readying his stance.

"You didn't ask me here to compliment me on my baseball skills, did you?" Jake said as he watched Jackson.

"No, not quite," Jackson admitted as his bat connected with the ball with a satisfying crack.

"Are you going to tell me why you're finally back in town? I mean, besides buying up even more property in Queensbay. I wish you'd leave some for the rest of us."

Jackson tensed. "I guess you spoke to Darby?"

Jake nodded. "I might have stopped by for a cup of coffee. Did the whole place really go silent?"

Jackson nodded. "I half expected them to start to chant something in a creepy whisper. It was eerie. No one said anything, I mean until…"

He stopped himself. What Lynn had done had been unexpected. And kind. Or maybe just ignorant. Maybe she had no idea why the whole town could hate him. She was a relative newcomer to town. Maybe the story of him and Ashley hadn't made it onto her radar yet. Of course, it was only a matter of time.

"Yeah, I heard Darby gave everyone a talking to after you left," Jake said.

Jackson swallowed. He'd have to thank Darby too. She'd been friendly with Ashley, but not once had she ever laid blame at his doorstep for what had happened, either then or now.

"I did have something I wanted to run by you," he said, deciding to change the subject.

"Ok. I'll listen." Jake, said promptly, being a good friend and not pushing the subject.

Jackson tensed. The idea was crazy, but it was important to him, something that he had realized as he built bigger and bigger buildings in places farther and farther away. He had often wondered why anyone would want to live in such places, had thought about all of the resources that were used to build them. And he knew there had to be a smarter, better way to do things. And that's what he wanted to do: build something that wasn't the tallest or the biggest; instead, he wanted to focus on something smarter, something that didn't rob the future to build it now.

"Green building."

Jake looked at him like he was crazy. "This is New England, Jax, not the tropics. People here go for more muted colors. You know, lots of whites, cream maybe."

"Not a green colored building. Green. As in environmentally friendly building practices. Solar power specifically. I think there's an opportunity here to help communities become more energy efficient."

Jake scratched his head. "This isn't the desert either. I know it's been a while since you weathered a New England winter, but for more than three months out of the year, we don't always get our fair share of the sun."

"It's a common misconception that you need year-round sun in order to use solar energy. In reality, solar panels are viable in just about any climate. Of course, they might not power your home or office building all year long, day in and day out, but even just a few solar panels can have a big impact. Or, even better than the roof of a house, let's say you have a big space, say like the roof of the parking garage at the mall...now there's space that just sits, useless old concrete. Why not turn it into a giant battery?"

Jake's arms were folded but he was leaning in and his eyes were narrowed, a sure sign he was interested. "You know, I've noticed a lot more of my customers asking about renewable and recycled materials when we're doing a job. I've even taken a couple of classes on green building so I can talk to clients better."

"It's a growing market opportunity—you can do good and make money at the same time. Don't you like the sound of that?"

Jake's eyes narrowed, in a considering look. "Of course I do. But what's in it for me?"

Jackson hefted the bat on his shoulder. "I figured I would be the sales and marketing guy. I have the deal with the manufacturer all lined up. But I don't have a crew ready to do the installs. But you might."

"So you want me to go into partnership with you—in this town?"

Jackson swallowed. This was the hard part. Years ago, that had been there plan; but then Ashley's death had made that impossible. Any association with Jackson might have sunk Jake. Jake had never said that, of course, but he must have known it.

"I know it's a lot to ask. I thought maybe it wouldn't be a big deal, but you were right, people in this town have a long memory."

"And I say screw them. I know one of the reasons you left was because you didn't want me to feel like I had to go into business with you. But I didn't care then and I don't now."

Jackson smiled in relief, felt his mood beginning to lighten. The reception he'd gotten at The Golden Pear had been much harsher than he expected. He'd been worried that Jake, being a smart businessman, would make the smart, businesslike decision and tell Jackson to go take a hike.

"I figured, I'll be out there, getting the word out, closing the deals, and then your construction crew can come in do the actual install. I can set them up with training and everything else you need. We can work out all the financial details as needed."

Jake nodded slowly, but Jackson knew he had him. Sure he could have gone through with his plan without Jake, but somehow it seemed right that they would do it together.

"Sounds like you have it all planned out. Got anyone willing to pay you for it?"

Jackson shrugged. "First client will be the Osprey Arms Hotel, of course. I convinced Chase to build in a solar powered roof. I figured that will make a powerful statement and be good advertising. Plus I hear the university is thinking of breaking ground on a new science and technology center."

Jake dropped his voice. "That's supposed to be hush-hush. But everyone knows, and all the construction companies are trying to get a piece of it. It's a big job. Why would they consider you?"

Jake's tone was friendly, curious, and Jackson felt the tension in his shoulders ease. Jake may not have officially said yes, but he was on board.

"I have an in. Not a guaranteed one, but the project manager is someone I know, used to work with. The university is apparently very open to the renewable energy idea and this guy has put in a good word for me, good enough so that I've scored a meeting with the planning board next week. But it sure would help my case if I could tell them I was a real company with installation capabilities and not just one man in a suit."

"Guess reports of your international playboy status were greatly exaggerated. You must have actually been learning something out there," Jake said, a smile creasing his tanned face.

"So you're in?"

Jake nodded. "I'm in. But as you said, it's a long shot." He paused and Jackson waited. "What if it doesn't pan out? Are you just going to pick up and go again? Because I won't give you a third chance."

Jackson shook his head, knowing that Jake meant what he said. "I knew it wasn't going to be easy, but I will stick it out here, no matter what it takes, no matter how hard it is. It's my town too."

"I can count on you?" Jake said, and Jackson knew all that was implied in that simple question.

"You can count on me."

Jake smiled and said, "Well shit and hot damn! How do we get started?"

Jackson let out the breath he didn't know he was holding. "I had a lawyer draw up some paperwork, about forming a partnership. I'll have him send it over for you to look at."

"Alrighty then. There's just one more thing. What are we going to name it?"

"Sanders and Owen Construction?"

Jake smiled, "I don't know, Owen-Sanders sounds more official, don't you think?"

Jackson laughed and almost could have hugged Jake through the mesh of the batting cage.

"We'll flip a coin, ok?"

Jake stuck his hand out and Jackson came outside the cage and shook it.

"Of course, now all you have to do is figure out how to convince the clinic to go quietly and you should be all set."

"I don't have to convince them of anything. I have the paperwork that says they have to be out," Jackson said stubbornly. If he wasn't going to back down in the face of town gossip, he wasn't going to back down on a business deal either. He had to be strong on both fronts if this was going to work out.

Jake shook his head and was about to say something when both their sets eyes were drawn to someone just entering the building.

Jackson watched as an all-too-familiar figure, striding with purpose and a bounce in her step, brunette ponytail swinging behind, passed them without seeing them and headed into the long corridor that separated the batting cages from the rest of the gym.

Jake gave him an enquiring look. "Speak of the devil. Perhaps you should see if you're more convincing this time around. Maybe the clinic will go quietly."

"No way," Jackson said, trying to keep the panic out of his voice. He didn't need another run in with Lynn Masters, especially not today. Every time he saw her, he came off looking like a heel. Jackson had never flinched in a business negotiation. His projects always came in on time and on budget. If he needed to be a hard ass, then so be it. It was one of the reasons why he'd been so successful so quickly. He had to remember that there was nothing personal in this. The building was his to do with as he damned well pleased, and he didn't need to be swayed by a bleeding heart doctor. And he didn't owe her anything for what she'd done at The Golden Pear.

All of that flashed through his mind before he realized just what Jake had in mind.

"Don't even think about it," he warned his friend.

But Jake just smiled and called out, "Hey, Lynn. How ya doing?"

Lynn, because it really was her, stopped, hesitated as if with indecision, then turned slowly around. She looked over at them and Jackson knew that she had seen them when she first walked in and had been doing her best to ignore them.

Now she looked at them both and finally said, in what Jackson knew was a deliberately cool voice, "Hello, Jake."

To Jackson, she only nodded before turning and heading in her original direction.

"Wow, you must really have pissed her off. I've never seen her not say hello to someone. Usually she's handing out hugs and lollipops as well," Jake said, his voice showing his amusement.

"Glad you're having some fun at my expense," Jackson said as he quelled the urge to slug his friend with the bat; instead, hefted it and stepped into the batting cage. His one thought was that perhaps Lynn had heard the story and realized she'd taken the wrong side the other day. No wonder she had looked right through him.

"Don't worry, the fun's just begun," Jake said with a laugh, and after a moment, Jackson joined in. It was good to be back home, even if his re-entry plans were not running quite as smoothly as he had hoped.

Chapter 17

"Phoebe!" Lynn cried out, opening the door to her apartment and wrapping her friend in a hug. "When did you get back?"

"A couple of hours ago," Phoebe said, her voice muffled by Lynn's arms. "Wow, I think you got stronger."

"Sorry, I didn't mean to swarm you. It's just that I missed you," Lynn said and realized that she had. Phoebe looked good, relaxed, and rested, with her summer tan still in place and her long blond hair pulled back in a loose chignon. She moved further into Lynn's apartment, an elegant vision in a flowing, floaty linen top paired with a long, clingy skirt.

"I missed you too. I have presents, so pour me a glass of wine," Phoebe said.

Lynn smiled, all of a sudden feeling less tired. The whispers were flying furiously at the clinic about the imminent closing and one nurse had already announced her resignation, saying she had found another job. Lynn had thought a workout at the gym after work would make her feel better, but seeing Jackson had only put her in a sour frame of mind.

Phoebe took a look around and tsk-tsked. "Wow, I'd like to say I love what you've done with the place, but I don't think anything's changed. Except maybe that mountain of magazines has grown."

"You were only gone three weeks. I'm busy," Lynn said. "But," and it was hard to keep the note of pride out of her voice, "I did what you said. I've been buying all those magazines about houses and marking the things I like, you know to help me find out my personal style."

So far, Lynn had only invested in a couch, low slung, slightly modern, in a neutral gray color, her a mattress and bed frame, a TV, and a couple of stools for the bar. Her clothes fit easily into the walk-in closet, so she hadn't even bought a dresser yet. The apartment was a basic white on white theme and while she knew a little color would be a good idea, she was enjoying the clean, clutter-free lines of it. For her, less was definitely more, but she wouldn't object to some pictures, bookshelves, and a knickknack or two.

Phoebe cocked an eyebrow at her and her eyes twinkled as she walked over to the pile of pages Lynn had torn out. She flipped through them, and Lynn waited in silence, finally deciding since it was her house that she could take off her grimy sneakers and shed the top layer of her workout clothes. She walked into her bedroom, dumped her clothes in the laundry hamper and found her favorite slippers, soft and lined with lamb's wool, put them on, and then threw on a clean t-shirt.

As she returned, Phoebe looked up and said, "Your style is kind of all over the place."

Lynn sighed. "I know. I can't decide if I like modern, or beachy, or country cottage. There's nothing ugly in those magazines, which I guess is kind of the point."

Phoebe pursed her lips. "You're definitely not country cottage. You're too simple for that."

"Excuse me," Lynn said as she went over to one of her cabinets and pulled out two juice glasses. She hadn't gotten around to finishing all of her shopping yet.

"I mean your personal style, your method of being, is simple. You care too much about and for other people to really focus on things. But it's not like you're Zen-like about it. You have too much energy and passion for that. But I don't ever see you collecting a bunch of things for the sake of it."

Lynn frowned, but she could see what Phoebe was saying. "I guess I'm more into experiences than things. You know, a great hike or good climb. An exciting vacation. A great run. A ski slope. Those memories get me more jazzed than any one thing."

Phoebe nodded, pondering. "You like old movies and books, but I don't see you as a collector of those since you have everything on your e-reader. You're a health nut, too, so you have all of that sports equipment."

Lynn laughed. "In my case, for the hiking and climbing, it's called gear. And like you suggested, I left most of it at my parents since I don't have a lot of storage space."

"Hmm," Phoebe said as she took the glass of wine Lynn handed her. She picked up the collection of magazine sheets and Lynn watched as she flipped through them again, deftly sorting them into separate stacks.

"What are you doing?" Lynn asked.

"You'll see. How's your new project at the clinic?" Phoebe asked.

Lynn sighed. "I think it's DOA. So much for making a difference." Phoebe had cheered her on through every stage of Healthy Kids Now, even encouraging Lynn to think up some sort of catchy nickname. Lynn didn't know if the name was catchy, but it had certainly made it more real to put a title to it.

"What do you mean? I think it's a great idea. Childhood health and wellness is such an important issue. I thought you had all the support you needed." Phoebe's wide blue eyes were clouded with concern.

"I did. That's not the problem. The problem is the clinic may not be around much longer."

Phoebe looked up from her sorting. "What are you talking about?"

"Two words," Lynn said. "Jackson Sanders."

"The elusive, ruthless, and enigmatic Jackson," Phoebe said. "Not even his own brother can explain him to me. Do tell."

So Lynn told and Phoebe nodded along.

"Chase told me about what happened to Jackson's fiancée," Phoebe said. "I guess it really tore him up. Chase isn't one to talk about things like that, but I can sense that Jackson's never really been the same since then."

Lynn took a moment to wonder what the old Jackson could have been like. Happy, carefree, a shorts and flip-flop-wearing beach bum? Somehow she didn't quite buy it. Jackson looked as if he'd been born in one of those expensive suits.

"Are you sure he won't change his mind? I mean, I know Jackson's not the friendliest person but shutting down the clinic, that's cold."

Lynn could only shrug in answer.

They had moved to the couch and were sitting facing each other, knees drawn up, bare feet tucked underneath. Despite the subject matter, Lynn was glad that Phoebe was home, here to speak with.

"What will you do?" Phoebe asked.

"I guess find another job," Lynn said, though in truth she wasn't so worried about that. There would probably be a space at the hospital, at least initially, and there were usually openings in private practices. But it was the loss of the opportunity to pioneer her Healthy Kids Now program that was gnawing at her.

She'd made a lot of progress already, collected a lot of data and worked one on one with dozens of kids. And she was starting to make a difference. Already some of her kids had lost weight, taken up a sport, started to do better in school. And best of all, they all felt great about themselves, filled with pride that they could make a difference in their own lives. But without the clinic she didn't know how she would keep the program going.

"What are you more upset about?" Phoebe asked after a moment.

"What do you mean?"

"The loss of the clinic or the fact that you won't get to work with all those kids?"

Lynn didn't hesitate. "The kids. I mean the clinic is great, but there are other places people can go for care. The hospital for one, or some of the other clinics in the area. A lot of them are in newer buildings, with better facilities."

"So maybe you're focusing on the wrong thing, if it's not the clinic that matters most to you," Phoebe suggested.

"And maybe you're taking his side because he's going to be your brother-in-law?" Lynn suggested, but without any anger.

"I don't feel there are sides here; but in any case, it doesn't seem to me like Jackson would care what I think. I have a feeling Jackson does what Jackson wants. But you," Phoebe fixed Lynn with a steady gaze, "surely, if you wanted to you could figure something out. You're a resourceful, successful, savvy woman."

Lynn sighed. "So I keep telling myself."

"What does that mean?" Phoebe laughed.

"I can't seem to have a successful date, my apartment looks like a dorm room, and every time I'm in front of Jackson I wind up looking like an idiot." The last part was out of her mouth before she could stop herself.

Phoebe's eyebrows rose and she sent Lynn a knowing look. "Interesting. I've never known you to care about how you appear to other people. Usually, you're not above strong-arming them into helping you with whatever cause you're working on."

"Apparently, Jackson is immune to strong-arming," Lynn muttered, deciding that she definitely wasn't ready to admit to Phoebe that she found her future brother-in-law attractive. A jerk, true, but an attractive one.

Phoebe reached out and patted Lynn's knee. "Well, there's one thing I can help you with. And that's your apartment. Here…" She picked up a sheaf of magazine pages. "I separated them into three different styles I think you'll like. All you need to do is pick the one you like best and then we can go shopping."

"Ok. I guess one out of three isn't bad," Lynn said, deciding that shopping might be just the thing to distract her from thinking about the way Jackson's shoulders looked in a pinstripe suit.

Chapter 18

"What the hell is going on in here?" Jackson looked up from the plans he had spread out on the desk to see his brother Chase, holding a six-pack and standing in the doorway of the top floor of Jackson's new building.

"And it's good to see you too," Jackson said, tossing down his pencil.

"Come here, little brother. You, back in Queensbay. I've been waiting years for this. Each summer I'd hope that you would come back, that we'd take the boat out for a spin. But each time, September would come around and we never get our sail in."

Chase, his big brother, grabbed him in a giant bear hug. Chase was shorter by a hair but more solidly built, a point he could never help but emphasize whenever he got the chance. Jackson relaxed, let Chase get his hug in, and then breathed again when his brother let him go.

"There was the time we met up in Norway and sailed the fjords. That was pretty spectacular," Jackson pointed out, though it had been cold enough to freeze the pickled herrings.

"True, but even here it's not too late. We still have a few good weeks of boating weather left," Chase said, his eyes flashing with eagerness. Jackson shook his head, knew that if Chase had the chance he'd be out on his boat all year round.

"We'll see. We have a lot to get started on," Jackson pointed out.

Chase held up his hand. "That stuff can wait. I still can't believe you're here on home soil."

"Don't get all misty eyed. Did you and Phoebe have a nice trip?"

"Couldn't have been better. Almost convinced her to elope with me on the shores of a beach in Indonesia, but I figured Mom and Dad would kill me. And Phoebe didn't want to disappoint all of her friends. We're planning something for the spring, maybe at the hotel, maybe at The Ivy House. Depends on how many people we invite."

"Don't you mean 'you,' not 'we?'" Jackson said. His brother collected friends the way other people collected lint in their pockets. If Chase was going to throw a party, there was a good chance he'd invite the whole town.

Chase rubbed his short, dark hair and looked a little sheepish. "Should I be blamed for wanting everyone to see how great she is?"

Jackson shook his head. Phoebe was smart, talented, and beautiful. And she happened to be the granddaughter of Savannah Ryan, a famous movie actress who had once had an affair with Jackson and Chase's grandfather. It had been quite the scandal a generation ago and hadn't exactly ended happily. But Chase and Phoebe had somehow managed to defy the odds and seemed truly happy. It made Jackson wonder if sometimes fate really did smile on some people.

"I would feel the same way if I were you."

"You know you'll be my best man. You and Noah, of course. I figured the women get to have all those bridesmaids, so I can have my brother and my best friend up there with me."

Jackson shook his head. "I can't believe you of all people are settling down. I mean, if anyone would have said to me that you would find *the one*, I wouldn't have believed it."

Chase laughed. "It's like role reversal. I'm the guy looking to settle down, and from what I hear you've been dating your way across the seven continents."

There was a pause. "Hell, I didn't mean it that way, Jax. I know if what happened to Ash…" Chase trailed off and Jackson waved his hand. Chase had been there for him, tried to get him to talk about it, but after being shot down so many times, usually knew better than to say anything about it.

"Hey, it's the past. Besides, I couldn't let you have all the fun. And now that you're off the market, just means there's more left for me."

Chase laughed with him. The lie slipped off of Jackson's tongue easily enough, but he could see Chase wasn't quite satisfied. Truth was he envied Chase, just as he knew that he couldn't go down the same path. Jackson knew he could never love like that again, never get so caught up in someone else that he forgot himself. Nope, he'd leave love to the stronger men of the world.

"I like what you've done with the place," Chase said, pointing to the hole in the wall.

"I decided I was ready start on the remodel," Jackson said and hoped that Chase wouldn't ask him more about his thoughts on relationships. In truth, after seeing Lynn at the gym, he had had felt the need to destroy something and decided that now was as good a time as any to start on the demolition part of his planned remodel.

"I can see that," Chase said, setting down the beer on the large piece of plywood set across two sawhorses, which was currently serving as a desk, worktable, and everything else in the place. An old boom box sat in the corner next to a large, super bright light. The radio was on the local classic rock station.

"I'll take one of those," Jackson told Chase, gesturing toward the six-pack. Without saying anything, Chase popped the tops off of two bottles and passed one over.

"You know, Jake could send a crew over here to do this for you."

"Feels good to take a swing at it." He looked over at the wall which was partially down.

"Hell yeah," Chase said, putting down his bottle and picking up the sledgehammer, hefting it in his hands. "Just tell me where."

Jackson indicated a stretch of the thin dividing wall he had started on, and Chase lifted the hammer, readied his stance, and swung a blow. There was a satisfying crunch as the thin materials crumbled against the onslaught.

Chase took a few more whacks and then stopped, looking at him. "So what is this all about? Why now? You stay away for years and now you're back?"

Jackson said nothing, just glanced down at the plans he had spread on his makeshift desk.

"I heard the Morans are selling their house, moving. Is that it? Is it because her parents won't be here anymore? You know they almost got divorced, but I hear they're giving it another chance and want a fresh start."

"I did hear that," Jackson acknowledged. "Mom told me. You know, even though she doesn't live in town anymore, she still manages to keep up on what's happening." Jackson ran a hand over his hair. "And maybe that was some of it. But finally, it was just time to come back."

Chase looked at him. "I always thought there was something you didn't tell me. I know you weren't there that night, cause you were crashed on the couch in the basement. You got that phone call and you left. And then you asked me to not say anything."

"I never asked you to lie for me," Jackson said.

"I would have," Chase shot back.

Jackson knew. He nodded.

"You weren't there, were you? With her when she died?"

Jackson didn't say anything, but he should have known Chase would have guessed the truth, or close enough to it.

"I was at the hospital," Jackson said, clinging to the one bit of truth among the lies.

"But there was no way you were driving that car, was there?"

When Jackson said nothing, Chase just shook his head, "Man, she sucked you into her drama one last time didn't she?"

Jackson knew his brother had never been a fan of Ashley, but after Jackson had kicked his ass over it one too many times, Chase had learned to keep his opinions to himself.

Jackson felt his pulse speed up, "You can't…"

"I can. She's dead but even when she was alive, Ashley Moran had her claws into you so deep and your head spinning you didn't know which way was up. I've known you all my life and I know what you were like before she walked into your life when you were sixteen. She said jump and you said how high."

Jackson didn't say anything, couldn't because it had been true. He had fallen under Ashley's spell until the very end, until faced with a truth not even he could ignore. Still, a promise was a promise.

"Well, now she's gone. I'm here—back, because I wanted to be, I'm ready to start over."

"Are you? Don't get me wrong. I want you here, more than anything. I just want to make sure you're not going to disappear on me, ok?"

"I told you, I'm here," Jackson said, one last time and knew it was true. He wouldn't let anything drive him away from his home again.

Chase, too, seemed relieved. "Well then, why don't we get started on getting you a real place to work." He hefted the sledgehammer again and aimed at the wall. Before he swung though, he turned and looked at Jackson. "By the way, why are you so eager to kick the clinic out? And aren't you letting the psychic stay? Seems like your priorities are all wrong."

Jackson gritted his teeth. He had made his decision and to back down now would only make him look weak. The clinic would have to go if only to prove that he,

Jackson Sanders, was a force to be reckoned with, not just Chase's baby brother.

"My building, my rules," Jackson said.

Chase shrugged. "Sure whatever you say. Though you know the clinic serves an important function providing important care..."

Jackson wondered just how many people the good Dr. Lynn Masters had given that speech to. His brother seemed to have it memorized.

"She's gotten to you too?"

"What, who? Lynn?" Chase smiled. "Quite the little spitfire, isn't she? Have you met her? You're staying next door to her, you know."

Jackson took the sledgehammer from his brother's hand, spread his feet, and swung. The walls trembled and a large hole bloomed from the impact. He handed the sledgehammer back to his brother, went over to the radio, and cranked up the volume.

Chase smiled but got the picture. The subject of Lynn Masters was officially closed, at least for now.

Chapter 19

"Thank you for meeting me." Lynn didn't know why she suddenly felt shy but she did as Caitlyn Montgomery Randall, looking luminous after having given birth just a few weeks ago, strode forward and shook Lynn's hand. Caitlyn was wearing a stylish dress and heels, and Lynn wished that she'd had something more dazzling to wear. She had scrounged together a pair of black slacks, a silk blouse with a small stain that she hoped wasn't noticeable, and her one pair of serviceable pumps for this meeting, trying for what she hoped was a grownup, 'I'm a professional' trust me look.

"My pleasure. I was delighted when you called. It's never too early to start planning for the future. But come, let's go to the conference room so we can talk."

The offices of Queensbay Capital were in a four-story building set back on the hillside that led out of town, one that looked ordinary enough from the outside. However, once you stepped off the elevator and onto the main floor, Lynn could feel the energy.

The whole office was light and bright, not what Lynn expected from an investment firm where people took money seriously. She had thought there would be lots of dark wood and old men in suits. Instead, most of the staff seemed on the younger side, and though there were plenty of suits, there was nothing stodgy about them. Colorful art, many of them waterscapes with a modernist touch, lined the wall, and instead of old-fashioned polished mahogany desks, they were all light blond wood or glass and metal contraptions.

There were tablets and sleek computers and there was just enough bustle going around in the air to make the place seem vibrant and electric.

Caitlyn, not slowing down at all, led her into a glass-walled conference room where a bank of windows commanded a distant view of the harbor.

"Thank you for seeing me on such short notice."

"Always a pleasure, Lynn. I hear that you took a permanent job at the clinic. How wonderful."

Caitlyn Montgomery Randall was a few years older than Lynn and had grown up in Queensbay. She was married to Noah Randall, a technology entrepreneur, who had also grown up in town. Now, she ran a successful investment firm, while her husband advised other start-ups. They'd just had a beautiful baby boy, Lucas, and they lived in a beautiful house on one of the bluffs that ringed the harbor. Lynn had been there once for a cocktail party, a fundraiser for the hospital. You could have hated them for their obvious happiness and good fortune, but you wouldn't. They were generous to a fault, and Caitlyn was vivacious and striking so that you couldn't help but be drawn into her orbit.

"Thank you." Lynn felt a moment of guilt. Caitlyn had offered to help Lynn get started investing when she was ready and Lynn had used that as a pretext for this meeting. Still, that wasn't the reason Lynn had come, instead hoping that Caitlyn's reputation as a philanthropist might serve her instead.

"I imagine this isn't quite a social call or a let's set up an IRA account type of visit." Caitlyn looked at her shrewdly, one eyebrow raised above her luminous gray eyes.

"Not exactly." Lynn felt a sense of relief that she wouldn't have to beat around the bush. "I am so sorry to bother you, but I couldn't think of anyone else who might be able to help. See, we're also under a time crunch. At the clinic, I mean; and I need your advice."

"What sort of time crunch?" Caitlyn asked.

"The landlord wants us out."

"Duane Peterson is kicking you out?" Her voice was filled with surprise.

"It's the new landlord. Jackson Sanders."

Caitlyn's face registered surprise. "He bought the building?" Her face turned serious. "I hadn't heard that."

"I think it was the first thing he did when he got here. I think Chase is pretty surprised too."

"Aren't we all," Caitlyn said in a low voice, almost to herself. Lynn wondered if Caitlyn's bewilderment had something to do with what Tory had told her about Jackson's fiancée.

She looked up, shaken out of her thoughts. "But I don't see how I can help with that."

"It's your advice I need. See, it's not so much the clinic I am worried about. I'm sure we're already looking for some new space, but it's about my program—Healthy Kids Now."

Caitlyn nodded. "I remember you mentioning it."

"I wanted to formalize it, set it up as a real program, not a business necessarily but maybe more like a charity. I have some money to start up with, and now that I've had some success, I want to put together a real plan that can be used by other clinics and hospitals in the area."

"Sounds impressive."

"It's a start. Really, it's not so hard, knowing what to do. I mean the information is out there, but there's almost too much of it. I found when I started to give my patients—the kids and their parents—some simple guidelines, like just one or two behaviors to modify at a time, there was a much higher success rate than berating them on all the things they were doing wrong. Soon I was seeing more active, healthier kids. I was sort of just trying it out at the clinic, but I want it to be independent of it, so if the clinic closes all of the work I've done isn't for nothing."

Lynn realized she had been sitting on the edge of her chair, so excited to talk about her ideas that she couldn't relax.

"You sound like you have this all thought out," Caitlyn said.

Lynn leaned back a little in the comfortable leather chair, trying to appear professional. "Thought is just about all I've done." It had been Phoebe who had inspired her to take this next step, and together they had decided that Caitlyn was the perfect place to start.

Caitlyn leaned forward. "I like it. I think you're on to something. Of course, there would be some start-up costs, even if, as you said, you want to incorporate it as charity. Nothing too substantial, but you will need to make it official, and you'll need a lawyer. Don't worry, I know someone who will be very reasonable. I also know a woman who started a non-profit to make school lunches healthier. I'll give you her name too so you can chat. She'll have a lot more practical advice than I can give you. And of course, you'll want to set up some banking accounts."

"I have the money." Lynn said, thinking of what her grandmother had left her. It wasn't much but it would probably be enough to get the project under way. And if Lynn had to move in with her parents to make ends meet, well then that's just what she would have to do, until she found another job.

"I know you do, after all you do let us manage it. But while I admire your desire to build this on your own, I think you may have more success if you reach out to others for support. And becoming an official entity will be a step in the right direction. It will make everything more official, but it will also make sure the rest of the world takes you seriously."

Lynn leaned forward in her chair. She had known that coming to Caitlyn would be a good idea. The woman knew everyone, or so it seemed. Inspired, Lynn asked for a pen and a piece of paper and started to make some notes so she wouldn't miss anything. For the first time in days, she began to feel a glimmer of hope. Maybe something good could come out of this situation.

Chapter 20

Lynn walked past the batting cages, trying to make it seem like she couldn't care less who was there. Overall, though, she was in too good of a mood, riding high off her strategy meeting with Caitlyn, to let the thought of running into Jackson Sanders bother her.

Still, there was no harm in being prepared for a rogue sighting, since it seemed to be happening quite frequently. Especially if she was going to do a workout that would leave her sweaty, she wanted to ready. Ready for what? She sighed. Jackson had made it clear that he thought she was a nuisance in scrubs. Smelly workout clothes wouldn't help her case either. Too bad Queensbay was only big enough for one health club. And there was no way she was going to let the fear of Jackson seeing her hot and sweaty keep her out of it. Especially since hitting the gym seemed to be the only action that was happening lately.

Somehow the twin thoughts of Jackson and hot and sweaty made her stomach do a flip-flop, and she had a brief, intense image of naked bodies twisting together. She wondered what he would look like out of his work suit. She'd hadn't caught more than a glimpse of him when he's been here with Jake, only that his shoulders had seemed broader than she remembered and the muscles in his arm had all but rippled when she had turned to catch him swinging the bat. She shut down her hormones with a groan. Really, you would think there was one only one thing she thought about.

Swallowing, she told herself to stop thinking that way, but still she breathed a sigh of relief when she saw no tall, lanky blondes at the batting cage; only some middle-aged dads and their kids. She planned on a good, long workout and didn't want to be disturbed.

She went to the locker room, changed, and headed out onto the main floor of the gym, to the rock-climbing wall, which in her opinion, was the place's best feature. She fairly tingled in excitement looking up at it now, noting the pattern of the toe and handholds. She had climbed it a hundred times, but that didn't mean she could be lazy about planning her route.

"Hey, Lynn. Haven't seen you in a while." Bode Weller, one of the gym's personal trainers, came over and gave her a hug. He had longish brown hair, bleached blond at the tips, brown eyes, and a body like a Greek Adonis. She let herself enjoy the hug for a moment, feeling his muscles squeeze around her like a python, and then gently pushed him away.

"Bode, how have you been?"

"Great," he said. "Even better now that I've seen you." He gave her a puppy-dog sad look from underneath his eyes.

"Oh please! Like you even noticed I was gone." She shook her head. Bode was one of the more popular trainers at the gym and had a regular parade of women, young and old, salivating over him. Lynn herself had looked at him quite a few times as well, but that was all. Bode was a little too relaxed and easy going for her to think of him seriously. And he was a notorious flirt, but she knew that she had no problem allowing him to practice his charm on her.

Unbidden, she found herself doing a little comparison of Jackson to Bode. He probably wasn't as bulky or a ripped as Bode, but there had been the hint of decent musculature underneath that nicely tailored suit. Of course, he was pretty tall, so that meant that any weight he did carry would be nice and evenly distributed, probably leaving him long and lean like a cat. She gave a mental shrug to clear the image of Jackson from her mind. She was here to focus, and to climb.

"Here, let me get that harness rigged up for you."

Lynn was perfectly capable of doing it herself but she let Bode check her equipment, smiling a little as his hands lingered in all the right places. After all, he was only doing his job.

"All set here," Bode said.

"Thanks," Lynn said, going up to the rock wall and locating her first hand grip. She'd been delighted to find that a gym with a large indoor rock-climbing wall was opening up near Queensbay. She'd been one of the charter members, figuring that if she couldn't go out and climb the real thing, this was almost as good.

Focused, determined, Lynn started her climb. She didn't try to do it fast; rather, she took her time, letting her mind both wander and focus. One part of her concentrated on the different handholds and footholds while the other half ruminated the other issues facing her.

Even though it looked like The Healthy Kids Now program might take off on its own, she was still left with the problem of the clinic closing. So far, Sadie had made no progress on finding a new place for them to go. Time was counting down and somehow she had managed to tick off the only person who might be able to help the situation. Jackson Sanders.

It was his eyes that gave her hope, she thought. Sure, most of the time they were indecipherable, like a cat's, but occasionally she thought she saw flashes of...what? Hurt, compassion? Maybe, but Jackson always seemed alert, tightly wound like a leopard or a lion. Waiting to pounce.

Lynn almost had to laugh at that. There was no one who would ever accuse her of being catlike. Or waiting to pounce. She was more like a puppy in that regard. Ready to play, ready for action.

She was almost halfway up the wall when she became aware that there was someone else on it with her. She could hear Bode coaching the climber from below, but she could also sense a presence, fast approaching.

It wasn't long before a hand, large and well formed, at the end of a long arm, appeared at her side. In a moment, the rest of the climber came into view and she swiveled her head to see who it was.

The surprise caused her to falter, and it was only when the large hand reached out and steadied her that she was able to catch her balance.

"Are you ok?" Jackson asked her.

It took another moment before her mouth and brain connected and started to work together again.

"What are you doing here?"

He looked at her from underneath his helmet. Yup, definitely the blue eyes of a predator, Lynn thought.

"I believe it's called climbing," he said, his leg pushing him up and propelling him forward so he was able to climb ahead of her.

"Is this your first time?" she asked. She would not have pegged Jackson as an outdoorsy type.

"No, not quite. But don't tell the instructor. He seems intent on giving me directions I don't need."

Lynn frowned. Bode generally knew what he was doing; and if he thought that Jackson needed instructions, then he probably did.

"I didn't figure you for a climber," Lynn said, looking up. She pulled herself up so she was more evenly matched with Jackson. *It's not a race,* she told herself, but it didn't seem quite fair he had come out of nowhere to pass her by.

"I hear it's excellent exercise," Jackson said, looking up and around for his next grip. Lynn watched his technique. It wasn't very refined but it got the job done. His big frame made it easy for him to find a foot or handhold and then it was just a matter of sheer strength for him to pull himself up.

She looked at him, could see how his back muscles bunched and tightened under his fitted t-shirt, the way his long, muscular legs moved with the rest of the body. Well, whatever he was doing for exercise, it was working nicely, Lynn thought, since there was nothing wrong with his body, especially the view from below and behind.

"You don't climb for real, I mean outdoors?" Lynn asked, picking up her pace. The top half of the wall was trickier than the bottom half, with the grips more spaced

121

out. She used her knowledge of it to pull ahead of Jackson, watching as his hands searched for a good position.

"You mean on real rocks? Not since I was a kid," he said, his voice holding just the hint of breathlessness.

"You should try it sometime, might loosen you up."

He gave a snort. "Does that mean you climb trees too?"

"Only when something's chasing me," she said, sending him a proud grin as she passed him and made her way to the top.

A rueful look flickered over his face, but he kept going, pulling himself up to the top more slowly.

Lynn looked around, surveying the space and catching her breath. Ok, so it wasn't anything like what she had climbed back in Colorado, but it wasn't so bad. And the Mountain State had never had a view quite like Jackson Sanders in it, either.

"Hey, guys. Time to come down; I've got some people waiting," Bode called from below. Lynn nodded and readied herself for the rappel down. Sure, there was no way this could compete with the real thing, but it was still no small thrill to let yourself leap out into the air, the only thing keeping you from free falling your harness and a piece of rope.

With a little whoop, she shoved off, relished the speed and then slowed herself down to a more respectable, rule-abiding pace.

"Nice work out." Bode caught her and then set her upright, his hands moving over her just a little as he set her upright.

Jackson landed neatly next to her, glancing between her and Bode. Lynn decided that she didn't mind the way Bode let his hand rest on her shoulder, not when she saw how Jackson was looking at them. Maybe this was the way to pierce Jackson's ice demeanor.

"Not bad for a first timer," Bode said offhandedly to Jackson. Lynn could feel Bode drawing up tight beside her, his arm still possessively around her. She nearly sidestepped but just to keep watching Jackson's reaction, she stayed where she was.

Jackson only said, "I'm a quick learner."

"Your form and technique could be a little better," Bode said quickly. "Maybe we'll just have another go at it, and then I'll critique you."

Lynn looked between the two men and decided she had better make herself scarce. "I'm just going to go over and use the weight room. Thanks, Bode."

"No problem." Bode shot her a smile and then said, "I was thinking maybe we could grab a beer together. My buddies and I usually hit Quent's Pub around eight?"

Lynn tried not to care if Jackson overheard this exchange or not. Bode had been bugging her to go out for a 'beer' for a while, but she'd always found some excuse, usually work related, to say no. But now her hours were more regular, so there really wasn't any reason she couldn't, shouldn't go out. If she told her mom she was going on a date voluntarily, then she'd be less likely to set her up on another blind one. She was fairly certain she could drag Tory along so she'd have backup. After all, Tory had told her stop over-thinking her relationships, and Bode had never struck her as much of a thinker. Maybe he was just what she needed. And there was the fact that Jackson was standing there, watching, as if he actually cared what she had to say.

"Sounds good," Lynn said, and glanced over at Jackson, and just caught the look that flitted across his face. Was he angry? Jealous? Whatever it was, he certainly wasn't indifferent.

She tried to hide her smile, and knew good manners needed her to say something. "I'll bring my friend Tory along, so Jackson, if you're not doing anything, maybe you'd like to join us?"

His blue eyes raked over her, took in Bode standing next to her, arms crossed.

"I have other plans, thank you," he said coldly.

Lynn nodded, but felt what? A small shiver of disappointment. Still, she turned to look at Bode, with his surfer-length brownish-blonde hair, bulging biceps, and pecs that practically danced on their own and decided that there could be worse ways to spend an evening than in the company of the very well-toned and defined Bode Weller.

"Well then, catch you later, Bode," she said as casually as she could, and walked away. She didn't dare look back, but she was certain she could feel two sets of eyes staring at her as she crossed the gym floor toward the weight room.

Chapter 21

Jackson didn't know why he disliked Bode almost on sight. Certainly it wasn't because he was jealous of the easy way he had gotten Lynn to agree to go out with him. Or the way Lynn had clearly been staring, ogling Bode in his sleeveless shirt and workout pants. But he just didn't like the guy.

He hadn't planned on running into her; at least, that hadn't been his primary goal in coming here. Sure, he knew that this was the only gym in town. The thought had crossed his mind that maybe, when he decided to go for a workout, there was an off chance he might bump into her. The thought bothered him, but he hadn't tried to stay away either. It was just that he wasn't supposed to care about her one way or the other. And yet he couldn't deny that he had been strangely gratified when he'd seen her walking in and stopping at the front desk. His eyes had followed her to the locker room and then before he realized what he doing, he had sweet-talked the receptionist into booking him onto the wall at the same time as Lynn.

He still didn't know why he had done it. The right thing to do was to stay away. He hadn't come back into town to start dating. Especially not his brother's fiancée's best friend. That would definitely be against his no-strings policy. And Lynn didn't even like him. She, who seemed to welcome the rest of the world with open arms, looked at him like he was one step above medical waste. He shouldn't need to work at this, he had a thousand other things to occupy his time.

Now, after listening to Bode gave him a lecture about climbing wall safety, Jackson was doing his usual gym routine, running, lifting some weights. He had kept an eye on Lynn while she did her own workout, seen her use some free weights, then do pushups and pull-ups, her toned little body moving effortlessly through the exercises. She was slicked with a bit of sweat, and her workout clothes, while not tight, clung closely enough to her curves so that he couldn't help wondering what she would look like without them on.

He watched as she disappeared into the locker room, presumably done for the day. Off to her date with that muscle head Bode.

He tried to put the thought of her out of his head as he finished up his workout. He headed over toward the water cooler to get a drink and then hit the showers, when he heard Bode's voice from inside one of the gym offices.

"Dude, climber chick is going out with me tonight."

Jackson froze, listening.

"What, you mean Lynn, the hot little doctor? She agreed to go out with you?" The other voice was raised in disbelief.

"Yeah, finally. She's going to meet me at Quent's tonight. Said she's bringing a friend; want to ride shotgun?"

Jackson thought it sounded like Bode couldn't quite hide the triumph in his tone.

"Think her friend is as smokin' as she is?"

The other guy's voice was eager and Jackson clenched his hands in anger.

"Of course. Hot chicks run in packs. But look, Lynn's mine—you get what you get."

"Fine, but man, I still don't know how you got that sweet piece of ass to say yes to you."

He heard Bode laugh. "Who could resist me?"

"She's probably only interested in you for your body."

Bode laughed again. "What do you think I want her for? An interesting conversation over wine and cheese? I'm just hoping she'll want to play doctor with me."

There was a bout of loud laughter, and Jackson swallowed the impulse to shove open the door of the office and take a swing at Bode.

He heard a sound and turned, trying his best to look like he was casually strolling away, clenching and unclenching his hands, trying to work off some of his anger, when Bode came up behind him, clapped him on the back and said, "Not a bad day for a beginner, dude. You know we're running a special here, fifty percent off your first month of training. I'd be happy to set you up with the paperwork."

Jackson let his anger settle down. It wouldn't do any good to take a punch at Bode. At least not yet. But there was no way he was going to let a guy like Bode prey upon an unsuspecting girl like Lynn. With her big brown eyes, that curly hair, and passionate personality, she was an easy mark for guys like him.

Barely sparing a smile for Bode, he disentangled himself, promising to stop by later, and made his way to the locker room, mulling over his options. Perhaps he might just stop by Quent's tonight after all.

Chapter 22

"What made you decide all of a sudden you wanted to go on a date?" Tory asked. They were at Lynn's apartment, getting ready to meet Bode and his friend.

Lynn was looking through her paltry selection of tops, trying to decide what to wear. She had lived the last eight years in scrubs and was slowly realizing that her wardrobe had suffered for it. She couldn't wear a repeat of her date with Nate. Hence the emergency call to Tory, who seemed to have perfected the casual chic look, for some fashion advice.

"What do you think about this one?" Lynn asked, holding up one of her favorites, a scoop neck, tunic-length top in a dark red.

"Hmm," Tory said getting up from the bed and coming over to Lynn's closet. "You didn't answer the question."

Lynn shrugged. What was the real reason that she had volunteered to go on a date? Was it to keep her mom off her back? Or had she only said yes to the date with Bode because Jackson had been standing there and she had the sudden, crazy impulse to see if she could get a reaction out of him? But that had backfired. Jackson had seemed to have cared less that she was going.

And why should he? He was what? The clinic's landlord. And a mean one at that. He seemed to have no room in his heart other than what was best for the bottom line. What did she hope to gain by talking to him so more? Just more of those icy, cold stares that sent shivers down her back. And there had been plenty of those today.

All she knew was that whenever she had looked up from her workout, he had been looking at her. He looked away of course, thinking he hadn't been caught, but she had been totally aware of him the whole time.

"Earth to Lynn…Since you agreed to go on a date, did you decide to take my advice? Does this mean you think Bode is really hot, or have you just decided that it's been so long something's going to rust shut if it doesn't get used?"

"Rust shut?" Lynn asked. "You know that isn't physically possible."

"I wasn't being literal," Tory said with a wave of her hand.

"Well it's not literally or metaphorically possible for it, as you call it, to rust shut." Lynn shuddered at the image, but she had to admit that Tory had a point. It had been a while and her hormones seemed to be in overdrive. She had thought it was because she had finally reached a place in her life, professionally, where things were going well. And that meant that the other part of her body wanted in on the action, even if the reason things were going so well was that she had neglected her hormones.

But now everything was turmoil and her hormones hadn't gotten the message that there was a much bigger crisis going on than their lack of activity.

"It's really been, like years? How have gone so long?"

"Med school is pretty demanding," Lynn said.

"It must not have been very good," Tory said casually as she plucked a blouse off a hanger, looked at it, and discarded it on the growing heap of clothes on the floor.

"What?"

"The sex, silly."

"It was ok," Lynn defended her experience.

Tory smiled. "Ahh, that's the problem."

"What do you mean?"

"Honey, sex isn't supposed to be ok, it's supposed to be good." Tory pulled out the syllable in the last word and gave Lynn a knowing look. "You need to up your expectations," she continued.

"And what should my expectations be?" Lynn asked.

"Great sex. That's it. Nothing else. Don't expect more than that, especially from someone like Bode, who let's admit, doesn't seem like much more than a pretty face, and you'll be fine. Probably better than fine. You just need to get laid, without all that other crap about hearts and flowers and moonlight walks into forever."

Lynn blinked. "That doesn't sound very romantic."

Tory shook her head. "That's the point. You need to start with baby steps, you know, personal pleasure, and then you can move onto romance. At some point."

"But…"

"Look, did you find Nate attractive, envision yourself doing the horizontal mambo with him?"

Lynn shook her head.

"Good, so you cut him loose right?"

Lynn nodded. It had taken some dodging and excuses about her crazy schedule, but Nate had finally stopped texting her.

"And Bode's easy on the eyes, right?"

"True," Lynn agreed.

"Well, unless you have someone else in mind?" Tory said, with a wicked smile on her face.

"What?" Lynn found her face flaming. How did Tory do that?

"Nothing, just working out a hunch," Tory said, her voice innocent, as she held up a sweater, considering.

"This isn't some game," Lynn said.

Tory smiled, her caramel colored eyes dancing, "Oh yes it is. And now it's time to play. Wear this one, with that skirt, and these boots and let's see if you can score a goal, slugger." She tossed the outfit on the bed and smiled.

"You're mixing your sports metaphors," Lynn said. She looked at the outfit Troy had picked out. Simple, casual and the v-neck sweater would show just a hint of cleavage. Maybe Tory was right. Not everything, especially guys, needed to be a matter of life or death. Maybe she just needed to enjoy the ride.

Chapter 23

Bode was waiting for them, and as promised, he'd brought a friend. Bode looked good, Lynn thought: a little more polished than he usually did at the gym. Tonight, he wore a pair of dark jeans and a charcoal-gray t-shirt that seemed like it had been poured on. She stopped and took a moment to drink in the perfection that was Bode Weller's pectoral region. His brownish-blond hair was slightly tousled and his dark brown eyes looked her over appreciatively as he pulled out a barstool for her.

Lynn introduced Tory to Bode, and Bode introduced them to his friend Greg and there was hand shaking and hellos all round. And then silence, except for the backdrop of music. Classic INXS was playing and there were more than a few people singing along.

"Been a while since I heard this song," Lynn said, looking to break the quiet.

"Yeah, well, it's Aussie night and Quent is running a special on beer from Down Under. Can I get you one?" Bode said, smiling at her.

Lynn nodded, and Bode went to go fetch the drinks. Tory and Greg eyed each other, and then Tory suggested they try a game of pool. Greg seemed thankful for something to do and Lynn was left alone.

She scanned the pub. There was a baseball game on one TV, football on another, and soccer on the third. None of them were big games, and no one was paying that much attention.

"Here's your beer. It's an Australian micro-brew, one that Quent swears by," Bode said, returning with two bottles of beer and a bowl of nuts.

He slid onto one of the barstools at their little table and she immediately found that somehow the stool had moved much closer than before. Bode's knee was touching hers and she pulled back just a little. Maybe she hadn't been on a date in a while, but she thought they should have at least one beer before he tried for close physical contact.

Undaunted, he leaned his head in. "It's a nice change to see you here, outside of the gym. You look good there, but you look pretty hot outside of it."

"Yeah, it's good to get out," Lynn said, fighting the impulse to lean back. Her pulse was racing but it wasn't her hormones talking. She didn't know what was wrong with her. Bode was nothing like Nate, the Civil War, vice presidential-loving accountant, who'd left her with nothing but the desire to run away screaming in boredom.

Nope, Bode was almost the exact opposite, and while Nate had been scrupulously polite about touching her, Bode was going in the total opposite direction.

She felt a hand brush casually against her thigh and she moved away. Bode sent her a lazy smile and she turned the talk to where he liked to go on vacation. They talked about other things and Lynn decided that except for an interest spending time at the gym, they didn't have much in common. It didn't seem to deter Bode though, as he kept reaching out, trying to close the distance between them, while she just as carefully tried to maintain it.

Finally, she decided she needed a break and excused herself to use the restroom. She was washing her hands and thinking through ways of politely breaking off the evening. First, she would need to give the signal to Tory, which was too bad, since she genuinely seemed to be enjoying herself with Bode's friend, Greg. Still, Tory was her wingman and that was the nature of the job.

She took a deep breath, counted to ten, and told herself she could do this. It was part of being a grownup, part of dating, being able to play the game right, let someone down so that they got the picture but weren't left with hurt feelings. How had Tory phrased it? "It's not you, it's me..." Time for a graceful exit speech, she supposed.

Lynn came out of the bathroom and headed briskly down the hallway into the main room of the bar. Out of her peripheral vision she caught a glimpse of something. She stopped just before she hit it, but still managed to connect with something cold and slightly wet.

"What are you doing here?" she asked, looking up.

Jackson stood there, looking down at her, a slight frown on his face, one hand holding a beer bottle away from her. There was a foamy head at the top, probably from the impact Lynn had had with it.

"Here, let me get you a napkin," Lynn said. She reached over to the bar, where there was a pile of small square, white napkins neatly stacked. She swiped a bunch and started to pat down Jackson's sleeve.

"Don't worry about it," he said, moving a little out of her reach. He was wearing a crisp white button down, a pair of dark wool slacks and dress shoes.

"I thought you had other plans," Lynn said, feeling silly holding the bunch of slightly damp napkins in her hand. She looked around and then set them down on the bar. She hazarded a look around. Unlike The Golden Pear, no one here seemed to take notice of Jackson and he seemed, relaxed even confident, with none of the tenseness that had radiated through his body the other day.

She knew she should get back to Bode, but her curiosity at finding Jackson here was getting the better of her.

"I did, but they fell through. I didn't feel like sitting at home, so I thought I would come out and watch the game."

"The game?" Lynn asked.

He pointed towards the baseball game.

"You like baseball?" Lynn asked, knowing her voice sound more surprised than was polite.

"Like, love it, used to play it."

"Really?" Lynn said, considering. So that explained the batting cage. She took a step back, assessing him. Sure, he was taller and lankier than a lot of baseball players and certainly a lot fitter than most of them, but she could see it now, a cap pulled low on his head, his eyes roving over the infield, assessing each player's position, just waiting for one of them to make the wrong move.

"Not since college, of course, but, yes I play it."

She nodded and was about to start back to the table where she'd been sitting with Bode, whose back was to her, intently looking at something on his phone.

"You seem shocked," he said, taking a sip of beer, his blue eyes watching her carefully over the rim of the bottle.

She shrugged, not wanting to admit that she had been giving him that much thought. "You didn't strike me as a guy who played a sport."

"I'm also a black belt in Taekwondo."

"Oh," Lynn said, trying not to sound impressed. So maybe she did need to rethink her assessment of Jackson Sanders. Not quite the priss she'd thought.

"How many sports do you play?" he asked.

"Soccer, for a team sport. But I grew up out west, so I ski, climb, hike, and bike."

"That's an impressive list. You sound quite active." Jackson said.

She looked at him quickly, wondering if he was being sarcastic, but he merely looked down at her. He seemed a little more at ease, a little more human now that he had ditched the full business suit. He looked almost cute, Lynn decided and then tamped down that feeling. He was evil. Ok, so maybe evil was overdoing it, but he was not a nice guy. She wasn't about to just forgive him for his decision to close the clinic because he decided to smile at her. She was a stronger woman than that.

"I like the outdoors. And climbing things. Trees, rocks, hills, that sort of stuff. Was that really your first time on a rock wall?" Lynn asked, curious to know.

He looked at her and the faintest of smiles ghosted across his lips. "Second, if you count the time when I was ten at Boy Scout camp."

"Really? You were pretty good."

"Thanks, but I was just following you."

The compliment threw her off guard. She wasn't expecting him to be nice and it was destroying the image she had of him.

"I should go, get back to Bode," she said, suddenly knowing she needed to pull herself away.

"I thought you said this was a group thing?" he said, his voice casual.

"Umm, sure it is. I mean Tory's over there with Bode's friend Greg, playing pool, but I guess it's ok, I mean, yeah sure, come on over." She knew she was stammering, but somehow Tory's quick guide on dating hadn't covered this scenario.

"I was just teasing. Go, enjoy your date. I am sure Bode's quite the interesting fellow."

"*You have no idea,*" Lynn almost shot back, then before she could say anything, she turned and walked away, knowing that her face was flaming.

Bode had swiveled around and watched her coming.

"What's he doing here?" There was a querulous tone in his voice. Lynn stopped, surprised to realize that Bode and Jackson were eyeing each other like a pair of roosters in a chicken coop.

Lynn threw one look over her shoulder. Jackson was watching her, and when he caught Bode's eye, raised his beer bottle in a mock salute. Bode stared back at him and finally gave the barest of nods. She watched the whole thing like it was some sort of surreal show, not sure what to make of the testosterone pissing match going on.

"He said he came to watch the game. His plans fell through," Lynn said, hopping up on the barstool. She looked. Bode had gotten her another drink, but she was sure she didn't want it. She was ready to go, before Bode and Jackson's visual sparring turned into something worse. Her brother, Kyle, had once explained that sometimes guys just didn't like each other, that it was just a guy thing, and that when that was the case you could never tell what would happen. It had never made sense to Lynn until she was in the middle of it.

"Really?" Bode shot Jackson another look, this one dark and dangerous, and Lynn put out her hand on his arm to calm him.

"It's a small town. Not too many places to grab a beer and watch the game if you don't feel like being on your own."

"Guess not." Bode gave a smile and seemed to shrug Jackson off. Lynn was glad but she was also wondering just how she could get Tory's attention and bring her back over so she could find a way to leave. She could feel a headache beginning to loom and suddenly she wanted nothing more than to go home, to her nice new bed in her nice new apartment, and go to sleep.

"Well, where were we?" Bode said and he leaned in closer. Lynn was pretty sure they had been talking about hiking in the Catskill Mountains of upstate New York, but Bode seemed to think they had gotten much farther than that.

His hand was sliding up her leg, inside the skirt that she was wearing. The shock of it had her frozen. His other arm snaked around her shoulders as he drew her in for a kiss. For a moment she didn't quite get what was happening and then when she did realize it, she wondered why she didn't like it.

She pushed hard on his chest with her hands, managed to say, "Bode, I think maybe you should stop."

He pulled back for a moment and shot a look of disbelief at her. "Stop? If you didn't want it, why did you come out with me? C'mon, not like we have a lot in common, except we both got good bodies and I would sure like to find out what yours feels like. I've been watching your ass climb that rock wall for weeks now and I'm ready to get my hands on it."

Lynn was too shocked to say anything, and Bode must have taken that as an opportunity because he went in for another kiss, his hand snaking its way even farther up her skirt.

Bode tasted like beer and his lips were rough and his hand insistent. She pulled away, but he didn't let her go, so she pushed harder. She fought down the first wave of panic. After all, they were in a bar, and surely he would take the hint and just let her go. And if not, she knew what to do: she'd taken a self-defense class at the clinic and she just needed to remember whether she was supposed to go for the throat or the eyes first.

She never got a chance to make a decision. There was a whish of air and a sudden moment, and she felt herself topple back, almost, but not quite, falling off the barstool.

"What the hell?" Lynn said, looking down at the writhing form of Bode. Jackson stood there calmly, almost as if he hadn't moved.

Attracted by the sudden commotion, Tory and Greg materialized behind them.

Bode rose to his feet and for a moment, Lynn thought nothing more was going to happen. But she underestimated

Bode's feelings on the matter. Without warning, he charged Jackson, who nimbly sidestepped him. Bode stumbled, almost fell, but Quent, who knew when trouble was brewing in his bar, caught him.

"Hey now, what's happening?" Quent's voice loud and commanding brought the pub to a standstill.

"It didn't seem like he was acting like a gentleman," Jackson said calmly. He looked Bode in the eye. "I believe the lady said no."

"Yeah, is that what you think? Then she shouldn't be such a tease!" Bode shot back. At this, Jackson moved toward him but was stopped by one of Quent's meaty hands.

"There's no fighting in here."

Jackson lowered his arms and took a step back. Lynn fought to catch her breath. It had all happened so fast. She hadn't meant for anyone to take Bode down, but still, the jerk hadn't gotten the picture.

"Come on, let's go," Tory had her arm and was pulling her away.

Lynn walked out of the pub into the cool night air, drawing a deep, deep breath.

"What happened in there?" Tory asked.

"I don't know…Bode, well he was kind of an ass. He put his hand up here, and I mean all the way up here, and when I told him to remove it and said I wasn't that kind of girl, he laughed and said why the hell had I gone out with him if I wasn't interested in sex, because it wasn't like we had anything else in common. And when he didn't take no for an answer, Jackson was there doing some sort of weird ninja trick that had Bode on the ground in no time flat."

"I saw that, and I have to say that was kinda hot," Tory said, nodding. "Imagine that, Jackson Sanders coming to your rescue. And sorry about Bode. Maybe you aren't ready to just jump into bed with someone."

"I didn't need rescuing," Lynn said, ignoring what Tory had said about Bode. Yes, her hormones were itching, but not for what Bode was offering. It had been a little too blunt. And he hadn't taken no for an answer the first time. She'd been just about to tell him that in no uncertain terms, the way she had learned in defense class, but Jackson had just been there, smooth, capable, kind of like James Bond. Ok, so maybe she didn't need the rescuing; but Tory was right—there had been something kind of hot about Jackson stepping in.

"I am sure you didn't, but still, it's not every day a girl gets caught up in a bar fight."

Lynn slowed her pace just a little, shook her head, "I'm not a girl. I'm a grown woman, a doctor; and the last thing I need is be caught up in some sort barroom brawl."

"Whatever. I still think it's kind of hot. And wow, the way Jackson was staring at you, like he couldn't tear himself away."

"Oh please," Lynn snorted.

"Well, it's about time he got over her. You know, he might just be what you need."

"I didn't need any help," Lynn insisted. "He was just being a gentleman, you know because I'm friends with his soon to be sister-in-law."

"Whatever. Anyway, here's my car. I'm going to head home now."

"You ok to drive?" Lynn said.

"I only had one beer the entire night," Tory said. "But let me drive you to your door."

Lynn was about to say no, that the walk would do her good, when a shadow fell upon them, cast by the old-fashioned street lamp.

They turned and saw Jackson walking towards them. He had put on his jacket and to Lynn, he looked tall, dangerous, and very suave. James Bond indeed.

"Ladies, can I walk you home?" he asked, coming to a stop before them.

"This is my car, I was going to head home, but since you and Lynn are heading to the same place, you can make sure she gets home safely," Tory said quickly, shooting a fierce look at Jackson.

"Lynn will be perfectly safe with me," he said to Tory, his voice stiff.

Lynn watched the exchange between Tory and Jackson, puzzled. There was an undercurrent here that she didn't understand, but then it didn't seem to matter because Jackson was looking down at her for confirmation and all she could do was mutter, "Umm, sure," suddenly feeling tongue-tied.

She gave Tory a quick, one-armed hug and watched as her friend jumped into her little Mini Cooper and peeled off.

And she was left standing in the street with Jackson.

"You were heading home, I presume?" Jackson said.

"Yes," Lynn answered, because she didn't really have anywhere else to be. Except for a date with her couch, the Hallmark channel, and some black raspberry ice cream with chocolate sauce.

"Should we go?" He held out an arm in the general direction of the harbor and she fell in step beside him, suddenly aware of the heat emanating from him.

"I guess I should say thank you," Lynn said. "I mean, I was handling it, could have handled it. In fact, I was going to try a move like yours, I mean not like yours, because wow, yours was pretty killer. I didn't even know you were there. Is that because you're a black belt?"

She stopped took a breath, realizing she was babbling. Nervous; why was she so nervous? Jackson had only ever made her irritated, mad, before—not nervous. Ok, so he had made her both. Irritated, nervous, jumpy; you name it, he had caused just about the full spectrum.

"Yes and yes."

"What?"

"Yes, I am sure you could have had handled it, but it annoyed me he wasn't getting the message fast enough. And yes, I was able to do that because I'm a black belt."

"Have you ever done that before?" she asked, not sure if she wanted to know if he made a habit of rescuing other women.

"In a bar?" He glanced down at her and she thought that maybe, for once, his eyes looked less icy, friendly even.

"Yeah."

"No, never in a bar. In competitions, yes. But then I haven't done one of those in many years."

"It doesn't seem like you're out of practice."

"I just finished what you started." His voice was gracious.

"Are you always so much of a gentleman or do you just like dropping guys with an axe kick?"

He stopped then and she was forced to stop with him. "If you're asking if I approve of violence, I do not. But I hate bullies even more. And Bode was bullying you."

"So you would have done the same for anyone?"

She wondered why she was disappointed when Jackson answered with a simple yes and they continued walking. She didn't know why she felt she needed to explain the situation to him, but she did.

"I'm really not the type of girl who goes all the way on the first date." As she said it, she knew it was true. She needed a little bit of romance, even if her hormones were screaming for some therapy. "And that's all he seemed interested in. I mean, he acknowledged that we have nothing in common except a certain level of physical attractiveness…I mean, he practically admitted he was only interested in my body."

"And that upsets you?" Jackson asked dryly.

She looked up at him. His eyes were shrouded in the dark, so she couldn't tell what he was thinking. She swallowed, all of a sudden nervous. She had never imagined walking in the moonlight with Jackson Sanders, and it was putting her on edge. Why did it have to be him that her underused hormones responded to? Why couldn't they do backflips for Nate the accountant, or even Bode the blunt?

They were almost at the harbor and the building that housed their apartments. A few clouds were rolling in, playing hide and seek with the moon. Tomorrow was supposed to be rainy, she remembered, the first real rain of the fall. It would be a good day to huddle in bed, figure out why her professional life seemed to be going so well but her personal life was in shambles. It was because she was book smart and guy stupid, she decided.

They were almost at the stairs that led up to the second-floor balcony. He got there first but stood back, letting her go ahead. She mounted the steps, going up them as quickly as possible, all of a sudden eager to get away from Jackson. Her body was too jumpy, her nervous system tingling—a sure sign her hormones were kicking up into overdrive.

So far, he had shown nothing but irritation or excruciating politeness to her, and she could only assume that his own body and nervous system were not in any way compromised. Like he said, he would have done what he did for anyone. *So don't read too much into it,* she told herself.

The light had been fixed, she noticed, and now there was no mistaking her door from Jackson's, especially now that she had put a new doormat in front of it.

"Here we are," she said, walking to her door, one hand fumbling for her key in her purse.

To her surprise, he didn't stop at his own door and go directly in. Instead, he came until he was standing close to her. As her hands fished the keys from her bag, she felt them tremble slightly. There was something distinctly unnerving having Jackson Sanders standing so close to her, his eyes staring at her face.

Without a word, he leaned in and for one breathless moment, Lynn had a crazy idea that he was going to kiss her, and though she wasn't nearly ready for it, she nonetheless would have wanted it.

Instead, he reached his hand out and took the keys from hers. In a swift, fluid moment, he opened the door to her apartment and the keys were back in her hand.

The distance was back between them now and she let out a breath, confused at what had just happened, or in any case had not happened.

"Have a good night," he said.

"Are you always such a gentleman?" she breathed.

"There's no reason we can't be polite to one another." His voice was steady.

"Yes, of course," she managed to stammer, then added, "thank you."

She waited, but there was nothing but an awkward silence stretching between them. Quickly, before she could embarrass herself further, she let herself into her apartment, shutting the door behind her. She leaned against it and closed her eyes, wondering why she had thought, even for a moment, that he might have wanted to kiss her, and that against all reason, she had wanted him to.

She was just about to move, think about undressing, getting into something comfortable, maybe make a cup of tea, when there was a quiet knock at her door.

Without bothering to look through the peephole, she opened it and there he stood, a sudden burst of moonlight tipping his blond hair silver.

"Yes?"

"I'm not always such a gentleman, Lynn," he said. And he moved in quickly, taking her face in her hands, his lips coming down on hers. It was as if an electric current sprang between them and she felt herself lifted up off her toes and into him, her arms coming around his shoulders as she pulled herself into him.

It seemed to go on forever as they hungrily devoured each other. She heard a sound, a wordless moan, and realized that it must have come from her.

All too soon, he broke free from her, took a step back, his hand firmly at his sides.

"Have a good night," he said. Then turned on his heel and walked to his own door and was gone.

Shocked, Lynn held the door open just a moment longer and then stepped back, shut it, and sunk to the floor, truly wondering what had just happened and how she was ever going to be able to sleep with her body wound up and as tingly as a kid with the chicken pox.

Chapter 24

Jackson paced restlessly in his apartment, wondering just what he'd done, trying to assess just where his feelings were going. He stopped, looking out the window at the harbor. The moon was out now, uncovered by the clouds, and it left a glittering quicksilver trail across the surface, which in the dark, looked still, heavy as if all of Queensbay Harbor was a cauldron of molten silver.

He hadn't meant to kiss her. Or had he? He rubbed his hand through his hair, knowing that he was lying to himself. Ok, so he had meant to kiss her, knowing that if he left and then came back it would definitely unsettle her. And he wanted her unsettled, right? He wanted to know that she was lying awake at night thinking about him. But why? She wasn't his type. He didn't have a type, couldn't have a type. He wanted no strings attached. He liked women who were taller, blonder. Not as enthusiastic. Detached. He remembered how passionately she had spoken about the clinic. He couldn't let himself become involved. He couldn't ever feel again.

He had sworn after Ashley that he wouldn't let his guard down, that he wouldn't let himself care about anyone. It had hurt too much, pushed him too close to the

149

edge. He was willing to offer his bed, companionship, but nothing more. Sure he'd been attracted to women, he wasn't a monk, after all, but he hadn't felt a powerful need for anyone, not like with Lynn. And she had answered with every fiber of her body, to that kiss. No, this was not good at all.

He sat down on the couch, suddenly tired. He looked at his hands. He hadn't landed a punch in a long time against anything more than a training bag. Bode had looked tough, all thick head and muscle, but that only meant he had fallen harder.

There had been a certain satisfaction in knocking the guy down, Jackson thought. He may not have wanted to get tangled up with a woman, but when she said no, you had to respect that. And Lynn had been making it clear that she wasn't interested in a casual, physical acquaintance. Nope, Bode had deserved just what he'd gotten.

And Lynn? She didn't deserve him, not if she really cared. And Jackson had a feeling she could be the type of woman who cared, very, very much.

Chapter 25

It did rain the next day. Lynn awoke early, to the soft patter of rain on the roof. From her window, she could see only gray, as if the whole of Queensbay was covered in a soft blanket. The rain, cloud, and mist hovered over the harbor so that the edges of the docks were ghostly outlines and the hills and bluffs that ringed the town were invisible.

She had the day off. She had been excited for it, but now it stretched in front of her, empty, and she didn't know what to with herself.

She could unpack some more boxes, hang some pictures up on the wall, but she only had one, a print Phoebe had given her. Maybe she should go shopping. There was a gallery or two in town with some affordable photographs. She could browse through their racks, pick up a modest purchase, treat herself to a carbohydrate-heavy lunch at The Golden Pear, maybe hit the library and check out a book she could read.

All of that sounded appealing, except for the weather and her mood, which matched it perfectly. Gray-blue. Lynn was not a melancholy person and she didn't quite know what to do with the feeling that made every action an effort. She rolled back on her pillows and stared up at her white ceiling. What had she been thinking agreeing to a date with Bode? She should have known he'd only be interested in sex. Ok, so maybe that's all she had thought she was interested in. But not in the first hour! He had hadn't even offered to buy her dinner, just a beer and a bowl of free mixed nuts. But at least he had been honest. An asshole but an honest one. She had gone on the date knowing full well that Bode wasn't her type. And that perhaps his only use to her was to make Jackson jealous.

Last night she had been kissed twice, which was twice more than she had been kissed in about two years. And Jackson's kiss had been by far the better one. She hadn't been kissed like that in a long, long time—if ever. It had been amazing: all her senses on overload, every nerve-ending exploding. Not even her first one with Todd Hammerschmitt, her eighth-grade boyfriend for all of two weeks, could compare. He too had needed something. Her science homework. After the big test, he had dumped her for Jessie Unger. Lynn sighed.

No, Jackson's kiss had made her knees go weak, her heart clench and then thump like a bass drum. There had been a roaring in her ears and she had felt every nerve in her body strung tight. It had been amazing. But it was just a kiss. She shouldn't read too much into it. Especially not from someone who was as emotionally damaged as he was supposed to be. He was the definition of fixer upper, and she needed to stay away.

But he had rescued her and walked her home. Had he thought he deserved a kiss for his knight in shining armor routine? She pulled the pillow up over her head and mouthed a silent scream into it. Just because she thought he was cute—there she had admitted it—there was no reason to start building up a fantasy around Jackson. Damaged goods—that's what Tory had all but said.

And now she didn't know what to do next. Her operating playbook had nothing on this. Was she supposed to leave the kiss in the past, pretend it had never happened, treat him coolly and professionally? Like a tenant to the landlord? Had it been a one-time thing? Or did he want to do it again? She curled and uncurled her toes, not able to stop remembering the feeling of being kissed by Jackson.

She knew what she wanted. She could kiss Jackson again and again and never get tired of it. Was it possible that for him it had been just another kiss? That it had all been one sided?

Exasperated, she tossed the pillow aside and swung her feet out onto the floor, deciding that she needed to exercise, burn off some of this energy. Maybe then she would come up with a plan, a strategy for how to handle Jackson without making a fool of herself. Then she remembered. Hitting the gym, where she was likely to run into Bode, was off limits, and with the gray cloak of fog, running outside along the beach was an equally bad idea. Last thing she needed was to sprain or break something.

No. That meant being indoors. Shopping and eating, maybe even a movie, Lynn thought, brightening slightly. She could go see what was playing. It had been a long time since she saw a movie in the theater. Something loud and full of action and explosions. Mindless entertainment. That's what she needed, something where there wouldn't be a trace of romance.

Chapter 26

He was coming out of the hotel when he saw her walking toward her car. She had on tall rubber boots, jeans, and an expensive-looking raincoat with a turtleneck poking through the collar. Her hood was up, protecting her face from the spit-like rain that seemed to envelope them.

"Lynn!" he called after her and he saw her stop, hesitate and then finally turn around to give him a tight smile.

"Hello," he said, coming to stand before her. He didn't trust himself to get close to her. She stood there, hands jammed in the pocket of her coat. He did the same and found himself suddenly at a loss for words. Maybe it had been a bad idea to greet her. Perhaps he should have just slunk away, hoping that they didn't run into each other. Which was a silly hope, since for the moment they were working and living in the same buildings.

"Hi," she said.

"Going out?" he asked.

"Yes," she said, and then the silence hung between them. He could have kicked himself, knowing this wasn't going as planned. Well, he hadn't really planned anything about their meeting. Just knew that there was a part of him that wanted to—no, needed to—see her again.

Since there seemed to be nothing more to say, he saw her turn, as if to go.

"Wait," he said, holding up a hand. "I just wanted to say…" He stumbled for a moment, trying to find the right words. "After last night, I mean with Bode. I wanted to say, that it would be fine if you wanted to use the gym at the hotel. No charge, of course. I checked with Chase. I know it doesn't have all the amenities of the other place, but hey, I figured it would be ok until you found somewhere else to go."

He stopped, taking a breath. Seriously, he had worked and lived in ten countries, could speak four languages passably, and now he was fumbling for words like he was in middle school talking to the first girl he'd met.

A smile, this one genuine, crossed Lynn's face. "Thanks, that would be great. I wasn't sure what to do. I mean, going outside is always an option, unless it's like today, so…" She trailed off and then ended with another, "thanks."

"Anytime." The rain picked up again. There didn't seem to be much point in standing out there, but he couldn't quite bring himself to get away.

"Ok. Well, I'm going to go run some errands," she said, and he watched as she started to back away, then turned and practically ran towards her car.

He stood for a moment more in the rain, watching her go, reminding himself that it was better this way.

Chapter 27

Lynn finished with her patient, a nine-year-old girl who had strep throat. The girl, who had been nervous when she first came in, was now relaxed and happy to know that there wasn't something really wrong with her.

She gave a prescription for antibiotics to the mom and lollipops to the girl and her little sister, who looked at her solemnly with big blue eyes.

She stood, stretched, looked around. It was late in the afternoon and the patients were starting to thin out. The clinic closed early tonight, so soon it would be time for her to go home, Lynn thought. A good thing, since she'd been here since early in the morning. It was a nice fall evening, and the rain, which had lingered all yesterday, had blown out to sea, and in its place was cool, crisp, fall weather. Queensbay seemed shiny and bright under brilliant blue skies dotted by puffy white clouds, everything looking as if it had been freshly scrubbed.

Maybe she'd get out in time for a run, or even a walk; anything, since just getting out would be good. Or she could hang some of the pictures she'd bought and invite Tory and Phoebe over to help out. That might help her keep the thoughts of Jackson out of her mind. The movie the other day had worked, up to a point. The point where the hero—a blond actor with blue eyes and chiseled features—had gone for the obligatory kiss with the female lead. Lynn had almost gotten up and left the theater, but she was in the middle of the row and still had half her popcorn left. So she suffered through it, telling her hormones to calm it down. Going back to work had been a relief, for at least there she could focus.

But now another quiet evening stretched in front of her. Yup, some girlfriend time, take out, a glass of wine would be just what the doctor ordered. Feeling better at the thought of spending time with friends, she headed out towards the small office/break room all the staff shared. She could grab a cup of bad coffee, or better yet some tea, and finish up her paperwork.

She heard his voice, before she saw him. Curious, she walked towards the sound. He was in the director's office, the door slightly open. She slowed and then decided to hurry past, since it was really none of her business what Jackson was doing here. After all, he owned the building, so he had every right to be here.

Sadie, who must have caught a flash of her passing by, called out to her, "Hey, Lynn! Come on in."

Almost reluctantly, she turned on her heel and went to the office. Jackson's presence seemed to overpower the small room. For a moment, all Lynn could sense and feel was him, his scent—the barest hint of good, clean soap and a lightly spicy aftershave. Her insides clenched and she willed herself to focus instead on the ever-pervasive smell of disinfectant, hoping to quell her dancing hormones.

She glanced between the two of them. Sadie was beaming and even Jackson looked as if he was pleased with himself.

"What's going on?" she asked.

"Mr. Sanders," Sadie began.

"Jackson, please," he interrupted smoothly.

Sadie flashed him a smile so wide that Lynn was almost blinded. "Jackson is offering us a new lease. A very reasonable one, that allows us to stay here for as long as we want, and he's promised to start to address the list of repairs and maintenance that Petersen never did."

"What?" Lynn asked, looking at Jackson in disbelief. "Why would you do that?"

"Lynn," Sadie hissed, "I don't think we should question Mr., I mean Jackson's, motives, now should we?"

"No, of course not," Lynn said, hurriedly, shoving her hands into the pockets of her white coat. She glanced over at Jackson who had stood and was gathering up papers, stacking them neatly, and then placing them inside a file folder, which he then placed into his briefcase. He was wearing one of his expensive suits again, one that showed off his broad shoulders. He looked like himself again, professional, aloof, unreadable.

Snapping the briefcase, he picked it up, shook Sadie's hand, and turned to Lynn. One look and her hormones swelled up like a tsunami and had her senses humming. It was his eyes. That had to be it. The way they could look hard and hurt and soulful, as if the mystery that was Jackson was all in there. They called to the healer in her, but he only gave a brief nod and even briefer smile.

"Doctor," he said smoothly as he inclined his head in her direction. "I look forward to working with both of you."

Sadie's profusion of thanks echoed in Lynn's ears as she watched Jackson leave the office. Ok, that was weird. It was like the kiss had never happened, like they hadn't so much as touched. So his offering her the use of the gym at the hotel had been nothing but being...gentlemanly.

How could he ignore her like that? Or worse yet, how could he make her feel like...a horny teenager, without so much as him feeling a tickle of attraction? He couldn't generate this much heat in her without some sort of answering reaction, could he? It had to violate the laws of chemistry, she decided.

"Can you believe it?" Sadie turned and addressed Lynn. "I mean it's like some sort of miracle. The board of directors will be thrilled. The terms are really quite favorable, and I believe that we'll really be able to make a go of it here."

Lynn barely heard her but nodded all the same. She waited a moment, not sure what to do, but then she rushed out, determined to get to the bottom of this. She had to know if the attraction she felt for him was mutual or if he really was so cold that nothing of it was getting to him.

Chapter 28

She caught up to him in the parking lot, where he was just getting into the driver's seat of his BMW.

"Wait," she said as she jogged over to him.

He rolled down the window and looked at her from behind sunglasses. "Can I help you?"

"Why? I don't get it. Did you do it because of me?"

"You?"

It came out like a slap. Lynn realized that she had just made a fool of herself. Hormones, adrenaline, the triumph of the male conqueror, that's what the kiss had been about. Jackson had defeated another man at her expense and her kiss had been the prize. And that meant anything between them had to be one sided.

"Well, I mean…" Lynn stammered, feeling her face turning bright red, before she clutched at the very rationale he had given her. "You said the clinic was paying below market rent and was a losing proposition for you and you wanted to refit the space into a luxury medical spa."

"Upon closer examination of the details, it turns out you have a solid history of paying your rent, which, upon further evaluation, isn't as below market as I thought. So I negotiated a slight increase and in return, I'll begin to address the maintenance issues. Plus, the medical spa is still interested but would prefer an upper floor, with an entrance in the rear, as their clients tend to prefer a bit of anonymity. So as you might say, I was able to work out a win-win."

"A win-win?" Lynn said, thinking over the explanation. "It seems like you made quite an about-face from your previous position."

"You know, Lynn," he said, pulling down his sunglasses and stabbing her with his piercing blue eyes, "I am not as inflexible as you make it seem. Yes, I'm a businessman and I try to make money. But it's not always about squeezing every single cent from people. Plus you always have to balance short-term with the long-term benefits. Sure, I could probably kick you guys out, fix the place up, and find someone who would come in and pay me more in rent. But then how do I know they're a business with staying power? That in six months they won't close up shop and I'll have an empty space until I find a new client? And besides, Queensbay is my home, always has been, and according to some medical professionals I've talked to, the clinic plays an important role in the town."

"Ok," she said, accepting what he said. He moved to turn on the car, and on impulse she reached out to touch his arm, feeling the electric connection that ran sprang up when their skin connected.

She quickly drew her hand back, saw that he had glanced down at where her hand had been and was now looking up at her. Maybe there had been something more to the kiss. On impulse, she said, "I suppose this deserves a thank you."

"I don't need a thank you. I was just being a good
citizen," he said but a dark look crossed his face. He had
felt it, she was sure, that same spark of connection. But he
didn't want to acknowledge it. She took a step back.
Whatever was going on, Jackson was fighting it. She looked
at him, but he kept his hands tightly fisted around the
wheels, eyes straight ahead. She shouldn't push it, shouldn't
push him. She'd be asking for humiliation.

"Well then, again thank you." She took another step
back, far enough away so that Jackson could safely pull
away from the curb without running over her foot. She
almost missed it, the look of relief that crossed over his
face, the way the tension eased out of his shoulders and
relaxed fractionally.

He looked up at her and his face was unreadable.
"Goodbye, Lynn," he said. And then he hit the gas and the
car took off.

Chapter 29

"Why do you think Jackson changed his mind about the closing the clinic?" Lynn asked Tory. They were in Lynn's apartment, at the breakfast bar, drinking coffee and eating bagels Tory had brought from The Golden Pear. Tory had promised to help her do some shopping for dishes and cookware, something she had been dreading, but Lynn was getting tired of eating off of paper plates and cooking in the microwave.

Tory swallowed her sip of coffee. "Oh, I don't think he grew a conscience if that's what you're thinking."

"What do you mean?"

Tory laughed. "It's because the poor man has been subjected to a steady stream of his friends and family telling him he was a bad person, a terrible citizen, and that if he wanted to stay here and try to forget the past, he needed to let the clinic stay open. First up was Chase—I heard him on the phone giving Jackson an earful, then later Noah Randall stopped by while Jackson was doing something at the hotel. I didn't hear that conversation, but I did hear the one in The Golden Pear where Caitlyn and Darby tag-teamed him about his Scrooge complex."

"Oh." Lynn didn't know why she suddenly felt so deflated. Why should she have thought that Jackson's changing his mind about keeping the clinic open would have anything to do with her? Of course, it made more sense that he would have considered how it would look if he closed the clinic. It had been a calculated move, a strategic decision; nothing to do with his feelings about her.

"What is it?" Tory asked, her voice suddenly sharply curious. "Did you think you had something to do with it?"

Lynn shrugged. She hadn't told Tory about the kiss she couldn't get out of her mind.

"You're not telling me something." Tory looked closely at her and Lynn felt a flush of embarrassment start to crawl up her skin under the intense scrutiny.

"You didn't, did you? Omigod! Did you sleep with Jackson Sanders?"

"I did not." Lynn's hand flew to her throat. "He just kissed me."

"Aha! Gotcha. I knew something happened and since you weren't about to tell me, I had to guess."

"It was just a kiss!" Lynn defended herself.

"He kissed you and you're only just now telling me about it?" Tory looked at her over her coffee and shook her head.

"Sorry that saving lives had to come first." Lynn said, a touch of petulance in her voice.

"There you go. That's always your excuse, you know. That whole 'saving lives' thing. What about me? You know, I fixed someone's hard drive at work the other day—saved a year's worth of data."

"That's impressive too," Lynn answered, doing her best to sound like it was.

"It's how I got the morning off. A little way of Chase saying thank you, plus I worked until four in the morning debugging the customer database last night."

"Wow. Guys must love it when you talk computer speak."

"Only the smart ones." Tory flashed a smile. There was a pause and then she said, "So he is getting over the late, great Ashley."

"Funny, because I don't think he's over her at all." Lynn said, putting down her coffee cup and pushing her bagel away. Suddenly there was heavy feeling in the pit of her stomach as she thought of something. Jackson might not be over Ashley. That would explain why he seemed so determined to ignore whatever was brewing between the two of them.

"Why, what do you mean? He finally came back to town. I mean, he's been away for years. If that doesn't say he's over her then I don't know what does."

"Then he has the most self-restraint of any guy I know." Lynn's mind flashed back to the way it had felt, with her back up against the door, Jackson's hands holding her, the way their lips had met.

"What do you mean?"

"That's it. It's like nothing happened between us. I mean he talks to me, but won't look me in the eye. I can't decide if he hates me or if he's afraid and wants to jump my bones."

Tory smiled. "I'd go with he wants to jump your bones. But supposedly he was pretty messed after the accident. Left town right after the funeral and didn't come back until now."

"What happened?" Lynn had to ask.

Tory shrugged. "I don't know exactly. I was at college so I only got secondhand information. The details were murky, even the newspaper articles were kind of vague. But apparently, it seemed like Jackson and Ashley were out for a ride, going too fast or something and the car crashed. Jackson walked away without a scrape and Ashley didn't."

"You mean people blamed him?"

"Yeah. Well, Mrs. Moran did and she went around town, doing all she could to smear Jackson's name. That's why he left. I mean, things were pretty brutal for him here, from what I gather. I mean, obviously Chase and his friends, his real friends, stood by him, but it wasn't easy. Of course, Ashley came out looking like a saint."

Lynn nodded, thinking that it explained the reaction Jackson had gotten in The Golden Pear. But she caught the underlying bitterness in Tory's words.

"You don't sound like a fan," Lynn said.

"I don't like to speak ill of the dead, but Ashley was one of those girls who had everyone fooled. She was blond and cute and a star soccer player. She raised money for homeless dogs and sick kids. She had a smile for everyone to their face and then a knife for their back. And she had her claws deep into Jackson. I mean, if he so much as said hi to another girl or hung out with the guys instead of being with her, she gave him hell. She was just a real, well, bitch."

"Wow. What did she do to you?" Lynn asked, curious.

166

Tory looked up with a slightly regretful face. "Let's just say I wasn't always the hot computer chick you see in front of you."

"Oh?"

"In high school I was a scrawny, glasses-wearing computer nerd, and Ashley was the sort of girl who ate my kind for breakfast and spat them out. Not that I wanted her dead, but I am not sure she deserved the storybook ending, or to be memorialized as a saintly do-gooder."

Lynn frowned. Jackson didn't seem the sort of guy who would go for a girl like that; but perhaps cool, blond, and bitchy was exactly his style.

"Well, I for one am glad you're a computer nerd, because seriously I do need your computer skills."

"Doesn't everyone," Tory said.

"I can pay you," Lynn mentioned and she saw Tory's eyes light up. She knew Tory enjoyed working for Chase and his company, but she also remembered Tory had mentioned wanting to start her own computer consulting business. When Caitlyn had told her she should get a website up and running for Healthy Kids Now, Lynn had no idea where to start, but trusted Tory would.

"Do tell." Tory said. And Lynn smiled. Now that the clinic was on steadier feet, Lynn was excited to take her program to the next level. Caitlyn and Phoebe had inspired her to start thinking bigger. She knew she couldn't do it alone, and she was certain Tory was the perfect person to help her.

Chapter 30

"What are you doing here?" Jackson's voice came out of nowhere and she almost dropped her hotdog. He stood eye level with her, but only because she was sitting on the third level of the bleachers. She hoped she didn't have any mustard on her face and fought the urge to send her tongue in an exploratory lick.

"What am *I* doing here? Why are *you* here?" she answered back, looking at him in surprise. Of all the people she had thought she might see at a girls' soccer game, Jackson was the least likely.

He nodded toward the players on the field. "Watching the game."

She looked at the soccer team and then back at him. "Do you often watch girls' soccer teams? Should I be worried?"

"No." He rocked on his heels, and she got the sense that he was embarrassed. She waited, hoping there would be more, so she held his gaze with a questioning one of her own.

"The coach asked me to stop by," he finally said, running a hand through his hair. It was longer than she had seen it, curling slightly over the edge of the collar of his leather jacket. She realized that he wasn't wearing a suit, just jeans and a shirt. Not that she was complaining. Jackson could wear anything, or nothing at all, she was willing to bet, and still be hot. Even his slightly odd behavior was doing nothing to quell her appreciation of that basic fact and the effect it had on her system.

"Are you going to stay and watch?" she asked, patting the empty bleacher next to her.

He gave a smile, but it seemed forced. "Sure."

He took the seat next to her, but perched on its edge as if he was ready to bolt at any moment. Still, his arm grazed hers and he didn't pull back, at least not right away. There was the faintest bit of pressure and she again felt the electric current running between them. He turned and looked at her, an intense, direct blue gaze; she had to look away, shift herself ever so slightly away from him to break their connection.

Lynn put her half-eaten hotdog down. She was still in her scrubs, of course, but she figured she didn't need to add a mustard stain to the patchwork of substances that had already landed on her today.

"You never answered my question. What are you doing here?" he asked, looking straight ahead.

"I'm just stopping by too. I promised that one," Lynn pointed out the girl in pigtails, "number thirty-two, Anna, that I would watch her play once this season."

Jackson watched. "Ok," he said and Lynn knew what he was thinking.

"It's not about how good she is. It's about the fact that she's here at all."

"And why's that?"

"Well, she's one of my first." Lynn said. He looked at her. "One of the first kids I put on my Healthy Kids Now program. Over a year ago, Anna was about twenty-five pounds overweight and drank soda for breakfast and thought a French fry was really a vegetable."

"Ok," he said, watching Anna more intently now.

"Over the past year, she's lost the weight, loves vegetables, exercises for thirty minutes a day, and got straight 'A's last quarter."

"All right, I'm impressed."

"Yeah, she's an amazing kid, now. But she was a tough case, stubborn; didn't want to listen to me, thought she was too smart to hear what I said. So I made her promise to motivate her. I didn't know if it would work, but apparently it did."

"What sort of promise?" he asked.

"If she made the soccer team, I would come watch her play. I think she kind of looked up to me, so I thought the promise would give her some encouragement."

"And did it?" Jackson asked.

"She's out there now. She's their backup player, so she'll only be on the field for another couple of minutes, but..."

"That's not the point," he finished for her.

"And since then, about fifty kids have gone through the program at the clinic alone. I'm working on making it more official, so that other places, like hospitals or schools and even other clinics, can use it."

"Really?" he said.

"You sound surprised?" Lynn countered. She was staring straight ahead, watching Anna, but she felt his gaze on her, so she finally turned and looked at him.

"Actually, I'm not surprised at all. Sounds like a good idea."

She looked at him, suddenly not sure what to say, so she just nodded and looked back at the field, hoping to distract herself.

"Go, Anna!" Lynn called as she watched the girl catch a pass and then dribble it up the field. She made it a respectable halfway before the opposing team managed to swipe the ball from her. But it was a start.

The whistle blew and the coach called for a sub. Anna, her pigtails flying and her face red, came off the field to a round of applause and cheers from her parents. She waved at them and came straight toward Lynn.

Lynn hopped down and gave Anna a big hug. "That was amazing!"

"You watched!"

"A promise is a promise," Lynn said.

A man trailed behind Anna. He had on sweatpants, a visor, and a whistle around his neck.

"This is my coach, Coach Dave," Anna said.

Lynn said hi, but realized that Coach Dave's attention was not on her, but behind her.

"You came," he said. She turned and saw that he was speaking to Jackson, who had risen and was standing uncomfortably behind them.

"Dave," he said moving forward. Lynn watched as Coach Dave pulled Jackson into one of those awkward one-handed hugs that guys always seemed to do.

"Well, Anna did an awesome job today. But let me tell you, without this guy we wouldn't have a field to play on."

Jackson shrugged, but Dave wouldn't be deterred. "Yup, let me tell you up until a few years ago this place was weed lot. But thanks to Jackson and his donation, now the kids have a place to play."

"Least I could do," Jackson said.

Lynn thought that Jackson was embarrassed, since the top of his ears were turning red. She looked around. She hadn't given much thought to the town athletics fields, but she supposed they were pretty nice as far as junior soccer and little league fields went. This field was tidy, neat and small-town picture perfect under a blue autumn sky, the trees ringing it wreathed in their autumnal coats of orange, scarlet, and yellow. There were bleachers, baseball diamonds, and separate fields for soccer. There was the snack shack building that had sold her the forgotten hotdog, plus a playground with little kids swinging and hurtling down slides.

There was even, now that she noticed it, a nice bronze plaque. She had to strain a bit to see the inscription, but then Coach Dave led Jackson over to it, keeping up a running commentary on turf versus grass, number of teams in the league, and other things. Lynn trailed along, watching the rigid set of Jackson's shoulders.

The plaque, when they got to it, affixed to the side of the snack shack, was impressive. It showed the relief of a female soccer player and underneath it read, "Dedicated to the memory of Ashley Moran, beloved athlete. Made possible by the generosity of Jackson Sanders."

"I told you I didn't want any recognition," Jackson said, turning on Dave. Lynn took a step back. She recognized the look in Jackson's eyes. It was similar to the one he'd had after he decked Bode.

Coach Dave slapped Jackson on the back, seemingly oblivious to Jackson's anger, "Oh man, I couldn't let that happen. Without your donation, none of this would have been possible. People deserve to know, man. It can only help you." At this, Coach Dave's hand dropped low.

Jackson drew up himself up so he practically towered above Dave. "I didn't do this to look good. The whole point was that I didn't want anyone to know. Take it down. I'll pay for a new one." Lynn saw that Jackson's mouth was set in a hard, thin line.

Coach Dave seemed about to say something more, but even he had the good sense to realize Jackson was upset.

"Whoa, sure thing, Jax. Whatever you want. Didn't mean to upset you. Just thought…"

Lynn took a step forward and put her hand on Jackson's arm. He turned to look at her, and she saw a flash of anger die down to be replaced by something else. Pain, regret maybe.

"I just don't want to make a big deal about it."

Dave, relieved that Jackson didn't seem like he was going to get any angrier, held up his hands. "Sure, no problem. Like I said, I'll get on it right away."

"Thanks." Jackson turned around and started to walk away. She put an arm out to stop him but he looked down at it, and then up at her and she saw his face was contorted in sadness. She wanted to reach out, to touch him, to smooth his hair and tell him it would be ok, like she did with one of her patients.

He seemed to read her mind because he took a slow step back. "Lynn, I am not one of your patients. What I have can't be healed with some aspirin and rest."

"I know," she started to say but he cut her off.

"No, you don't know. I don't know what you've heard…" He swallowed. "You might think you do know, but you don't, you can't. No one else ever will. I came back home because I couldn't, didn't want to stay away any longer. But not everyone is happy I am here. And I can't drag you down with me, so this," and he held out his hands to encompass her, "can't happen. It's not a good idea," he finished, almost as if he were telling himself.

He took another step back and she stopped, not following him and taking a deep breath. Really how much clearer could he be?

"Ok," she said.

Surprise flashed across his face and she felt a small thrill of satisfaction. Maybe he was disappointed. If so, it would give him something to think about.

There was a call behind her, from Anna, telling Lynn to come watch.

"I have to go. I made a promise," she said.

He looked at her sadly, his hands jammed into the pockets of his coat. "So did I."

Chapter 31

"Looks like things are moving along here," Jake said, leaning in the doorway.

"That they are," Jackson said. He had gotten most of the demolition done on the upstairs space and it was now mostly an open, raw space.

"You've been pretty busy here. You know you could have called me, I would have gotten a crew to come on down, take care of this for you," Jake said.

"I didn't mind doing the demo work myself," Jackson said.

Jake walked in, taking a good look around, testing things like support beams.

"I heard you renewed the lease for some of the tenants," Jake said casually.

"Yeah, Madame Robireux wouldn't be moved. I think she practically threatened to put a hex on me."

Jake shook his head, "That's not who I'm talking about."

Jackson shifted some papers on the sheet of plywood he was still using as a desk.

"Oh, the clinic? I ran the numbers another time and it seemed like it was more beneficial to keep them. I even got them to agree to slight rate increase, and in return I'll start to make sure that all the maintenance items that were neglected under Petersen get addressed." He decided not to mention how he'd been bombarded with all the reasons on why not to close the clinic from Chase, Noah, Caitlyn, and Darby, just to name a few people.

"That's awfully nice of you," Jake said, his voice deceptively innocent.

"What is it?" Jackson finally asked as the silence stretched between them.

"I was just wondering if a certain brunette spitfire about, yay high," he held a hand up to his mid-chest, "had anything to do with it."

"You mean Lynn Masters?"

"Yeah. You know, the lady in the scrubs and the white coat, cures people for a living?"

"I'm not doing it for her. I'm doing it because they're a paying tenant."

"Wouldn't be the first time you did something just because of a pretty face," Jake said, his arms crossed, legs wide apart.

Jackson looked up from his laptop as a sudden thought occurred to him.

"Hey, why are you so interested in Lynn and me? There's nothing there you know, but I didn't think I was crowding in on your territory."

The thought had finally penetrated his brain that maybe the reason Jake was giving him a hard time about her was that he had eyes for Lynn himself. If so, that meant Jackson would have to back down, because that was the guy code, right? Which wouldn't matter since Jackson had no intention of going anyplace with her, did he?

To his relief, Jake gave a little laugh, "No, not my territory. But she's a nice girl. And friends with your brother and Phoebe."

"I know that. And I've barely said two words to her," Jackson said, keeping his voice neutral. Sure he had kissed her; but in truth, they'd never had much of an actual conversation.

"Oh, so you didn't get into a fight at Quent's over her? I just thought I'd heard something about that. You know, you could have let me know; I would have been your backup."

"It wasn't a fight," Jackson said, running his hand through his hair. "The guy didn't stand a chance."

Jake smiled. "That's the Jax I know. I heard you took down that meathead with one swift flying tiger kick."

Jackson shook his head, but he was smiling. "And I keep telling you there's no such thing as a flying tiger kick. The guy was a jerk. Lynn made it clear she didn't want to anything to do with him and he couldn't take no for an answer. That's it."

"Heard you walked her home too," Jake said, throwing himself onto a folding metal chair that Jackson had brought in so he wouldn't have to sit on a box.

Jackson wondered how Jake had found out. Maybe from Tory? "We happen to live next door to each other. It was only natural that I walk her home, make sure that the meathead, Bode didn't get any crazy ideas about following her."

Jake shook his head. "Always the gentleman, Jackson. You know, you'd better be careful."

"What are you trying to say?" Jackson asked, going still.

"I would just hate for things to get messy, bro. I mean you just got back. I don't want you walking out all over again, over another girl. It's not that I don't think you deserve a shot at happiness, but Lynn's a good woman, made a lot of friends—mostly because she's healed them."

"Are you saying she's too good for me?"

"No, I'm saying that you still have a perception problem my friend. Right or wrong, you're still that guy who was driving the car the night his fiancée died."

"And how does that affect my relationship—though there isn't one—with Lynn Masters today?" Jackson was aware his tone was icy.

"People won't want to see her get hurt." Jake shrugged.

"What makes people think I would hurt her?" Jackson asked.

Jake shrugged again. "You've got a reputation, that's all; and she's popular girl. I just don't see it working for you too. So don't let her get under your skin."

"Good thing I'm not looking for anyone to get under my skin."

Jake smiled. "I thought that's what we're all looking for."

Jackson threw a pencil across the table. "Enough. Are you here to grill me on my non-existent love life or do you have another reason for bothering me on an otherwise perfectly good workday?"

"Just so happens I might have a project for us. Turns out one of my clients wants to make her house energy efficient and was thinking about solar panels on her roof, and she started talking to me about these things." Jake a took crumpled piece of paper out of his pocket. "And asked me if I knew anything about them."

Jackson took the piece of paper. It was an article from a magazine about a relatively new type of solar roofing panel. He thought it was a promising way to go and had planned on including them in his product lineup.

"What did you say?"

Jake smiled. "Told her of course I did and that our green building division would be happy to work up a quote."

"Green building division?" Jackson said.

"Well, that's if you think you're ready to be in business."

Jackson felt a wave of relief rush over him. He hadn't known just how much he wanted Jake to be in on this with him.

"Long overdue," Jackson said, holding out his hand, and Jake shook it.

"Better now than never."

Chapter 32

Lynn didn't consider herself a computer whiz, not on par with Tory, but honestly, once she had the last name, it didn't take much searching. The local paper had devoted quite a bit of space to the story. Ashley Moran had been a beloved hometown girl, just as Tory had said. She had been a star high school and college soccer player. She had come back to Queensbay after graduation, where she was coaching the school's junior team. According to the paper, she had liked the beach and boating. Classmates remembered her as pretty, involved in school activities. She'd been a good student...blah, blah, blah...All the usual accolades had been heaped her way. And she'd left behind her parents, a younger sister, Lindsay, and her fiancé, Jackson Sanders.

Lynn sighed and pushed the laptop away. So Jackson had been one half of the town's golden couple. That was the baggage that Tory had been talking about. To have been there when it happened, to be a witness to that. No wonder he'd run away.

She got up, walked over to the breakfast bar, and poured herself another cup of coffee. She had to be at work in half an hour and still needed to take a shower.

There was no sense in dwelling on Ashley Moran. It had just been her natural sense of curiosity, she told herself, that had made her look the story up.

But now that she knew, did it change anything with Jackson? He had said they weren't a good idea, but Lynn didn't know if it was because he wanted to protect her from his history in the town or if he had recognized there was something between them and was fighting against it, for whatever reason.

And she had to admit, there was something about the wounded look in Jackson's eyes that spoke to her. Occupational hazard, but she knew she was driven to try and fix people who were hurting. He called to her, and she was pretty certain that the feeling wasn't one sided. But she didn't know what to do about it.

Chapter 33

"I need to see a doctor," Jackson managed to say, through the pain. The woman at the front desk looked up from her computer, coolly assessing him over her half-moon glasses.

"Take a seat; someone will be right with you."

She handed him a clipboard too.

"But I'm bleeding," he said. Maybe he should have driven himself right to the emergency room. It had looked like a lot of blood when the glass had sliced through his hand.

"You're able to walk and talk, so it can't be that bad. Just keep it elevated."

Jackson's mouth dropped open and then he shut it. It hurt like a bitch, but it didn't seem manly to admit that. After all, there was one kid waiting, holding an ice pack over a swollen elbow, who just sat there, legs swinging, not crying or bellyaching.

Stoically, he took a seat. Filling out the paperwork proved to be a problem, since he had to balance the clipboard on his knee and try to fill in all the little spaces with his personal information. He gave up after a moment, and that was all it took.

"Next." Suddenly Lynn appeared in the doorway, hands jabbed into the pockets of her white medical coat.

The woman at the front desk nodded at Jackson and he stood quickly. The move dizzied him and he felt the clipboard drop. He swayed and then she was there, an arm wrapped around his waist.

"Lean into me," she said, guiding him through the door to the back area of the clinic.

"I'm fine," he said impatiently. The dizziness had passed and he felt better, or as good as one could feel with an open wound.

"Keep that hand elevated," was all she said, leading him onto a hospital bed. She dropped him down and then closed the curtain.

He looked at her. Her rich brown hair was pulled back in a ponytail, but a few stray curls escaped, curling around her neck and along her the elegant line of her jaw. She was wearing perfume, nothing heavy, but a light, citrus scent. He closed his eyes and breathed it in. She smelled good, like an angel.

He felt himself being laid down on the exam table while she held his arm up. He opened his eyes, saw her start to unwrap the bloody towel and then he had to close them again.

"How did it happen?" she asked, her voice calm, businesslike, and strangely soothing. If she wasn't upset, it couldn't be that bad. Still there was no hint of warmth in her eyes, and he wondered where was the friendly bedside manner he imagined her having.

"I was working on the upstairs space, trying to get one of those windows unstuck, and it came loose, broke, and the glass got my hand."

She was looking at the cut, face unreadable.

"You were fixing something?" There was a trace of amusement in her voice.

"Sure. Why do you sound surprised?"

Her chocolate brown eyes fixed on him and he was aware that his stomach jumped and not because of the pain. He had kissed her, unplanned, without finesse; and since then she hadn't been far from his mind.

Sure, he could try and lie to himself that it didn't matter, but he was done with that. Part of coming back home had been to start with a clean slate, professionally. He hadn't given a thought to his personal life, only knew that it would be a bad idea to get mixed up with Lynn. She was too passionate for one. And she knew too many of the same people. Ending things would be messy.

Still, he constantly thought about kissing her again, and what it would be like to keep kissing her and let it lead them to where it was meant to be. It must be the blood loss, he thought. He had told her to stay away, that she would be better off keeping her distance. And he meant it. If only it would make it easier for him.

She took a step back as if understanding something of what was in his eyes.

"You just seem like the type to hire someone to do the manual labor, that's all."

"Looks can be deceiving," he managed to answer. "I've worked construction, hands on and around the globe, since I was sixteen. I might be more used to managing people now, but I still know how to use a hammer."

"Are you sure about that?" she answered, but there was a lightness in her voice, an almost teasing quality, and he took hope in it, giving her a smile. She hovered close to him, still looking at his hand, the space between them narrowing until he could feel her breath on him. She looked at him, unblinking and he couldn't look away, knowing at that moment that everything he had told himself about staying away from her was a lie. The attraction between them was thrilling and he thought he would slowly go crazy if he tried to ignore it. But she would have to play by his rules.

Whatever was flowing between them ruptured when a nurse came into the exam area and said, "Suture tray, Doctor."

He saw Lynn take a deep breath and step back. She was back in her doctor mode.

"You need stitches. You're lucky the cut didn't go too deep. I can do it here if you want; or you can go to the emergency room, but you'll likely have to wait."

"Ok."

"Ok, what?"

"You'll do it, right? I mean, sew me up?"

She smiled. "Yes, I can do it. I can even give you something for the pain."

His eyes took in the big glass jar of lollipops. "And a lollipop."

"Only if you're a good patient." The teasing note was definitely in her voice, and despite the pain he found himself relaxing.

#

Her hands were steady. She made sure of that. True, most of her patients were several feet shorter than this one and desperately scared when she had to do something like this. Jackson wore a grim expression, but he was still as she gave him the anesthesia and then stitched up the nasty gash in his hand. He kept a steady gaze on her, his blue eyes reminding her of the sky on the first warm spring day. Something between them had changed, she was sure—some realization on his part of their connection. And this time, instead of freaking him out, he seemed calm about it, accepting.

He was dressed casually, in jeans, work boots, and t-shirt, and smelled faintly of sawdust and soap. The nurse was in and out, and so normally, where Lynn would have kept up a steady stream of chatter with the patient, in an effort to calm him instead she found herself tongue tied, supremely aware of him.

She felt him watching her and finally felt compelled to say something. "You're renovating upstairs?" It was better to stick to small talk.

"Starting to," he said.

"Who's moving in there, the medical spa?"

"The what...?" His brow puckered together. "Maybe. But it's for me."

"You?"

"I need some office space," he said.

"You're doing the work yourself?"

"Some of it. I guess I won't be after this, though."

She hazarded a glance down at him. He hadn't shaved in a day or two and there was light blond stubble on his face. It went well with the dressed-down look.

"No. Probably a bad idea, since you'll have to keep the sutures dry. And the hand will be sore for a while but there shouldn't be any permanent damage."

She finished off the operation and added the bandage. She realized she was still holding his hand and that he made no move to take it from her. From out in the waiting room she could hear the sound of a kid crying, a high-pitched wail, which probably meant a fever. There was the noise of the DVD player that was on a constant loop of kids' cartoons and a steady hum of soothing voices and cranky kids. Other patients were waiting yet she couldn't quite tear herself away from him.

All of that was pushed to the background, and somehow all she could hear was the thud of her own heart and a curious thrum in her own ears. In her hand, she could feel the warmth of Jackson's, feel the beat of his pulse. His eyes held her and she felt as if the ground shifted beneath her, as her stomach jumped and flopped. It was a heady moment, as if a bolt of lightning had hit her, and Lynn took a step back.

He had baggage, she reminded herself. He was older, a sophisticated world traveler. They probably didn't have much in common. Still, her heart was racing and she felt like she could look in his eyes and never get tired. She wanted to know if he could ever look at her in the same way.

"All done?" he asked in surprise.

"Yes," Lynn said. His question broke the spell and she took the moment to turn her back on him, setting down her instruments on the tray, ready to strip off her gloves. She turned to find him standing there, looking down at her.

"I guess it's my turn to thank you."

"You can consider us even," Lynn said. It came out more sharply than she meant it to, but she had a sudden urge to be rid of him. She couldn't stand this push and pull with him. Either he was interested and going to act on it, or he wasn't and they could both be miserable and get on with their lives. But she wasn't going to beg.

"Listen, about the other day," he started to say.

She held up a hand. "You don't need to explain."

"But I think I do. You know, so you can be fully aware of the situation," he said, stepping closer to her. She felt the nearness of his presence, felt as if all the air were being sucked out of her. Years of medical school, years in the ER treating all sorts of life and death situations and now, here was a guy making her feel like a witless first-year med student.

"You don't have to tell me anything," Lynn said. She didn't want to be told that there was no way she could compete with a dead woman.

"Probably because you already know," he said, his voice was laced bitterness.

"What?"

"It's a small town. Not too many secrets. I am sure you probably know I was engaged to be married to someone—Ashley Moran."

Lynn nodded, but Jackson seemed not to see it. "She died in a car crash, and well, some people felt I was to blame for it. But you probably were able to figure that out from what happened at The Golden Pear. After Ash died, it was too hard to stay. I left town and pretty much broke off all contact with anyone from here. My own family, my brother, my best friend."

She had a vision of a younger, grief-stricken Jackson taking flight from town, a backpack slung on his shoulder.

"And now you're back?"

"I'm back."

"Why?" Lynn asked. Jackson was so close she could see the way his jaw clenched.

"Because this is my home, and it's where I belong."

"Oh," Lynn said. There was strength in those words, conviction. But she wasn't sure. It might mean that he was ready to move back to Queensbay, but did it mean he was ready to move onto something new in the relationship department?

He stood still, waiting, but Lynn didn't know what to say.

She was saved by the bell, or rather by another emergency.

"Doctor, things are backing up out here, I think we have a broken arm. Do you want me to re-route some of them to the hospital?"

She tore her gaze away from Jackson. She had a job to do, she reminded herself. Her personal life would have to wait.

"No, we're done here. Please take Mr. Sanders up to the front desk, go over discharge procedures with him."

"Very well. This way, please."

Jackson held back, looking at her for a fraction of a moment, as if searching for an answer. He nodded, gave a rueful smile, and then started to follow the nurse out of the exam area.

He paused, turned and gave her a grin that had her heart skip a beat and her stomach drop and do a flip. "Doctor, there's something you forgot."

Affronted, she said, "What are you talking about?"

"My lollipop. You said if I was a good patient, you'd give me a lollipop."

"A lollipop?"

He nodded and smiled.

She gritted her teeth and walked past him. He took up so much space in her small exam room there was no way that she could go around him. So she had to brush past him, letting their arms touch. The shock went through her body, straight through. She wouldn't have thought he noticed, but he must have because he kept looking at her.

"Lemon? Strawberry? Cherry?"

He gave her a drop-dead gorgeous grin. "I'll take the cherry."

She almost dropped the bottle before she was able to hand him one.

Chapter 34

It had been a bad idea. It had been Tory's of course, because Lynn never would have agreed to this without some serious trash talking from her friend. She hadn't played softball in a while but she remembered enough of it to keep from making a fool of herself. By the fifth innings she even felt she was acquitting herself well. She caught a fly ball and knocked someone from the opposing team out. She'd had more fun than she thought possible playing the game. They'd even managed to squeak out a win.

And that was why she found herself at Quent's doing shots with two guys. It was the shots that were a bad idea, not playing softball. One was named Bob, the other Jeff, she was certain; or maybe their names were Brett and Jerry. The tequila was making them both seem funny, and even Jerry looked mildly attractive. Not Jackson attractive of course, but it had been days since Lynn had seen him and her hormones were in a crazy overdrive cycle, which the tequila was doing nothing to mitigate.

"Wow, I can't believe I got you out!" Tory sidled up to her and threw an arm around her shoulder, carefully turning her away from Brett and Jerry, who were busy reliving the last innings.

"That was fun. Let me know the next time you need a pinch hitter. Or a relief pitcher. Or a whatever."

"So do you think either one of them is cute?" Tory asked, her voice dropping low as she took a sip of the beer she was nursing.

Lynn laughed until saw that Tory was serious. "What do you mean cute? Like *doing it* cute?"

"Yeah, what else? Look, you need to get over Jackson, and the best way is to get right back in there."

"There's no getting over Jackson because there's nothing between us," Lynn pointed out. She had thought that maybe, after she had seen him at the clinic, after that intense moment of connection, that he had rethought the wisdom of staying away, but apparently he was stronger than she thought.

Tory shook her head. "Look, if you're attracted to him and he's attracted to you, and he's not going to give into it and you're not going to push him on it, then you need to move on."

"Hold on there." Lynn spun on her barstool. "Are you saying you think I should give him a push?" Lynn asked.

As she thought about it, she realized that she had always let Jackson pull back, never really shown him what he was giving up. She had let him kiss her once, and then like a dumb damsel in distress hadn't followed up on that, and instead had let herself wait around for a second chance.

Lynn narrowed her eyes, focusing on Tory, who was peeling the label off her beer bottle. "I thought you said he had too much baggage."

Tory shrugged. "I'm not talking about getting into a long term relationship with him, but I'm sure if you gave him a little push you two could find a way to amuse yourselves. After all, you're the one who said it's been a while. You just don't want all of your lady parts freezing up on you, you know, from disuse."

Lynn punched Tory on the arm. "I already told you, that's medically impossible."

"In theory," Tory shot back, rubbing her arm where Lynn had whacked her.

Another round of shots appeared. There was a shout, a happy one, and Brett and Jerry downed their glasses. Two pairs of eyes turned to look at Lynn expectantly. She smiled, reached for the glass and hesitated.

Her stomach lurched at the smell; she didn't want it. Brett and Jerry looked disappointed, but not angry when she made her excuses, gathering up her sweatshirt. She didn't bother to say goodbye to Tory, just knew she needed to get out and get some fresh air.

What had she been thinking? That she was going to meet the right guy in a bar? Seriously. The night air was cool and she walked toward the water and her apartment. Bed sounded good, and so did her old flannel pajamas, along with a cup of ginger tea to ward away any ill effects of the alcohol. And besides, what Tory had said, about giving Jackson a push, was bothering her. Why was she being so patient with him? She'd never be so passive with one of her patients if they were sick, if they needed something; so why was she letting Jackson dictate the terms of their…thing?

"You're muttering to yourself." Jackson appeared almost silently by her side. She jumped, surprised. He had seemed to materialize out of nowhere, but she realized she was closer to their apartment building than she thought, almost in the parking lot. She glanced over. His car was there, the headlights dimming as if he had just pulled in, gotten out, and locked it.

"You've been drinking," he said.

"I had a few drinks. Well, a few shots," she amended. She couldn't help it, she was honest by nature. The thought almost made her start to giggle but she clamped down tight on it. Jackson was standing, looking down at her. From that angle his shoulders looked impossibly broad, his arms thick and muscled. His blue eyes were icy again and perhaps just slightly disapproving.

"Shots? Are you crazy? You must weigh a hundred and ten pounds soaking wet. You can't possibly handle shots."

"A hundred and fifteen," she corrected him. "And I can do shots." She hiccupped, giving lie to her words. Bed was sounding better and better, she thought, and then she looked at Jackson. An entirely different kind of thought crossed her mind. Perhaps the answer had been staring her in the face all along. Maybe Tory was right, maybe she just needed to give him a push.

She swayed a bit, only a little of it fake.

"Here, let's get you home," Jackson said, slipping his arm around her and directing her toward the Annex. He quickly guided her up the stairs and once again opened the door for her. She spun around on the doorstep, fixed him with a look that she hoped screamed 'Come hither,' and invited him in.

She sensed the barest moment of hesitation in him as he thought about it, discarded his concerns, and crossed the threshold.

She had made some improvements to the apartment. She now had dishes, wineglasses, a corkscrew, and even a bottle of wine or two.

"Thanks for helping me. Can I get you a drink?"

She didn't wait for an answer. She had no intention of drinking much more, but Jackson stood there, standing stiff, like a deer caught in the headlights. She may not need one, but he definitely looked like he needed something.

She reached into a drawer and easily found the corkscrew since it was just about the only thing in there. The bottle of wine was in the new wine rack she had bought, a small iron thing with leaves and scrolls on it.

She pulled two glasses down and poured some into each of them.

"You're not going to let me drink alone," she said. All of a sudden, whatever tipsiness she had felt at the bar was rapidly fading in light of the adrenaline and anticipation thrumming through her body.

"I guess not," he said, and he came farther into the apartment and took the glass she handed him.

She swallowed her wine and realized that she wasn't sure what to do next. Small talk? Try to look sexy? All well and good, until she remembered she was wearing a grass stained t-shirt and a pair of athletic pants.

"How's the hand?" she finally managed to say.

He held it up and waved it at her. "Great. I went to my regular doctor like you said. He was impressed, said you had done a great job."

"Thanks," she said and took another small swallow. She looked at the bottle. It had been a gift from someone at the clinic, and even though she was no expert, she was pretty sure she had just offered Jackson Sanders, global world traveler, one hundred percent bona fide rotgut.

She watched him take his own sip and saw when he tried to hide his wince at the taste. He gently set the glass down on the table. She wondered if she should say something about changing into something more comfortable? Did women really do that anymore? What would Savannah Ryan, her favorite movie star of all time, have done?

Lynn suppressed a sigh. Someone as elegant and glamorous as Savannah Ryan wouldn't have been caught dead in a pair of grubby track pants and a stained t-shirt. If possible, it was a step down from her usual attire of grimy scrubs.

Jackson cleared his throat, and made to get up. "Well, if you're ok, I guess I should be going."

Lynn decided it was a what-the-hell-moment. As he started to rise, she moved over to him and put a hand out squarely on his chest. His smooth, muscled, very hard chest, which she could feel through the thin fabric of his shirt.

"No you don't."

"I don't?" he said, confusion in his voice.

"You can't go," she stated, aware that her adrenaline was zooming and her hands were shaking just a little bit. Ok, make that a lot.

He looked down at her, his eyes dark, unreadable. He was tense, she could tell as she didn't move, didn't let anything come between them this time.

"You can't go until you kiss me," she said.

"Lynn, you've been drinking," he said, gently putting his hands over hers. She decided not to take no for an answer. She pushed herself closer to him. She didn't have far to go because he was reaching down for her, his lips rushing to meet hers.

He faltered and then gave in, his mouth covering hers. She wrapped her arms more tightly around him, pulling him in close to her, needing to feel him, feel something. Her fingers found the waistline of his pants, and her fingers sought the button.

Suddenly she found herself pushed away, almost flung back to the other end of the couch. Stung, she curled her feet up, wrapped her arms tight around her.

He was sitting there, his eyes heavy with lust, his breathing labored.

"What's the matter now? Do gentlemen not take advantage of girls who've had a few drinks? I thought that was the basis for just about all sexual intercourse in the western world."

He closed his eyes, took a deep breath and his whole body seemed to still. "Actually, they don't. Lynn you're hurt, you're a little drunk. This isn't a good thing. I don't want to be something you'll regret in the morning."

"How can I regret what I've never gotten?" she said angrily, almost unaware the words had come out. "You think you make all the rules here. But you know what? You can't keep ignoring what's between us."

"Lynn," he said, his voice rough and low with warning.

"No," she said, feeling bold. She wasn't going to let him sneak away with an excuse, she was going to push it.

"Don't try to talk yourself out of it. Just answer me this simple question."

"What?"

"Do you like kissing me?"

"Yes," he breathed. "I like it a lot."

"Then why don't we just go with it."

"Because…"

"I don't care about your past, Jackson. I just care about now. We're two grownups who are attracted to each other. Can't that be enough for now? What if I told you that I am not looking for forever? Just for right now."

"Is that all you really want, Lynn? Something for right now?"

"Yes," she said, knowing part of her was lying. But it was for a good cause, because what she wanted most right now was him. And she didn't care how she got him.

"So you're saying you're willing to have sex with me right now, even if I told you that it would be a bad idea. That I'm not the type of guy who's in it for the long term? That whatever happens between us is a no-strings-attached kind of deal?" He took her hands and looking deeply into her eyes, he kissed one hand, then the other.

"Yes," she whispered. "Will you spend the night?"

He shook his head and give her a slow, wicked smile that more than anything he had done sent her heart pounding and her senses tingling. "Not this night. I would rather you have a clear head for this."

"For what?"

"Just because we can agree to no strings doesn't mean we shouldn't have some expectations. Or anticipation. Or even some romance. When was the last time someone took you out on a real date?"

"What?"

"Not Two for Tacos or Aussie Night at Quent's."

She blinked, struggling to remember. "A while. I mean never. I mean, a guy took me for burgers and milkshakes once," she managed to say.

Jackson laughed. "Then I think it's even more important that we do this right." He paused and his face went serious. "Lynn, I'm not the kind of guy who believes in happily ever after, but I do believe in making the most of right now. And while there might be no strings attached, a gentleman, as you like to call me, still has certain standards to uphold."

"Oh," Lynn said, trying to find the strength to breathe, realizing that she was finding this unbearably sexy. Jackson got up, leaned down and brushed his lips across her forehead, sending an electric thrill through her.

"Does that mean you're going to sleep with me?" Lynn tried not to sound like she was begging.

"Oh, don't worry, I intend to do a lot more than sleep with you," he said, and it was all Lynn could do to keep her mouth from popping open.

"And now, I think you better start sleeping it off. I'll see you tomorrow."

Lynn could barely nod as he gave her a grin that had a bolt of desire shooting down her body until her toes wanted to curl in delight.

Chapter 35

The pounding in Lynn's head woke her up at the same time as the pounding on the door registered. She sat up, aware that she was still in her clothes from the night before, still stretched out on her couch, a blanket twisted around her legs.

Snippets of last night came back as she struggled to her feet, automatically going towards the door.

"I'm coming, I'm coming," she shouted at the unknown knocker, then muttered, "What the hell."

She opened the door to a glorious, sunny, fall day and Tory, her hair shining in the sun like a brownish-gold mane, framed by a backdrop of the glimmering water of the harbor.

"Man, you do look like crap. Maybe trying to meet a guy in a bar isn't the best approach." Tory kept up a running stream of conversation as she dropped a brown paper bag from which a delicious smell wafted up.

Lynn's stomach lurched, which reminded her that she had skipped dinner in favor of tequila shots. She wasn't sure if eating now would be a good thing or not.

Tory hiked herself up at the breakfast bar, uncapping a cup of steaming hot coffee. "Don't worry, I'll share this with you while you brew a cup. The breakfast sandwich is from The Golden Pear by the way. Practically guaranteed to fix whatever ails you."

Lynn, just nodded, went over to the kitchen cabinet, found a glass, and poured some water and drank. It slid down her throat, doing a little to push away the cotton ball feeling in her mouth.

"What happened to you last night?" Tory asked.

With a sigh, Lynn pulled up another stool. Tory pushed over the cup of coffee and the breakfast sandwich.

Over coffee and an egg sandwich, Lynn told Tory about what had happened with Jackson.

"Wow, so Jackson came to your rescue again, and decided you were too drunk to have sex."

Lynn thought back, her memory hazy. "It was perhaps just about my most mortifying moment."

Tory shook her head, was silent for a moment, "No, that's when your prom date doesn't show up because there's a comic convention in town."

Lynn thought for a moment. "Yeah, that's bad too."

They were silent for a moment. "So now what?" Tory asked.

Lynn thought. Just what had been Jackson's words...? *I'm going to do a lot more than sleep with you.* She shivered at the thought and felt herself tighten at the memory. A threat? A promise? Either way it had been hot. Hot enough that she could almost forget he was probably still in love with a dead woman.

"I guess he wants to go on a real date. He said that while he doesn't believe in happily ever after, he does like to show a girl a good time...or words to that effect."

Lynn's insides quaked just a little as she thought about what that might mean.

Tory nodded. "At least that's a few points in his favor. He has a job, a car, he's good looking, and he wants to feed you before he sleeps with you. Sounds like a winner to me. Of course, he still has enough baggage to make Paris Hilton look like a light packer, but as long as you know it's a no-strings-attached deal, you should come out of this just fine." Tory seemed to be saying it to reassure herself. She looked at Lynn with concern.

"What do you mean, just fine?"

"I don't want to see you get hurt."

"You're the one who told me I should change my expectations, just go for sex. That's all I've been thinking about for weeks now. I don't think I can turn back now even if I wanted to. What's so wrong with Jackson?"

Tory shrugged. "It could get messy. I mean, he's smooth and polished and you won't feel like he's just in it for the sex. Not until it's too late. And he can definitely afford to buy you dinner. But when it ends, you'll still have to run into each other all the time. Queensbay's a small town. But he'll probably send you flowers."

As if on cue, there was a knock at the door. Lynn got up calling, "Who is it?"

"Delivery," a disembodied voice called back.

Lynn went to the door and came back with a long, white box.

"Oh man, please don't tell me!" Tory said.

Lynn opened the card, looked at it, and felt a smile come over her face.

"OK, so who are they from?"

"Jackson."

"See what I mean? A classy type of guy. You're right. What could be better for you to reopen your foray into the world of sex? An over-muscled man-boy or someone who is going to treat you like a lady and then rock your socks off?"

Lynn nodded. "If Jackson Sanders is so hot and eligible, then why would he be interested in me?"

Lynn held up a hand when she saw that Tory was about to launch into a tirade. "I'm not throwing a pity party, but don't you think he's used to a different kind of woman? I walk around in a uniform that's basically a pair of pajamas. I'm knee deep in snot and vomit half the time. Unless my mother's cooking, I eat ramen noodles and drink cheap wine."

Tory shook her head. "Maybe it's time you thought of yourself differently."

"So what are you saying I need to do?"

"Nothing. I'm saying Jackson must like you just the way you are. So don't sweat it."

Tory looked at the flowers and looked at Lynn. "Ok maybe sweat it a little bit. When you're not working, perhaps it's time we upgraded your wardrobe from scrubs and yoga pants to some tailored pieces and a few more dresses. You know, if he's going to play the grown up game, maybe you should too. Like the gift wrap that will drive him crazy to get to what's underneath, if you know what I mean."

Lynn thought for a moment. "Scrubs really aren't sexy are they?"

Tory shook her head. "Not in the least."

"They are comfortable."

"So are sweatpants, but those aren't real clothes either."

Lynn opened up the box. There were a dozen long-stem yellow roses nestled there. She picked one up, smelled the beautiful, delicate fragrance, and put it down. If this was Jackson's idea of dating, then she was all for it.

Chapter 36

She ran into him just as she was coming out of the hotel gym and almost tried to avoid him. Sweats and scrubs. She couldn't seem to catch a break in the sartorial department when he was around. She remembered what Tory had said. It mattered what she felt like on the inside. Fine, then time to summon her inner sexpot. She closed her eyes, but before anything came to her, she had been spotted.

"Hello," he said.

She stood up a little taller and smiled. He smiled back and she took it as a good sign.

"Hi." There was a pause while she thought about what to say next. He took a step closer to her and she found herself tongue tied. Stay cool, she reminded herself.

"I guess you're feeling fine if you were at the gym," he said as his eyes swept over her tank top and shorts.

"Yes, actually I am. I mean I still have a bit of a headache, but thanks to you—and breakfast—I am feeling better."

He moved closer to her so that they were almost touching. One hand reached up and he took his finger and ran it along her shoulder.

"Lifting weights?" he asked.

She nodded. His light touch sparked the senses all over her body and she told herself it had to be just the leftover adrenaline from her workout.

"Who knew muscles could be so sexy?" he said, his voice pitched so low she almost couldn't hear it.

"Oh," she said and then tried to regroup. "Thank you for the flowers. They're beautiful."

"I figured you could use something to cheer you up," he said. His hand moved up and touched the few strands of hair curling loose from her ponytail. Yup, definitely not the adrenaline, she decided. Her heart was pounding so loud it was a wonder he didn't notice it.

"What are you doing?" she managed to ask.

"I was hoping to get you worked up," he said simply and looked at her, his eyes dark, intense.

Lynn sucked her breath in sharply.

"Is it working?"

She managed to nod.

He leaned down and whispered, with mock seriousness, "So I assume what we discussed last night is still agreeable to you?"

"Very agreeable," she murmured. He took a step back, breaking their connection and she acutely felt the absence of it.

A big smile spread over his face and he said, "Then I would like to take you out on a date."

"Do we have to?" Lynn tipped her head back and managed to make her voice light.

He wagged his finger at her. "No you don't."

"Don't what?"

"Don't sell yourself short. I told you drinks at a pub and Taco Tuesdays does not a date make."

"It does in my book," she said.

"Well then, you've only dated boys."

"And you're not?"

He took a step forward again and she almost jumped in surprise. Careful not to touch her, he bent down and whispered so only she could hear, "I am most assuredly not a boy, and what's more I can take my time to appreciate you."

"Oh," came her breathy response.

"We're going to do this my way. Now, I would like to take you out on a date."

"Yes," she answered simply, because really, what more was there to say?

He leaned back, looked at her. "Wonderful. Shall we say Friday night, then? I'll pick you up at eight?"

"Friday?" Lynn said, "But that's days from now."

"You waited this long, surely you can wait just a little longer? I promise it will be worth it."

"Very well, then." Lynn smiled and decided that two could play at this game. "I'll see you on Friday, then."

"Friday," he said. "And not that you haven't upped my appreciation for scrubs and yoga pants, but I was planning on going to a slightly fancier place," he added.

"I do own other clothes," she lied, giving him another smile. Then she turned on her sneakered heel and went out the door.

He watched her, telling himself that he was jumpy for no reason, that it was just a date, and that he had been on dozens of them before, with women who were a lot more demanding, a lot more sophisticated than Lynn Masters. But not one of those had left him with the tight little curl of anticipation and desire quite the way the thought of spending time with her did.

He wasn't sure just when he decided he couldn't stay away anymore. He was aware that he had been fighting it, fighting her since he had first seen her, and that every time he had been around her, she had grown harder and harder to resist. And that kissing her was like nothing else, so that all the senses seemed to rush from his head, and that it felt right. Ever since he had woken up in that hotel room, aware that he had been dreaming of coming home, he had been living on instinct. And his instincts about Lynn were pushing him toward her.

Chapter 37

It started before she even knew it, in the days leading up to their date. Her cup of coffee at The Golden Pear was on the house, courtesy of Jackson. A tray of cookies showed up at the clinic, to be shared by everyone. There was even a note slipped under her door, with the words 'Can't wait until Friday' scrawled in heavy black ink. The note itself was written on thick, creamy cardstock, with Jackson's name engraved on the top.

Lynn's every nerve thrilled in anticipation as she thought about Jackson and the way his hands had felt against her skin. He hadn't even kissed her again and yet she couldn't stop thinking about him. About the way his shoulders had looked, wide and strong the day at the gym. Or the fluid way he moved, whether he was in a business suit or a pair of jeans. Then there was the way he smelled, of clean soap, with the slightest hint of spicy aftershave. Or the way his blue eyes fixed on her and seemed to read all the secrets written inside of her.

To make it worse, she heard from him, with his presents and his notes, but she didn't see him, or even hear him really. She fought the urge to go to his door and knock, telling herself that she needed to be mature, patient, to allow this game to play out. But she'd barely seen a light on in his place, and try as she might, she hadn't heard a sound, not even the low hum of the television.

So she threw herself into work, focusing on the clinic and refining her plan for her Healthy Kids Now project. Things were progressing nicely and Caitlyn Randall had even promised to help her throw a fundraiser, catered by Darby at The Golden Pear. Work distracted her, but that calm was shattered whenever Tory texted her with questions like what was she going to wear, how was she going to do her hair.

Finally, Lynn gave in and agreed to go shopping with Tory on Thursday night, which was why she was now stuck in the mall, in a too-small dressing room, under unflattering light.

"How dressed up did he say to get?" Tory asked.

"He just said to 'wear something nice,'" Lynn called out, after she stared at herself in the mirror again, deciding that the black dress she was trying on made her legs look too short.

"Hmm, well does that mean you even have to wear a dress?"

"I want to. Don't you think I should? I mean it sort of covers all bases."

"It means easier access," Tory said, a shade too loudly. Lynn poked her head from the dressing room.

"Will you keep it down out there?" she hissed.

"What?" Tory shrugged, her eyes wide and innocent looking. "You know that's what you're thinking about."

"Am not," Lynn said.

"That's just because you've never done it right. If you had, then that's all you would be thinking about."

"I've done it right," Lynn said, wondering just how she had gotten into a conversation like this.

"Really, so you've had incredible, toe curling, over the top orgasm sex?"

Lynn felt her face starting to flame red. She wasn't a prude, but still.

"Ah, I can tell by your silence that you haven't."

"I had a good experience."

Tory shook her head. "If that's all you've had, then you weren't doing it right."

"If sex was that good, nothing else would ever get done. After all, sex is a biological imperative, survival of the species. It's not really about pleasure," Lynn said.

Tory just smiled. "If you think that, then it just proves that you've never done it right. So on Saturday morning, when you're thinking it over, you'll call me and tell me what you really think. Because you will be calling me, pronto, and giving me all the details. And I mean everything."

Lynn said nothing but shimmied into the final dress Tory had selected for her. It was short, but not too short, and a deep, scarlet red. It picked up the dark red highlights in her hair and made her brown eyes dance.

She was silent, admiring herself, the way the dress dipped down into a V in the front and then flared slightly over her hips and out, giving the skirt a kicky bounce.

Tory, made curious by the silence, popped her head into the dressing room and Lynn saw her smile in approval, "Oh, now that's the one."

"Yeah," Lynn said. "I think I found it."

"Great. All we need is to find some underwear," Tory said.

"I have underwear," Lynn pointed out.

"Not the kind I'm thinking of." Tory answered.

"How do you know?"

"A perceptive guess. Come on, let's pay for that and hit Victoria's Secret. I think there's some black lace with your name on it."

Lynn gulped, wondering what she had gotten herself into. Black lace and scrubs didn't exactly go together. But she took a deep breath. A grownup wears grownup underwear, she told herself.

Chapter 38

Lynn tried not to pace. But she was nervous. Her hands felt sweaty and her heart was fluttering. Jackson had slipped one more note under her door, a simple 'see you later,' but all day she had been thinking of him.

She checked the watch. Almost eight. She had declined Tory's offer to come over and help her get dressed, but she had called once in a panic about what to do with her hair. Finally, they had decided on half up and half down, with some tendrils framing her face. The curls, which she had pumped up with the help of her curling iron, fell in luxurious waves down around her face, skimming her shoulders, and touching the bare skin of her back.

Checking herself in the mirror one more time, she sighed in relief. She looked good, she decided, better than good. She had followed a video on the Internet about how to give herself sultry, nighttime eyes using makeup, and the woman staring back at her was nothing like the scrub clad med student she was used to. No, finally she looked like a woman, a sophisticated woman. It was something, she decided, that she could get used to.

There was a knock on the door and she nearly jumped out of her skin, then told herself it was just a date. She had been on them before. Ok, so not many, but she knew how they were supposed to go. They would talk, they would flirt, and they would kiss, and perhaps, hopefully, more. Because this time, she was sure that's what she wanted. Jackson.

Another knock came, and Lynn snapped to attention. "Coming," she said, shaking herself loose of her thoughts.

#

Jackson fingered the collar of his dress shirt, then stilled himself. He wasn't the type of man who made nervous gestures. He had carefully schooled himself to stay calm, to never betray any of the nervousness he felt. In business, appearing calm under pressure was half the battle, and he had earned the respect of more than one grizzled business veteran because he never panicked.

Just why then did his heart leap up when the door opened and Lynn stood there? She leaned against the doorjamb, almost tall in high heels, her petite body looking lean and long in a red dress that hugged her in all the right places. It dipped invitingly low over the swell of her breasts and he wrenched his eyes up, looking at her face.

"You look…amazing," he finished lamely, realizing that she did. There was something slightly different about her, as if she had grown up in the few days he had carefully avoided her. Her dark eyes were smoky with expectancy and her hair curled around her face, begging him to touch it.

She smiled and he was reassured, seeing in it the same girl he had come to know.

"Right on time," she said. "Would you like to come in or should we just go?"

"We can go. I mean, everything is ready," wondering why he suddenly felt tongue-tied.

She nodded and turned and he saw that the dress scooped low in the back, revealing that she probably wasn't wearing a bra, and that her back was toned and muscled. She moved, even in her high heels, with a grace he found compelling. She went over to the breakfast bar, picked up her purse and a jacket.

He came in then and said, "Let me," holding out his hand for her coat. Wordlessly she handed it to him, and he held it so she could step into it.

He let his hand brushed against her cheek, the skin on skin contact sending a delicious tingle of delight through him. Her breath caught, the only indication that she felt it too. She turned and faced him, her head angled up towards him, and he gently brushed his hands along her cheek again.

"Lynn," he said.

"What?" she asked.

He allowed himself to bury his head briefly in the waves of her hair, smelling her shampoo which gave off a flowery scent with a hint of citrus.

"If we don't leave now, we might not ever get out of here," he said.

"Oh," she said as she understood what he was saying. "Maybe that wouldn't be so bad," she said, her voice low and enticing.

"Oh no you don't," he answered, pushing her gently away. "I said I wanted to take you to dinner, so that's what we're going to do."

"What about what I want to do?" She moved closer to him.

"I think that's your hormones talking, and since we're both adults here, we'd be silly to listen to just our hormones."

"As a doctor, I have to tell you that hormones are a powerful force of nature."

He took her hands looking into her eyes. "Don't worry. I have every intention of making sure that our hormones are fully satisfied. You're not getting out of this, Lynn, unless you want to, but we need to make sure we take it slow."

"I thought that's what we have been doing."

"You know there's something to be said about the anticipation," he said, pulling her toward the door. "Or were you the type of kid who went searching for your hidden Christmas presents?"

"Absolutely. And I ripped the paper right off. I bet you were the type of kid who saved all the wrapping paper."

"Folded it too," he said with a wink as he closed the door shut. He still held her hand as he walked her down the catwalk to the steps.

"So where are we going?" she asked.

"My date. I'm not ruining the surprise," he said.

#

They drove out along the coast, away from Queensbay. She was glad that they weren't going to the Osprey Arms, since it meant that they'd be less likely to run into anyone they knew. She felt it was important to have him all to herself.

"This is Sean Callahan's, the chef at the Osprey Arms, other restaurant," he explained as the lights of his car lit up the tower.

"A lighthouse?" she said.

"Yeah. Pretty cool, right? Sean Callahan and Chase were so successful with the Osprey Arms that Sean decided to open this place up. It's out of the way and specializes in locally sourced food. It's only been open a few weeks, but I hear it's getting some great reviews."

"I've heard about it, but haven't been," she said, thinking that this sure beat the heck out of Salsa Salsa.

He pulled up and a valet appeared, opening her door. Remembering to swing her legs out first, before the rest of her, she managed to gracefully exit the car.

"Does the light still shine?" Lynn stopped, looking up at the tall stone tower.

"No. They built an automatic beacon farther out on the coast, years ago. The local historical society bought it from the government but they were having trouble maintaining it, so when Sean and Chase suggested that they rent it and fix it up, everyone was happy."

He put a hand on the small of her back and ushered her into the building.

The tower had a stone house attached to it, what must have once been the lighthouse keeper's cottage. It looked bigger, roomier inside, and she wondered if it had been expanded to accommodate the restaurant. The ceiling stretched up the full two stories and in the corner, you could see the iron stairwell that must lead up to the tower itself.

Whatever windows that had been there had been replaced with large, solid paned ones that looked out over the water. It was dark now, and in the distance lights were winking on, perhaps from the distant shore of Long Island, but more likely from boats still at sea. Without thinking, she felt drawn toward the window and she stepped over to see that they overlooked a cliff that dropped down to a rocky shore.

"Impressive," she said.

"Isn't it?" Jackson said beside her and she heard the pride in his voice.

She had heard that he and his brother were partners on a lot of their projects and she wondered if this was one of them. If so, he had the right to be proud, she thought, taking in the space more carefully. It was light and airy, with beams flying overhead, and a giant hearth, where a fire crackled merrily. It smelled of wood smoke, leather, and richly spiced food. Tables were scattered, simple, rough-hewn, solid wood ones. The whole place seemed inviting and she thought, quietly expensive. This much simplicity cost money.

"How about we take a walk?"

She glanced unconsciously down at her shoes.

He smiled. "I meant a climb. We can go up to the top of the tower."

"Really?" she said, feeling like a kid at Christmas. "The view must be amazing."

"It's nothing to turn your nose up at."

With a hand at the small of her back, he guided her towards the steps and they started up. Luckily, the lighthouse had already been built on a raised bit of land, so the tower itself was short—relatively—for a lighthouse. They made it to the top after climbing the tight, circular staircase. All the way, she was breathlessly aware of Jackson at her back, never too close, never too far away.

Small windows punctuated the sides of the walls as they climbed up, affording glimpses of the dark sky, but the real treat was when they finally ascended to the top platform. It was enclosed in glass and the giant light, while its powerful reflecting lenses, stood dark. There was a small door that led to a parapet outside and Jackson opened it with a key he pulled from his pocket.

"It says 'Do Not Enter,'" Lynn pointed out.

"I know the owner. Besides, the best view is from out here. You're not afraid of heights, I take it?" he asked, his voice light.

"I like to climb rocks," she pointed out as she stepped out onto the iron catwalk. It was covered over with weathered planks, for which she was glad, since it meant that she wouldn't catch her heel.

The moon was on the rise and the sky was dotted with the first stars of the evening, and she could hear the boom of the surf and the surge of the wind in equal measure.

"It's beautiful," she said, taken away.

"Not as beautiful as you," Jackson said. He stood next to her and she leaned into him, thankful for his tall frame and the shelter it provided from the wind. He put an arm around her and she nestled into his warmth, feeling the heat surging between them.

"Truly," he said, his lips somewhere near her ear, "you look amazing tonight." His lips grazed her cheek and she turned towards him, the sudden need for him overwhelming.

"Even doctors can clean up when we have too," she murmured, her neck arching, her lips searching out his. In a moment they met and their lips brushed each other, touched, and then his mouth covered hers and he kissed her.

Their tongues met and she encircled her arms around his neck, standing up into him. His hands came around her waist, pulling her closer while they kissed. She twined her hands in the hair at the back of his neck and allowed herself to lean into his long, lean body.

A moan, which must have been from her, escaped and she welcomed the heat and hunger as she felt his hands, hot on her back.

"We should," he said, finally pulling back, "go back down for dinner."

She nodded, marveling at how his light eyes were darkened with desire. He came in for one final kiss, then took her hand and all but dragged her back into the relative warmth of the interior platform.

He led the way down the stairs this time, the descent leaving her breathless, though not from the exertion. Her stomach was flip-flopping, clenching in anticipation and, she realized, something else, deeper. Two-sided attraction, she decided, was a very powerful turn on.

Dinner proceeded smoothly, with the two of them seated at a cozy table near enough to both the roaring fire and the window. Light music filled the air, and the place started to fill up, the volume going up, but never enough to be distracting.

She was jumpy, too nervous to eat much, but what she did eat was delicious. A crab cake appetizer, a fresh greens salad, and then grilled salmon.

"You know, you don't have to be nervous," Jackson said, somewhere between the salad and the main course, as his hand reached out for hers. She let him cover hers, feeling the warmth and the strength.

"I'm not nervous," she lied.

"Oh really?" he arched one eyebrow.

"Ok, maybe a little. It's just that it's been amazing so far. You, the drive up here, the tower, the food."

"You've never been out to dinner?"

"Of course I have; it's just that you know most med students are, well, a little on the impoverished side, so we usually go for places where the drinks come in plastic cups and the food is usually served in red plastic baskets."

"Truth be told, I've been known to enjoy dinner served in a plastic basket too," he said.

"I find that a bit hard to believe," she said.

"It may have been a while, but there's nothing wrong with it. I just wanted to show you that you're special. That you deserve this."

She looked at him, with his blond hair, the sculpted cheekbones. "You don't have to, you know. I mean this is nice and all, but..."

"Don't," he said.

"What?"

"Don't talk yourself out of what you deserve. Lynn, you're beautiful, accomplished, and hell, I'm betting you've saved a life or two; you're funny, intelligent, and strong;

and, well, the list could go on. You deserve the best, so please allow me to treat you that way."

She was speechless, reaching for her wine and taking a sip to cover her emotions. He was right, she thought. She had never demanded much from the guys she had dated, mostly because she had been too absorbed in pursuing her career.

"Thank you…but I'm not impressed," she added.

"Then I guess I'll have to try harder," he said, a playful smile lighting up his cheeks.

"Ok, so you know I'm a doctor and like working with kids, so why don't you tell me what you like to do besides follow me places and play with power tools?"

He shrugged. "Jake Owen and I used to run a lawn mowing service in the summertime, then we got into painting houses, then handyman stuff, all while we were in high school. I went off to college but we kept it up over the summers. Then one year I got an internship with a big construction firm in New York City. As project manager. You know, learning how to build skyscrapers while managing time and budget. I loved it and they offered me a job after college. I was supposed to do it for a year or two and then Jake and I were going to go into business for real, start a full service construction business. Sort of expand on what his dad had started."

Jackson toyed with the stem of his wineglass and Lynn waited.

"Then the company offered me a chance to go to London, to work on a project there. I took it and for the past couple of years I've traveled, managing building sites in Dubai, Hong Kong, even Australia for a while."

"Sounds like you were quite the nomad," Lynn said. She noticed that he didn't mention why he'd left in the first place. Fine, if he didn't want to talk more about Ashley, then she could live with that.

"I was."

"Why did you decide to come back?" she asked, hoping that a question like that wasn't off limits.

He looked down, then up, and his blue eyes were dark but his expression was rueful, "Look, don't think I'm crazy or into this hocus-pocus stuff, but I woke up in my hotel room one morning and all I could see was sand and tall buildings, hot, dirty, dusty. And I thought I had to get out of there. I'd been having a dream, of water, of boats, of Queensbay. I knew it was time. Like I was finally called home."

She looked at him. "For real, you felt a calling?"

"I can't explain it but I just decided to accept it. So far, things have been working out," he said.

"And just like that you quit?"

"Well, almost. I gave them a decent amount of notice, but I also felt like I learned as much as I needed to, plus I sort of got more interested in green construction and remodeling older buildings—you know, bringing things back to life. My employer builds things on a massive scale. I want to do something smaller scale, more environmentally friendly, maybe even self-sustaining energy-wise. Right now, it seems like the next big wave will be solar power, really getting it to catch on, with all sorts of construction, big and small; and I want to see if I can be a part of that."

"So back to Queensbay? What are you going to do now?"

"Well, Jake and I are joining forces. I'm redoing the old Sail Makers' building—in case you haven't noticed," he said with a wink. "And Jake and I will get started on renovating the Osprey Arms soon. It should keep me busy for a while."

"And after that?" Lynn asked curiously, wondering if there really was enough here to keep a man who lived all over the world busily.

"I have my eye on a few projects in the area. Some big, some small. I'm sure I will find things to occupy myself."

Lynn sighed. "Sounds like pretty soon you and Chase will own half the town."

Jackson laughed. "We won't be that bad, but to be honest, Queensbay was on a long, slow, slide for a while. Chase and I, well, we're happy to help bring it back to its former glory."

Her eyes narrowed. "Not you too?"

"What do you mean?"

"Let me guess, you got in early on Noah Randall's IPO?"

He laughed. "Chase and Noah have been friends for a long time. I just rode on their coattails; but yes, it was one of the best investments I ever made."

"And now you and Jake are going to be swinging hammers together?"

Jackson smiled. "Something like that. Truth, I'm more of the sales and marketing guy. And Jake only swings a hammer these days when it's for a friend."

There was a pause but before Lynn could ask another question, he said, "Perhaps you'd like to check out the dessert menu? I've heard the chocolate cake is amazing, as is the upside down walnut apple pie."

Lynn sensed that Jackson wanted to change the subject and decided that it was all right. After all, she wasn't sure he'd want to hear her talk about the correct way to perform a tracheal intubation.

"I'm game for it, if you are."

"Challenge accepted," he said.

She excused herself just after dessert, going to the ladies' room and closing herself in the stall. Dinner was almost over, and this was it, she thought. She hadn't been sure if it would be his place or hers, but she had made sure that she had fresh sheets on her bed. She leaned against the door, savoring the prospect. She was nervous yes, but more than that she was ready, her body humming with excitement.

She let herself out of the stall, stood at the sink. The wind on the tower hadn't done too much damage to her hair, but she rearranged it so the dark waves fell down on her shoulders. She wanted this, she thought, wanted this with him. She took a deep breath, to steady herself, telling herself she was ready.

Jackson was waiting for her, her coat draped over his arm. As he helped her into it, her skin tingled from the brief contact. He took her hand and led them outside. The valet jumped to attention and his car was there in a moment.

He guided into her the passenger seat, and she leaned back in the soft, buttery leather as he got in. The car pulled smoothly away, heading down the coast road back towards Queensbay.

She didn't know what to say, her tongue feeling thick. She almost jumped when she felt his hand reach for hers. He took it gently, brought it to his lips, and kissed it.

Comforted by the gesture, she found her voice. "Thanks for dinner. It was lovely."

"My pleasure," he said, throwing her a glance. They were almost to back to town and he pulled smoothly into a spot. She looked up. The third-story window of her apartment was there, with the small light she had left on, a beacon in the dark.

Before she could open the door, he was there, his hand reaching for her. She let herself be pulled up and into him. She half expected him to kiss her, but he didn't, just letting her linger in his arms while he sent her a lopsided smile that caused her stomach to curl in a tight ball.

She led the way up the steps and when she reached into her purse for the key, he took it from her and in a smooth gesture, unlocked the door and opened it up for her. The door swung wide and she stepped in, turned. He was still standing outside the door, not coming in.

"What are you doing?" she asked.

"Saying good night."

She felt her face fall. "Don't you want to come in?"

"Not tonight," he said.

She took a step back as if she had been slapped. He held up his hands. "I didn't mean it that way."

He stepped closer, but still stayed well outside the door. "More than you know, I want to come in, but then I might not be able to leave."

"Isn't that what you want? It's what I want." Lynn was tired of beating around the bush.

He looked at her, his eyes dark, unreadable. "You know it's what I want. And I'm glad it's what you want to. And believe me, I intend to get there with you."

"Then why don't you come in?"

He took a deep breath and a step back. "Because I'm enjoying the way things are going, Lynn. And truth be told, it's a little fun to watch you beg."

"I'm not begging," she said as she stepped forward, closing the distance between them, "I believe you respect me, if that's what you're worried about." And she did. Whatever happened with Jackson, even if he didn't believe in happily ever after, she knew that he would appreciate her, care for her while it lasted.

"You know I do. But I want you to be sure. That you understand the rules. We're attracted to each other, we want to be with each other..."

"And that's it. I got it, no strings attached. But seriously, I'm not sure how much longer I can wait," she told him, as her insides clenched in frustration. Ok, there, she was almost begging.

This time he let her get close to him and she kissed him. He didn't respond at first and then his mouth came down on hers, covering hers with hot heat and possession. His hands twined in her hair and she stood up on her tiptoes. Before she knew it, he had backed her up against the wall in her apartment and was kissing her back, pressed into her. Her brain couldn't think, lost in the heat and passion. She felt the tingle of excitement spread through her as she wrapped her arms around his shoulders.

He pulled away. "Like I said, you should have no doubt that I want you. But, not like this."

She looked around. "We could go inside. I have a couch, a bed…"

He smiled down at her, a suddenly wicked smile that had knees trembling. "Don't worry, I have plans. Do you trust me? I want it to be special. You said, after all, that it's been a while."

"I didn't say that," Lynn said.

"You didn't have to," he said with a sly smile.

"I don't need a trip to Paris or anything like that."

"Now there's an interesting idea," he said as he nuzzled her neck. "But I was thinking that we'd spend the day together tomorrow."

"Ok," she said, surprised and delighted. "I can do that."

"Meet me at the docks, tomorrow, say ten o'clock. How about we go for a boat ride?"

"A boat ride?" she asked. "Isn't it cold out?"

"Dress warmly. I want to show you something."

"Ok, a boat ride. Should I bring anything?"

"No, I've got it covered," he said. "I'll see you tomorrow."

"Fine. If you think you can wait that long." She said it as a challenge, wanting to see if it would make him reconsider.

"Oh, I'm not sure that I'll get much sleep tonight. But like I said, I'm a patient man; I can wait."

She realized she wasn't going to get any more than that from him, so slowly, tantalizing, she closed her door.

She waited, leaning against it, to see if she could hear him. There was a shifting of weight, the slight creak of the floorboards underneath him and then she could sense movement against the door, almost feel where he had placed his hands. She lifted one up, to where she imagined his was.

"Lynn, go to bed. Trust me, I'll be waiting for you tomorrow," his voice came through the door.

And then she heard him go.

With a sigh that did nothing to calm the adrenaline coursing through her, she turned and faced her empty apartment. She had a feeling it was going to be a long night.

Chapter 39

"What do you mean nothing happened?" Tory screeched so loudly that Lynn had to close her eyes. "He took you to the Lighthouse, voted the most romantic restaurant in all of New England, and you barely even kiss good night?"

Lynn sighed. She had finally managed to get to sleep but then she'd an embarrassingly vivid dream and she had woken in the midst of tangled sheets, damp from head to foot, with an aching knot of frustration tied up tight within her. She hadn't been able to sleep after that, and when she got the early morning text from Tory, she had agreed to meet her for a quick cup of coffee before her plans with Jackson.

"He said he's being patient."

"Sounds like he's teasing you," Tory said, and Lynn could almost hear the wheels of her brain turning.

"Though, that's not necessarily a bad thing. I mean, talk about the buildup! You must just be about to explode. I mean, your underused lady parts facing an eruption of cataclysmic proportions."

"Will you shut up!" Lynn said, looking to see if anyone else had heard. Joan Altieri, the proprietor of The Garden Cottage, a local store that sold fancy home goods and knick-knacks, seemed awfully engrossed in her morning paper, which must have been racy enough to have the tops of her ears turning pink.

Even Darby Callahan, all eight and half months pregnant of her, seemed to be hovering near them, wiping a neighboring table down with an unusual thoroughness.

She had thought that meeting with Tory would help calm her, but Lynn was as jumpy as a flea with eczema, and Tory's voice was a little too loud for comfort. It was a small town and if Joan and Darby knew about her and Jackson, it wouldn't be long before all of Queensbay, including her parents, found out. Besides, given what half the town thought of Jackson, maybe keeping their relationship quiet was the way to go.

"What, it's not like everyone isn't after the same thing here. You're due for a good healthy dose of robust exercise."

"Seriously, is that all you think it is?" Lynn hissed.

"It's not the only thing, but it certainly makes this business of living a little more exciting... You know," Tory said, breaking off a piece of her chocolate croissant, dunking it in her coffee, and then holding it half way on route to her lips, "Jackson may have you right where he wants you."

"And what does that mean?"

"Awfully worked up. And focused on one thing. Wow, look who has the one-track mind."

"I do not have a one-track mind," Lynn protested.

"Whatcha thinking about now?" Tory said as the chocolate croissant disappeared between her lips.

Chapter 40

After her breakfast with Tory, she walked slowly home and waited until it was time to go. Her mother had called and left a message, asking her to call her. Lynn was certain that her mother had made it into the café and had heard the gossip.

Lynn decided her mother could wait, but wasn't surprised when her mother sent her a text: *"be safe...and by that I mean use protection"*

Feeling the flames of embarrassment light up her face, she didn't know how to respond to that, so she ignored it. It was the pitfalls of having two parents who were doctors themselves. No beating around the bush when it came to bodily functions. And safety first, always safety first.

Now she was walking along the docks of the marina, enjoying another beautiful fall day. There was a chill in the air but she hardly felt it through her sweater and fleece, which was warm enough to withstand an arctic storm.

Jackson had sent her the slip number so she could find him and as she passed boats big enough to take up residence on, she wondered just how much money Jackson had made investing. He had said boat, not yacht, she was sure of that.

However, the directions led her just past a sleek white motor yacht with tinted windows, around a sloop large enough to have sailed around the world to something much more charming.

"This is yours?" she asked looking it over. Jackson stood in the little cockpit of a gleaming, varnished, antique wood runabout. The hull was a golden brown and the brass trimmings shined bright. Jaunty striped cushions were on the two captain's chairs and the small bench that ran along the back of the cockpit. Everything was orderly and precise in the little boat, which rocked slowly in its slip.

"All mine," he said. He was wearing jeans, boat shoes, and a fleece pullover that hugged his broad shoulders. The sun glinted on his fair hair and there was a definite note of pride in his voice.

"She's beautiful," Lynn acknowledged. Living on the coast might be new to her, and boats somewhat uncharted territory, but even she could see this boat was a classic, something that must have been lovingly restored.

"Thanks. I did most of the work myself, years ago. Well, everything but the engine," he admitted.

"Was it a lot of work?" Lynn said.

"You bet. She was a wreck, literally. Washed up on the shore. I was the first to find her and when the owner decided she was too far gone to fix, I had a hell of a project on my hands. Chase has been looking out for her for me, but I haven't been out since I got back into town."

Lynn could tell that Jackson was just as excited as she was about the prospect of a day on the water.

"Do you need me to cast off?"

"That would be great." Jackson started the engine, and it gave off a low, throaty putt-putt as it idled. Lynn walked to the bow of the boat, untied the line, and then walked to the stern. She loosened it and then did as graceful a flying leap as possible onto the boat, while holding onto the stern line with one hand.

Jackson's arm, the one not manning the steering wheel, caught her and pulled her close. He gave her a quick kiss on the cheek before turning his attention back to the water in front of them.

Lynn thought about the butterflies in her stomach and willed them away. It was a beautiful day, warm for October, and the sky was a clear, deep blue, with large, white clouds scudding across it. In the sun it was lovely, but she was glad she had dressed warmly. There was more than a hint of the changing seasons in the air, of unsettled weather and longer, darker nights.

Jackson guided the boat out through the closely spaced vessels moored close to the marina and then out into the channel. Soon most of the boats would be pulled in for the winter, but there were still a fair number to navigate through.

"You never told me where we were going," she said, raising her voice to be heard above the sound of the engine and the wind. She had pulled her hair back into a ponytail, but some strands whipped across her face and she tucked them behind her ear.

"Here and there," Jackson said.

"Here and there?" Lynn asked. "You don't seem to be a here and there type of guy."

He shrugged. "Not on dry land. But the water's a different story. I thought we'd explore the harbor. Have you been out?"

"Once, with your brother and Phoebe, on Chase's sailboat. My dad's thinking of buying one, so Chase gave him the tour."

"Ahh, Chase and his sailboat. Now tell me," Jackson said as he pushed down on the throttle and the sleek little boat jumped ahead, "Which do you like better..."

Lynn laughed as her hair whipped wildly around her head.

He even let her drive, or steer, the boat. She stood up, so she could have a clear view of the water ahead of them, and he nestled himself behind her, his body blocking the wind, his weight a comforting presence as he showed her the controls, taught her how to pick out a spot on land and use that to guide her.

They moved past the hulking wreck of the Queensbay Show House, its tattered 'Save Me Now' banner flapping in the wind, and then up the shoreline into a sandy cove, and then back out into the main harbor.

She was having so much fun she didn't notice that the white clouds had piled up into a mass of smoky gray ones and that the sun was covered by a milky film that stole its warmth.

"Is it going to rain?" she asked, glancing up as she shivered.

Jackson followed her gaze. "Most likely. But that's ok."

Lynn looked back over her shoulder. It was hard to judge distances over the water, but she felt even if they made all out for the marina, they were still looking at getting a good soaking before they landed.

"I don't think we'll make it back to the marina in time. Don't suppose you have any foul weather gear on board?"

There was a small stowage area in the bow of the boat but it wouldn't really provide much in the way of shelter, Lynn thought.

"I might, but we won't need them," Jackson said, his hand coming down over hers as he slowed the throttle down and nudged the wheel in the direction of the shore.

"We're going to go to the beach?" She knew she wasn't keeping the surprise out of her voice.

"Not quite. We're heading for that dock there. We can tie up there and catch some shelter."

"Won't the owner get mad?" Lynn asked.

Jackson shot her a smile. "He's an old friend. He won't mind."

Lynn was about to argue that they couldn't just go barging in on someone when the first large raindrop splattered on the windshield in front of them. Already the wind had turned colder, more cutting and she thought that it would be nice to get inside.

"Want me to take her in?" Jackson asked, and Lynn handed over the wheel. She set out the bumpers along the gunwales and picked up the bowline, waiting. Jackson guided the boat quickly but gently and cut the engine so they floated up to the dock. Just before they touched, Lynn was out, tying the boat down. The rain was starting to come down a little harder now, the flat surface of the harbor awash with concentric circles as each raindrop landed and disappeared.

Quickly and without much talking, they secured the boat together. He lifted a cushion and she saw there was a compartment under one of the benches. From it he pulled out a bright yellow rain slicker and tossed it to her. She wrapped it around her and in a moment, Jackson was with her on the dock. He grabbed her hand and they all but ran up the long walkway towards the end where the dock landed on the sandy verge.

She looked up. They were along the bluffs of the harbor, where the elevation went almost straight up. She could catch a glimpse of a structure amidst the trees above.

"Hope you don't mind a bit of a climb," he said as he pointed to the set of steps that zigzagged up the steep incline.

"Not a problem." The rain goaded them on and the climb was over before she had even realized it began. The steps opened up to a wide lawn and Lynn got the impression of a low-slung building that hugged the hill it was built into. There were windows, lots of them, and strong, sturdy beams made of warm brown wood and dark metal. Staying close to her, Jackson hurried her up the slope, then to a set of stairs that led to a wide-planked deck that ran along the front of the house.

Still shielding her from the rain, he slid open a door and they plunged into the silence of the house. Lynn stood, letting her racing pulse slow as she took in her surroundings. Windows. She got the impression of lots of windows and open space, metal, and wood trusses. It was sparsely finished because she realized that most of it was new. There was the faint smell of raw wood and new paint, even as there was the smell of something else, like cinnamon and vanilla mixed in as well.

"Is this a new house?"

With a slight shushing sound and a click, the slider door locked into place and Jackson turned to her. "Not quite. It's been completely renovated though. It used to be a traditional ranch, a bit boxy, with nothing special except for this."

He motioned and she was drawn to the window. The sky was completely overcast now, a gunmetal gray that turned the surface of the water to a leaden pewter shade. The rain, which had started in large, single drops had now turned into a single sheet of water pouring down. She shivered, feeling the dampness, glad that they didn't have to go out there again, at least not right away.

"Here," he said, dropping an arm around her shoulder. "Let me start a fire."

He led her down to a sunken living room, where one wall was dominated by a fireplace, surrounded by mellow gray fieldstone. The chimney, in the same stone, went up to the vaulted ceiling above. A sectional couch, in a light cream color, sat across from the fireplace.

Grateful, Lynn sunk into it, while Jackson crouched by the hearth. As she stripped off the raincoat and her damp fleece, she could see that a fire had already been set— paper, kindling, and some nice fat logs. All that needed to be done was to set a match to it. Jackson took a long narrow container, opened it and a match appeared. He struck it on the bottom of the tin and the flame jumped to life. Cupping a hand around it, he maneuvered it closer to the fire and touched it to the paper.

In an instant, the flame caught and there was a crackle as the fire settled in. Almost immediately, she could sense the warmth coming from it, and she moved along the side of the couch to get closer to the blaze.

He turned and looked at her, throwing her a smile. The light in the room was soft and gray, a reflection of the world outside. His blond hair caught the red of the flames as he leaned back on his haunches.

"Sorry about that. The weather wasn't supposed to turn this early in the day. I thought we had until late afternoon."

"Is it supposed to rain for a while?" Lynn asked.

Jackson got up, and reaching past her picked up a soft wool throw in a dark chocolate color. He draped it around her shoulders and she soaked up the warmth.

"Until late tonight."

"I guess we won't be going back out in the boat for a while."

He looked at her. "Not if we don't have to. There's supposed to be a decent amount of wind, with the rain heavy at times. It's not that far back to the marina but there's no sense risking it if we don't need to."

"So we're stuck here?" she asked, the realization of the possibilities suddenly dawning on her.

He came up to the couch and leaned a little closer to her. "In a matter of speaking. We're not that far from town, you know. Pretty sure there's a car in the garage, if you want to go home?"

"Your friend, is he coming back anytime soon?"

"Friend?" Jackson said and his face showed a moment of confusion. "Oh, you mean the owner."

Lynn, nodded, wondering why she suddenly felt shy.

"No, I think we're safe from any interruptions," he said, his voice rough.

She felt a flash of desire, of anticipation and tried to hide it by stretching out her legs.

He smiled, as if sensing her unease. "How about something to eat? And some music?"

"Maybe some music," Lynn agreed.

"Good idea. The stereo system is over there. I'll check the kitchen and we'll meet back here?"

Relieved she had something to do, they got up, and Lynn went to the shelf that held the radio. It looked like all she had to do was turn it on. A small screen popped up, allowing her to select a type of music. She scanned through the choices, settling for classic rock.

Satisfied, she turned and wandered back towards the kitchen. This floor seemed to be taken up by one large room that was divided into a kitchen, an eating area, and the sunken living room. Beyond that, there was a set of stairs leading down and a hallway beyond that. She imagined that the rest of the house, things like bathrooms and bedrooms, all had to be down there.

The kitchen was brand new. Dark granite counter tops contrasted with lighter, amber colored wood cabinets. The appliances sparkled and were all top of the line. Lynn knew, since her mother was a spectacular cook and coveted ones like these.

"It still smells like a new house in here," Lynn said snagging one of the stools that ran along the counter.

"Yes, the renovation just finished. Mostly. There's still a few things to do, but it's livable."

"I'm surprised the fridge is stocked," she said, craning her neck for a better look.

"Always be prepared," Jackson said, emerging with a bottle of champagne.

She looked. He had already set out some cheese, crackers, and grapes.

He opened a cabinet without hesitation and pulled out two champagne flutes. She watched as he set them down and expertly opened the bottle. There was a small pop and the white bubbly liquid dribbled into the glasses.

She took the one handed to her. He held out his glass and they clinked. She took a sip, the bubbles hitting her nose.

"You seem awfully familiar with everything in this place," she said.

He gave her a smile and lifted one eyebrow. "I have a good memory."

"Really?"

"I helped build the place."

"With your own hands?"

"Not quite. Let's just say I had a lot of input into the design."

"And the absentee owner?"

"It used to be my grandmother's. She needed to downsize so I bought it from her. At first, I was renting it out, but about a year ago the tenants moved and I decided it was time to remodel a bit.

"I can't quite see a grandmother living here," Lynn said.

"Exactly. Don't get me wrong, I love my grandmother. But the place was stuck in a seventies time warp. I added an addition, finished out the basement, and of course, transformed the space into something a little more modern. I always loved the view, sitting out on the deck."

"Not many people would be able to have the vision to take something like what you're describing and transform it into this."

"Do you like it?" Jackson asked.

"Like it?" Lynn said. "I love it." And she realized she just might have found her style. Everything called to her, from the muted earth tones of the furniture to the darker shades of the wood. Even the exposed steel rafters, painted a dark gray, blended together. The space was not so much sparsely as carefully furnished, with just enough of everything and no extra clutter. It felt restful, simple.

"It's not too modern? My mom took one look and I swear she was ready to give me her glass figurine collection to make it homier."

"Well," Lynn said, looking around, considering. "It definitely looks a bit like a single guy lives here. I mean your TV takes up one whole wall. And while you do have a few books around, they all seem to be on serious subjects."

"I read mostly on my e-reader," Jackson defended himself.

"And there's nothing living here. Not even flowers, which technically aren't living. What about a plant? Shouldn't you have a fern or something?"

He laughed. "I'm a guy. Plants seem awfully girly. And you have to remember to water them."

"Yeah, I'm not much good at keeping things alive— well, except for people," she amended.

"Good thing then," he said giving her a look that had shivers spiraling down her back.

"What about your apartment at the marina?"

He laughed. "I was just there temporarily while they finished some work in here. Chase keeps one for family and friends. I don't really like staying in the actual hotel, so he let me use it."

"That's why it seemed like you haven't been there for a while," Lynn said, thinking that explained the unusual quietness she had noticed.

"Not this week. I've been staying here."

"Did you plan all of this, as a way to get me into your bachelor pad?"

"I can't control the weather, you know. Like I said, I thought the storm was going to come in much later. I figured that we'd have a nice trip around the harbor, maybe anchor, enjoy something to eat, and then I would casually suggest we check out a property I was working on."

"So you did plan for us to wind up here?" Lynn said.

He smiled at her, leaning closer to her. "I told you I had a plan."

His face was just inches from hers. She closed her eyes, breathing in his scent of soap, fresh air, and rain. He smelled good and she could feel heat rolling off of him, surrounding her. She wanted him to kiss her, wanted to wrap herself in him. The weather was cold and dark, and in here it was warm and cozy. Logically she knew Queensbay was only a few miles away, but it felt as if they were in a separate place.

"You shivered," he said, concern in his voice. "Come," he took her hand and pulled her to him. His lips brushed the top of her hair, and he led her back to the couch and the warmth of the fire.

"I'm not fragile, you know."

"I know," he said, his face hovering in front of hers for an instant, so close she could almost feel their lips touch.

"Why are you afraid of hurting me?"

"Who says it's not the other way around," he said, and it took a moment to realize what he was saying.

"Me, hurt you? What are you talking about?"

His blue eyes held hers, dark in the gray light. She could hear that slash of the rain against the windows and saw that the storm had moved further in toward them, sheathing the house in a gray cocoon.

He looked out the window and a rueful smile broke over his face. "Let's just say I think too much about you already."

She felt her stomach jump and flip-flop as she felt the need to be near him. She wasn't sure what she wanted beyond this, the ability to lose herself for a few hours. Anything else could wait.

"Can't we just enjoy the now? Unless of course, you don't find me attractive in that way," she said, easing herself closer to him and looking him in the eye.

Her hand rested on his shoulder and she trailed it with the faintest of touches down the strong length of his arm.

"Lynn," he all but growled.

"What?" she asked, all the innocence she could summon in her voice.

"Don't do that if you don't mean it."

"I mean it," she said, turning so she faced him. She reached first, pulling him closer to her, closing her eyes, bringing her lips to his. There was the barest moment of wavering before his mouth clamped over hers, hot and full of need. His arms came around her, pulling her in close, so she was all but trapped.

The electricity, the crinkle of attraction sparked between them and she found herself melting into him, reaching up to find the soft, silky feel of his hair, pulling him closer to her. He broke the kiss for a moment, his eyes searching hers. She could see the need, the want in them, and she shifted her weight so she was pressed into him, giving him the invitation he needed.

His head came down again, but he scraped his lips over her neck, up her jawline before going to take her mouth again. She moaned and moved her arms down the length of his back, feeling the play of the muscles there.

He leaned over her and she surrendered, leaning herself back onto the couch, allowing her hips to press up to meet him, feeling his own need there.

His hands found the V of skin where her sweater dipped down. She shivered at the dynamic thrill that came over her. His hands worked their way down, finding her nipple through the thin wool of her sweater, the slight pressure working it to attention, sending a flash of desire straight through to her groin.

Slowly, his hands moved further down, to the strip of exposed flesh between the waist of her jeans and the hem of her top. He put his palm there, the full force of the heat of his hand like a brand on her skin. She gasped and he moved it up, under the sweater, along her bare skin until he reached her breast again, this time his fingers slipping under the fabric of her bra, finding her bare nipple, which he rubbed until she could feel it puckered with desire.

Casually, as he kissed her, she could feel his other hand dip into the waist of her jeans, skim along the flat surface of her stomach and then press against her mound. She moaned, feeling lost with lust and desire.

She needed to be in contact with him, she thought, reaching up and pulling his fleece off. He had on a shirt underneath, the stiff, starched cotton molding over him like a second skin. Her fingers fumbled for the buttons, her fingers clumsy in her hurry.

She looked up, saw the laughter and desire in his eyes. Not shy anymore, she lifted herself up, then in a smooth, fluid movement, took off her sweater. He breathed in sharply, his eyes on hers, as he finished off the buttons of his shirt for her. The shirt discarded, they sat there, looking at each other, drinking it in.

Her eyes roved over the broad sweep of his shoulders, to his smooth chest, down to the flat, defined abs of his stomach. She reached out and trailed her fingers down them, ignoring his sharp intake of breath.

"You're sure?" he asked.

She leaned up, pulling him down. "I'm sure," she said as she wrapped herself around him.

Taking that as all the permission he needed, she felt him undo the buttons of her jeans and felt them being slowly pulled off. She shivered as his warm hands replaced them.

She was only in her bra and panties, and his smile was wolfish as he kissed his way up from her ankles, his hands trailing along behind. She felt as if all her neurons were alive, her body filled with a current of desire.

His hand brushed against the silky cloth of her panties. She flexed her hips, but he bent his head down, his teeth scraping against the fabric of her bra. His hands came up and smoothly he flicked open the clasp and she sprang free.

The pad of his thumb circled her nipple, tight with desire, and then she felt his hand slip down, teasing again as he found her panties. He slipped his hand in, slowly, tantalizing, until he found her spot, already wet. He stroked and she felt her need rise up, hot and fast.

She threw her head back and surrendered to the feelings flowing through her. He kissed her neck, his breath warm and hot on her skin. Her hips rose in an involuntary response and her whole body tensed and hummed, drawing tight as her body gathered itself. She grasped him, feeling the hard muscles of his back, her mind emptying of anything but the sensations running through her.

She felt the wave crest over her, felt her body draw tight as a bow as he pushed her towards her climax, her whole body quivering. It came, pushing her over the edge, the waves of satisfaction rolling off her. And then she wanted more. Her hands found the fly of his jeans, and she fumbled, pushing, rolling them down.

As if sensing her impatience, he used a free hand and together, she felt the jeans roll off, until he was left in his boxers, his need for her obvious though the fabric.

"Are you sure?" he asked again.

"Yes," she practically sobbed. She wanted him. There was a moment while he fumbled in the pocket of his discarded jeans and he drew out the square foil wrapped package.

She took it from him and surprised, he leaned back. But she opened it and took her hands to pull down the fabric of his boxers. He was more than ready for her, she thought, as she rolled the condom down the shaft, taking her time.

She glanced up and saw that he had his eyes closed, his jaw clenched.

"Is everything ok?"

He looked down at her. "If you keep that up, I might not make it much longer."

Laughing, she held her hands up. Taking that as her surrender, he grabbed them and pulled them up over her head. Immobile, she looked at him. He released her, his hands trailing down her body until he reached her hips. She angled them up and he entered her, slowly at first and then as the heat and the feeling grew between them, faster, with more assured thrusts.

She felt her blood tingling, her body quaking as her need rose again, her body ready to meet his desire with her own. She grabbed his hips, guiding them in and out and they found a steady rhythm. She watched his face, saw the climax building in him until she felt it tear through him into her and she allowed herself to follow, both of them reaching the edge and tumbling over it together.

He sank down onto her, a delicious, heavy weight, as she felt her hammering heart start to slow back down.

The silence weighed upon them and she wasn't sure what she should say. Tell the truth, that it had been the most incredible sex of her life, or play it cool and act like toe-curling sex happened to her all the time.

"Wow," he breathed. And then, "I'm sorry. I didn't mean for this to happen on the couch." He rolled off of her, but the seat cushion was wide enough so that he was able to pull her close to him. The throw found its way onto them and she snuggled into him, feeling content, the warmth of his body sealing her happiness.

"I don't think where mattered, just why it took so long," she said, then realized she had forgotten to play it cool. At least she hadn't begged to do it again.

"Good things come to those that wait," he said, and she could hear the smug satisfaction in his voice.

"Then you can just keep those things coming," she said, her fingers tracing lazy circles along the muscled ridge of his arm.

"I am sure that can be arranged," he said, and she felt his lips touch her hair, his hand slide down to leave a streak of heat down her back.

It was still raining out, the storm in full force, the house now fully enveloped by a wall of gray clouds. The music played on the hidden speakers and the fire had burned low. Their glasses of champagne sat forgotten on the coffee table...Lynn felt like she wanted to take this moment and hold it in time. She felt like something had shifted, that everything had changed.

She felt the lassitude slip from her as Jackson's hands became more insistent, felt the curl of desire flare up in her stomach, realized what she wanted as she tilted her head up to meet his, felt and met the heat of his kiss. Yes, she was going to enjoy the moment.

\#

Her stomach rumbled, and he found her one of his button-down shirts to put on, and she wore that, her panties, and nothing else as he made something to eat. She hadn't checked the time, didn't know, with the gray clouds, whether it was lunch or dinner; but it didn't matter. She knew neither one of them had any intention of going anyplace.

"You're not a bad cook," she said, tasting the pasta he had cooked with simple efficiency.

"Pasta's not that hard," he said.

"You should meet my mother: the woman can do wonders with pasta." It was out of Lynn's mouth before she could stop herself. She felt a flush of embarrassment, knowing that she had broken the first rule of casual relationships. Never mention the family, especially when they had agreed up front that this wasn't serious.

"I didn't mean it like that. I mean you don't have to meet my mother. In fact, it's probably better that you don't, you know, because who knows what she'd think? Or worse yet, what she'd say to you."

Lynn realized she was babbling, so she took a deep breath and pretended to be very interested in the linguine and vegetables that she had wrapped around her fork.

She felt his gaze on her and looked up, relieved to see that his expression was more amused than angry.

"Meeting your mother..."

"Look, I didn't mean it that way. Or that she would say anything bad. Or who knows, maybe she would. All I meant is she's a good cook. Usually no one can resist that.

But it's probably better that we keep this on the down low, if you know what I mean."

She almost missed the sudden tightening of his expression, but then it was replaced with his usual unreadable look.

"The down low?"

"You know, quiet. It's that, well, I mean, some people might think, you…"

"Of course," he said, taking her hand and pulling it to his mouth, and brushing his lips against it. "I understand perfectly. Better not to have too many people intruding into our relationship, right?"

"Exactly," she said, not sure why she felt deflated he had agreed so quickly.

They ate a bit more in silence, then Jackson looked out the window. "It seems that the rain has stopped," he said.

She looked up and saw that the sky had lightened up, flashes of blue showing through ragged tears in the gray clouds. Drawn, she got up and walked to the bank of windows. The whole world looked wet and a breeze had kicked up, frothing the water of the harbor with whitecaps. The sky out to the west showed rays of sun breaking over the horizon. It was late in the afternoon, almost evening.

He came behind and wrapped his arms around her, and she sunk into his warmth, savoring the smell of soap and spice that had come to mean him to her.

"We don't have to go. Tomorrow the weather will be much better and we can take the boat back."

She turned, running her hand up his arm and up to his cheek. "Are you asking me to stay the night?"

"Well, considering I haven't even given you a tour of the whole house, I thought it might be nice."

"Are you just trying to get me into your bedroom?" she asked.

He waggled his eyebrows at her. "That might be part of it."

She turned, linking her arms around him. "I can't think of a better way to spend a weekend."

Chapter 41

She stayed through the weekend. They did little but watch old movies, play ping-pong on the table he had in the basement, and make love. They snatched bits of sleep and he cooked their meals from his well-stocked pantry. She ignored all of her text messages from Tory and her mom, only saying she was ok but busy. The weather for the most part stayed cloudy and gray and she felt safely tucked away in their private little aerie.

Monday morning came all too soon and he drove her down to the village. It wasn't a long drive by any means, but suddenly she was nervous, as if their weekend was ending and with it something more. They would say goodbye of course, but she wondered if it meant goodbye, it was fun, now it's time to move on; or did it mean goodbye until we can do this again? No strings attached had been the agreement but she didn't know how far that extended.

Her stomach felt strangely nervous, jumpy as they rode down from the heights overlooking the Sound and into Queensbay proper.

It was early in the morning. A fine gray mist clung to the trees, even though the sun promised to break through.

A hint of colder weather was in the air but she didn't want to think about it. Children were standing in clusters, waiting for their school busses, moms in various states of dress watching over them, most of them clutching coffee cups that sent up clouds of steam into the air.

"Penny for your thoughts," he said.

She gave herself a start. She hadn't realized she'd been looking out the window, drifting away. She looked over at him. He seemed relaxed, comfortable, sitting there in a dark pair of suit pants. He had on a crisp white shirt and jacket but hadn't bothered with a tie.

"Nothing, really. Just watching the kids."

"Remembering what it was like?" he asked.

She nodded. "I always liked school. But we moved a lot when I was young, or it seemed like it, since my dad finished up his training and then served in the army. Fall was exciting but it was sort of like a rollercoaster. Not the excitement of new beginnings, or the change of the seasons, but something more akin to, oh my god, will I fit in, will the kids be nice to me? You know, your standard kid stuff."

He shot her a smile as he slowed down behind a school bus. "Yeah, I know what you mean. Fall was always the time for new clothes, new shoes. It was football season, too, so that was always fun."

"I guess it must have been different, growing up in the same town, going to the same school, year after year," she said.

"There wasn't that sort of rollercoaster anticipation about it, I guess; but you're right, there is something about fall and new beginnings. I always loved the smell of wood smoke, how as the leaves thinned you could start to see everyone's houses. You get your last days out on the water, and then you'd spend your time getting the boat all shipshape."

She laughed. "For a guy who's been all around the world, you seem pretty comfortable with the small town traditions."

"What can I say? I'm a small town guy at heart."

Jackson had said the past was the past, but here in his small town, everything must remind him of her. What had Tory said about Ashley and Jackson? They had been inseparable all throughout high school. Lynn tamped the thought down before she could think any more about it.

They were in the village now, almost at her apartment. She needed to get home, grab her scrubs, and hop into the car to get to the clinic She checked her watch. Just enough time.

Jackson pulled into an empty spot. Lynn swallowed. Best to be brave, to be a grownup, thank him for the good food, the good sex, and all that, and then appear like she could care less if they made plans to see each other tonight, tomorrow, or next month. That had been the deal, right?

She put her hand on the door, ready to bolt out of there with a hurried goodbye, but he was quicker, sliding out of the car and to her side before she could open the door.

He did it for her and held out his hand. Always the gentleman, she remembered as she stood up. The gray skies of the weekend were definitely burning off. It would be sunny today, a wonderful, sunny gorgeous day. A perfect day to be dumped.

"Thanks," she said, not trusting her voice to say much more.

"Do you want me to walk you up? I can drive you to the clinic, but you probably want your own car there."

She nodded, her throat feeling constricted. But it had to be said.

"Thank you for the lovely time this weekend. Perhaps..." she didn't get any further than that because he had both hands on the side of her cheeks and he was looking down at her with a slightly amused expression.

"Did you just call what we had lovely?"

Unsure, she managed to stutter out a yes. He smelled of soap, a hint of spicy aftershave, and his nearness was doing things to her she didn't quite expect.

"Well it was..."

He kissed her, his mouth hot on hers, demanding. It was a full-bodied, full-sensory kiss. His hands twined around her hair and she relaxed into him, wrapping her arms around his broad shoulders, pulling them to her.

"Better than lovely," she said. They came up for air and he looked at her, his eyes hazy with lust.

"Are you sure you have to be at work in half an hour?"

Her head fell back as his lips nuzzled along her throat.

"Absolutely sure," she said.

"When are you off again?"

"Thursday," she said.

"You'll see me then?" he asked, his voice insistent.

"Yes," she managed to whisper, feeling a hot joy spread through her. He wanted to see her, and well, he wanted her.

"Good. Dinner?"

She nodded, "My turn to cook for you."

He raised an eyebrow. "I thought you told me you lived on ramen and coffee?"

"I did. I suddenly found myself interested in developing a more sophisticated palette. Trust me?"

He held up his hand, the one she had stitched up. "With my life...and my stomach."

Suddenly giddy, she laughed, found the strength to break free. "I really do have to get to work," she said.

"I'll watch to make sure you get in," he said. "Wave from the balcony."

Assured, feeling loved and strangely sophisticated, she took a step back, nodded, and tried not to skip as she made her way up to her apartment.

Chapter 42

"Well, well, well." Jackson drew up short as his brother's voice floated behind him.

"Look at who you just drove home. Were you playing doctor?"

Jackson spun around, his hands balled into fists. "That's not funny." He knew Lynn hated jokes like that, and besides there had been nothing funny about what they had just shared.

Chase held up his hands in surrender. "Sorry, brother. I'm just a bit surprised."

"And why's that?" Jackson said, folding his own arms across his chest. They were in the upstairs suite of rooms of the Osprey Arms that Chase had been using for himself before he had moved in with Phoebe. Now it was going to become project central and Jackson had come to discuss plans and budgets with his brother.

"I don't know." Chase ran a hand through his short hair, visibly frustrated. "I just haven't seen you with a girl in a while."

"You haven't seen me in a while, period," Jackson pointed out. "There were plenty of girls along the way. I enjoy being in a relationship, treating a lady right. As long as we both understand the rules."

Chase raised an eyebrow.

"That it will end eventually. I don't intend to settle down and get married."

"Good for you," Chase said, clapping him on the back. "It's bad for your health to keep it all bottled in. I just didn't realize that you were, you know, ready."

Jackson steeled himself. Chase was his brother and probably knew him as well or better than anyone, including Jake. Still there were some things he couldn't even tell Chase, that Chase couldn't know.

"It's been a while. I'm allowed to move on," Jackson said, defending himself.

"I know, and that's great. I mean we all loved Ashley and it was terrible what happened, but..."

"But what?"

"Well, it just seems sudden, you know. You moving back here, which is great, but getting caught up again with a girl, too? Maybe you should take it one step at a time."

Jackson's eyes narrowed. "I already told you, I'm quite comfortable with relationships. Is there a problem with Lynn in particular," he asked, his voice dangerously low.

"Not at all. And that's the point. She's a nice girl."

"She's not a girl," Jackson pointed out, remembering the way her body had moved under him. There had been nothing but a passionate, sexy, strong woman in bed with him the past weekend and he had loved every second of it. Her strong, tight, lithe, athletic body had surprised him in many, many ways. He sucked in a breath and focused on the lecture his big brother was giving him.

"Fine, a woman. But she just got out of med school, just moved out on her own. Hell, I don't think she's ever had a real boyfriend."

"So?" Jackson stilled, watching with hidden amusement as his brother grew more and more uncomfortable. He didn't plan on enlightening Chase that Lynn wasn't as innocent as she seemed.

"So, just don't mess her up," Chase said.

"What?" The word came out of Jackson in a burst of surprise.

"I just mean she's a good friend of my future wife, and I like her and I'm looking out for her."

"You think I would hurt her?" Jackson asked.

"Not on purpose, no, but I don't think Lynn's a casual type of girl, if you know what I mean. And what I saw you two doing out there seemed pretty intense. Are you ready for that, ready to be serious?"

It was Jackson's turn to run his hand through his hair. "Who said anything about being serious? We were just having some fun," he said, echoing the words Lynn said to him.

"That looked like more than fun to me, brother. And look, I know you too. You may say that you can have a casual relationship, but that's not true, not when it really matters. So just be careful for both of your sakes. I don't want to have to pick up the pieces again."

"And what's that supposed to mean?"

"Look, I get it. You were messed up after Ash died and you had to get out of here. But there were whispers and the Morans kept coming around looking for answers. I defended you even though I didn't understand why you left. This was your town too."

"And I'm back now. And Lynn and I are, well, we're taking things as they come." Jackson felt the flash of anger, wishing that people would have enough sense to mind their own business. But that was part of living in a small town. Your business was never fully your own. There were too many interdependent relationships riding on it.

Chase nodded. "Good. You know I hate pulling the big brother act, but you're family, and Lynn's a friend. I just don't want to see it get messy."

"Hey, it's just a mature relationship; no strings attached," Jackson said, knowing even as it came out of his mouth that he was already beyond that, no matter what Lynn said she wanted. Chase was right.

Chase gave a rueful smile. "Somehow it never quite works that way, does it?"

Chapter 43

Lynn checked the index card again. Her mother had written it down in her neat, precise handwriting. The recipe was the Holy Grail, the one her grandmother had passed down through generations of Masters women. A guaranteed man-pleaser, the recipe was supposed to have been the one that had won her grandfather's heart, at least according to Lynn's grandmother.

The ingredient list had looked deceptively simple, she thought, looking at the packages of food crowded over her counter. She and Jackson hadn't seen each other in four days, Lynn thought, not that she was counting, and she had invited him over for a home-cooked dinner. He had asked what he could bring, and she had made what she thought was a sophisticated response. "A bottle of good Bordeaux."

Her mother had said it could go well with the dish. She had wanted to say more, but Lynn had told her that she was being safe and her mother had backed off, knowing that there was only so much honestly you could have with your adult daughter.

Now, as Lynn looked at the recipe she wasn't quite sure where to start.

"At the beginning," she could almost hear her mother say.

All that had seemed well and good as her mother had passed over the card, but now the terms like sauté, blanch, and make the garlic dance had her bewildered. Her mother had offered to show her how to do it, but Lynn confident that this cooking thing couldn't be too hard, had passed on the offer.

So now there was nothing to do but make a start of it. She grabbed one of her new knives, pulled an onion from a bag, and started dissecting it.

The videos helped, she decided. Lynn had caved and used her tablet to search up definitions, techniques, and just about everything having to do with the recipe. She was led down a rabbit hole of videos and articles about fresh versus dried herbs, the proper way to handle a knife, and whether salt was really necessary to make water boil.

It was fascinating to watch, knowing there were people out there who treated cooking as a science. Her mother had always approached it as more of an art, but now Lynn had a better appreciation for how many different steps must have gone into putting a simple weeknight dinner on the table. When she glanced up at the clock she had to stop herself from cursing. Jackson was due here, literally at any moment, and there was an explosion of flour in one corner and what looked like the results of a nasty accident involving decapitated tomatoes in another. The first batch of garlic had burned, and though she'd bought enough to keep a nest of vampires away, there was a lingering, slightly over-roasted smell in the apartment.

And she was still wearing scrubs. She was about to make for the bedroom when the doorbell rang.

"Just a minute," she said and looked around. There wasn't time to do much of anything she thought. Perhaps clean up the flour? There was a short knock, as if to highlight his impatience.

"Ah hell," she muttered and went to open the door. He was standing there, wearing a dark suit, no tie, shirt open at the collar. She thought he might have gotten his hair cut, but she had no time to think because he crossed over the threshold and pulled her toward him, covering her mouth with his, a kiss full of intensity and desire.

All thoughts of a dirty kitchen faded from her mind as her senses took on a life of their own. Perhaps her Nonna was wrong about food being the way to a person's heart. Perhaps all it took was a kiss. His scraped his lips against her chin as she pulled him into her apartment.

She was vaguely aware of the door shutting behind them and of the way his arms encircled her, lifting her up onto her toes, closer to him.

"I missed you," he said as he set her down. She licked her lips and took a step back to gain a measure of steadiness. She told herself that she shouldn't get used to that, that this was, by mutual consent, a fling, meant to be passionate but ultimately destined to flame out. Jackson had all but told her he wasn't ready to love again.

"I can tell," she said.

He smiled down at her and with a fluid gesture, held out a bottle of red. "You said Bordeaux, correct?"

She nodded, taking the bottle and setting it down on the kitchen counter.

"What are we having?" he asked.

"Well," she looked around, and his eyes followed her gaze. "It's supposed to be chicken cacciatore. And I was supposed to have showered and dressed. And not made it look like I was murdering tomatoes."

He looked at her and she was certain that his mouth was twitching, but he said nothing as he went into the kitchen and peeked into the pots and pans.

"It's an old family recipe," she offered.

He took up a spoon, stirred something, and then held it up for a taste.

"Wait," she said, panicky, "Me first. I don't want to poison you."

"Do you really think it's a possibility?"

"There's a first time for everything," she said darkly. She went over, took the spoon from him, and inhaled. Ok, so it didn't smell so bad. Sort of like tomato soup. Sure, not like when her mother was cooking it, but maybe it would taste fine.

Tentatively she took a taste. "Omigod," she said, dropping the spoon and going to fan her mouth.

"What?" he asked.

"Hot," she managed. She needed water, or milk, but she was certain she didn't have any of that, so she went over to the sink, quickly grabbed a cup and switched on the tap.

"How bad can it be?" Jackson asked. She turned in time to see him dip the spoon in, lift it to his mouth, and then take a big swallow.

It took a moment before he too started to cough and sputter and his eyes water. Wordlessly, she filled the glass full of water and handed it to him. He drank it one gulp.

"Were you supposed to use red pepper flakes?"

She nodded. "That's the secret ingredient. The recipe called for a pinch, but I thought I should measure it." She held up the measuring spoon.

He looked at it and burst out laughing. "That's a tablespoon. That's more like a fistful."

She looked at the spoon, looked at the mess, and then because he had started to, she went along with him and soon they were both laughing.

"Maybe you should stick to medicine," he said.

She punched him lightly, but he was too quick for her and caught her hand, using it to pull her towards him. He wrapped his arms around her so his chin nestled on her head.

"We could always go out," she suggested, trying to quell her laughter.

"Or," he said, taking her chin with his hand and lifting it up, "we can just stay in. I'm not that hungry." He dropped his mouth and his lips brushed against her ear. She felt her body respond, a thrill coursing through her. Her Nonna definitely had it wrong. Food had nothing on this.

His mouth moved to hers, insistent, demanding. She reached up into him, hearing herself moan. She wanted this, wanted him. Everything seemed to slip away as his arms came around her. She could taste the sauce on him, the scent of spice and to her it seemed to mean danger. She knew that she shouldn't let herself be so caught up in this, so caught up in him, but when his arms came around her and he pulled her to him, everything else seemed to fall away. For so long she had been focused on her goal that she had let nothing distract her. Now, when Jackson was around, everything but him and her need for him, faded away.

His arms slid down her shoulders, around her back so that he cupped her backside. In one fluid movement, he lifted her up so that her legs were wrapped around him. His teeth raked down her neck.

"Didn't you say you just had a new bed delivered?" he said, his voice a low growl that made her clench tighter around him.

"Something like that," she said.

"Sounds to me like we better go break it in, make sure it's up to standard."

He swung her around and before she knew it, he was carrying her from the living area, down the short hall into her bedroom. She managed a wild glance around, wondering what sort of shape it was in. Thankfully, she had put all of her clothes away and all there was was the bed and its new cover, soft, inviting.

He lowered her down on it, and she felt her head hit the pillows, her hair splaying out around her. She looked up at him. He took off his jacket and tossed it aside. Before he could start on the buttons of his shirt, she rose up, pulled him down and kissing him, began to undo them, one at time. She let her hands roam over his chest as she pulled the shirt away, let her fingers soak up the feel and play of his muscles, feel the strength underneath them.

She tossed the shirt in the corner and her hands hovered over his waist and played with the buckle of his belt. She could feel his want through the soft fabric of his pants as she brushed her hand over him.

He hissed in through his teeth and looked down at her. "Be careful of the game you're playing," he said.

Her fingers fumbled with the belt buckle and she had to use two hands before it slid free. He stopped her before she could go any further.

"Your turn," he said, and the warmth of his fingers burned on her skin as he grabbed the bottom edge of her top and pulled it over her head.

"At least those are easy to get out of," he said with a laugh, as his finger caught the waist of her pants and tugged them down. She was thankful that she had thought to wear matching underwear and bra today.

He smiled, his finger flicking the nub of her nipple under the red lace of her bra. She could feel it harden in response as her back arched up to him.

"Racy, lacy red lingerie. Under scrubs. Will wonders never cease?" he said as he kissed the spot between her breasts and then trailed kisses down the flat surface of her stomach.

"Just like they say, don't judge a book by its cover. Or a girl by her scrubs."

His fingers teased around the edge of her panties and then slowly, almost unbearably slowly, he slid them in to find her wet, moist center.

"Don't worry," he said as his eyes darkened, watching as her body responded to his touch, "I like the whole package."

She almost lost it then, pushed over the edge but she fought the need, letting him stroke her until her desire built up in her, pulling her, pushing her to a crest. She reached for him, her hands finding his fly, and this time he didn't resist as she slid his pants off, tugging them down so he could shrug out of them. He stepped free of them and then tugged down the waist of his boxers so she could see that he was ready for her.

He unhooked her bra and lowered his mouth down to her nipple and took it with his tongue, gently flicking it to rigid attention. His hands slipped her panties off and she couldn't wait any longer, as she moaned his name and raised her hips up to him, almost there. He entered her quickly and together they moved in sync.

She felt her whole body thrum and hum with fulfilled pleasure. She wrapped her legs around him and rose up to meet him. Together their eyes met and he locked his gaze on her. They moved together, finding their rhythm, and together they rode up and over the wave.

#

They lay tangled next to each other. Lynn felt her heart racing and willed it to calm down. Next to her, Jackson was lying, strong, quiet, the sheet pulled halfway up around him. He lifted up one arm and smiled at her and she felt her heart melt. He was a nice guy, she reminded herself, nothing more. In fact, he couldn't be. She had to remember that before she let herself get too caught up in him. Still, she could imagine lying next to him, like this, on a regular basis.

It was his stomach that gave him away.

She laughed. "I guess I never fed you."

"I appreciate you for your other talents," he answered, a wicked tone in his voice as his hands lightly traced the line of her hip.

"I suppose we could always order in," she said.

"I'm pretty sure Giovanni's pizza delivers," he said.

"And thank goodness for that."

Chapter 44

The fire crackled warm and bright. Lynn looked around the assembled faces and smiled. Logs and chairs were pulled up in a circle around a huge bonfire that had been built on a little slip of beach below Noah and Caitlyn Randall's house. The log next to her was empty, but not for long as Jackson lowered his long form down next to her.

"I brought you a lobster, corn, and some clams," he said handing her a plate. She put her cup down, setting it into the sand so it wouldn't spill.

"Wow, this looks delicious. You cooked this all in a hole in the ground?" she asked.

"Yup, that's the beauty of a proper New England clam bake. It's a bit late in the season, but when you said you'd never been to one, I couldn't resist."

The firelight flickered, casting long shadows across their faces but she could see his smile and catch the twinkle in his eye.

"So, Doctor. How's the food?" Chase asked, settling down easily onto the log next to them and putting an arm around Phoebe, who gave him a kiss on the nose. Across the fire, Caitlyn Randall, lounged in a real chair, while Noah brought her a plate. Caitlyn was smiling but Lynn caught the looks she kept shooting up toward the house, where baby Luke was supposedly sound asleep, under the watchful eye of a trusted babysitter.

Beyond the fire, Sean Callahan, tended to the big hole in the ground from which all their food was emerging. Also in a chair, Darby, looking like a veritable Madonna, sat, her hands across her full belly, smiling every now and then as she felt the baby kick.

Tory was there, with a guy from the rival softball team. Jake Owen was here as well, but flying solo, which didn't seem to bother him at all.

Someone had set up a radio and a steady stream of upbeat music, a mix of classics and contemporary hits, played on.

Lynn held up the lobster by the tail. "What am I supposed to do, just crack it open?" she said, eyeing the hard, spiny shell with curiosity. She figured she was pretty adventurous when it came to food, but somehow she had never eaten a whole lobster before.

"Do you mean," Tory said in mock horror, a hand over her heart, "that you've never eaten a lobster before?"

Lynn looked around the assorted faces of the group, all of whom were looking at her as if she had tentacles and claws herself.

"Well," she said as she began to defend herself, "it's not exactly indigenous west of the Rockies, is it?" she pointed out.

Jackson laughed and pulled her to him, giving her a kiss. "I take pity on you. I will help you slay the big bad lobster."

There was a round of laughter as Jackson picked the lobster up from her plate. He started to explain the proper methodology of eating a lobster to her but she looked up, distracted, feeling someone's gaze on her. It was Chase and his dark eyes were looking at them, staring as if he was seeing something he didn't quite believe. The intensity, the speculation in the gaze made her uncomfortable. All of a sudden, she wondered if it had been such a good idea to make hers and Jackson's relationship public so soon.

It was Jackson who had wanted it; he'd looked so hopeful when he asked if she'd mind, as if he was afraid she'd say no, worried that she would be nervous to be with him. Lynn had told him to stop being silly. As far as she knew, there had been no further incidents like the one at the café, and what's more, she didn't care. All that was in the past, as far as Lynn was concerned.

So with a glee that she hadn't expected, Jackson had organized this party and said it felt good not to be sneaking around. She hadn't tried to dwell too much on what that meant for the definition of their relationship, but she knew she was starting to believe that what was between them was more than a casual thing.

Phoebe caught Chase's attention and it shifted from them. Lynn decided to ignore the shiver of foreboding that ran down her back and turned her thoughts back to Jackson.

It was getting late and the bonfire was starting to wind down. Caitlyn and Darby had left together, climbing the stairs up to Caitlyn's house, Darby moving slowly, saying she needed a real chair and a real bathroom, while Caitlyn had assured everyone they were welcome to stay.

Noah, Jake, Sean, and the rest of the couples were scattered around, on logs or blankets, digesting the enormous meal. It was getting cold, Lynn thought, the warmth of the day slipping quickly away as night settled fully down. The water was a soft whisper of waves lapping gently at the shore. Off along the coast, the lighthouse, the real one, flashed its light in a steady rhythm and the far shore was defined by a flickering line of lights. Conversation was dwindling and when Jackson whispered in Lynn's ear, she nodded, ready to go as well.

He stood up, sand spilling down from him. "I'll start to gather our things," he said.

"I just want to take a quick look at the water," she said and picked her way carefully along the rocky shore, the light from the moon and the fire her only guide, to the water's edge. She hugged her arms tightly around her. She was wearing jeans and a warm coat, but still the air was chilly, and on a whim she bent down and ran her hand through the water. It felt surprisingly warm.

As she rose up, she felt a presence next to her. She looked up, expecting to see Jackson, but it was his brother Chase.

"Don't be fooled. It's way too cold for skinny dipping," he said. His voice was light but even in the shadows she could tell that his face was serious.

"How would you know?" she shot back.

"Experience. You can't live in Queensbay and not be tempted. It feels warm because the water retains the heat of the summer well into the fall. It's always warmer in October than in April, no matter how hot a day you get in the spring."

"Is that something you did a lot?"

"What, skinny dipping?" Chase gave a low chuckle. "Among other things. Small town. We had to find a way to assume ourselves."

Lynn waited. She was friendly with Chase, but there was no way to mistake this for a casual encounter.

The silence seemed to stretch between them so that she had to ask. "Do you have something to say?"

"You seem to be getting along very well with my brother," Chase said.

"I might be," Lynn answered.

"That's good. He needs that."

Lynn waited, sure she knew what was going to be next. A big brotherly warning about not hurting Jackson or he would have to kill her. Or something like that. But what Chase said next surprised her.

"Just be careful, Lynn."

"What do you mean?" Her voice was laced with surprise. Of all the things he could have said, she had not expected that.

He turned to her, his voice pitched low and filled with concern. "You're a nice girl, Lynn, a good friend. I don't want to see Jackson hurt you is all."

"How would he hurt me?" Lynn asked.

"I don't know if Jackson's really ready to love someone again. But you are. You're one of the happiest, most passionate people I know. And you think you can fix people, and most of the time you can. But my brother, I'm not so sure he's fixable or that he'll be able to give you what you deserve. I am only saying this as your friend,"

Chase said as Lynn took a step back as if she had been slapped.

"Love…Who said anything about love," her voice started out high, but she caught herself and ended in a whisper.

"I see how he looks at you and how you look at him. He's happy; I'll give you that, and I thank you for that. I never thought I would see him that way again after what happened."

"You mean her," Lynn said.

"Yes, Ashley. It destroyed him. And truth be told, I don't know if he's whole yet."

Lynn wanted to scream in frustration. At every turn with Jackson she felt haunted by a dead woman, Jackson's silence about it doing more than anything else to confirm the presence of the saintly, deceased Ashley in his heart than anything. She felt always like it was one step forward and two steps back. Or maybe this was what Jackson had meant all along. He was perfectly capable of being a great boyfriend. But he would never give his heart to her. She ran a hand over her hair, ending in a tug on her ponytail.

She wasn't sure what to say, and thankfully, didn't have to because Jackson came up to them, threw an arm around her shoulder and snuggled her close to him. She leaned into his warm, hard body and let herself be warmed by the dazzling smile he sent her, and thought that maybe she should be happy with what she had. A sexy, attentive man who made love to her but didn't love her as much as she loved him.

"What are you doing out here with my girl, brother?"

"Just advising her against taking a dip," Chase said, laughing easily.

Jackson leaned down, scooped up a rock, and tossed it into the water. In the silver moonlight, Lynn watched as it skipped three hops and the dropped down into the surface, sending its concentric ripples outward.

He looked down at Lynn. "You do have a sense of adventure," he said and his voice was lightly teasing as he shot a look toward Chase.

She took a step back, already sensing what the brothers had in mind.

"It's colder than it looks," she protested. But she was too late.

She screamed for help but it was two against one. Phoebe and Tory came running to her rescue but the girls were outnumbered. Somehow they all managed to end up in the water, fully clothed, wet and shivering but laughing.

#

Later, warm and snug in bed, with Jackson sleeping beside her, Lynn struggled to find her own sense of peace. She and Chase had never finished their conversation but his message had been clear. Jackson was still in love with his dead fiancée. She looked over at his sleeping form, gently tracing the smooth muscles of his back. He shifted but stayed asleep. True, he had made no promises to her, only that he would treat her like a grownup. That she would enjoy herself. That she would feel sexy and sophisticated. And with him, she did. But not once had he mentioned love. And just where did that leave them? Or leave her? Did she truly love him? Or was she just in love with him, in love with the way he made her feel? Was there a difference? And why now, after guarding herself so carefully, making sure there were no distractions, had she fallen for a man who couldn't love her back?

She reached out, wrapping her arms around him, and pulled him close, as if she could divine his intentions through the heat of his body. He stirred, turned toward her so that he was pulling her close to him. Even in his semi-awake stake, she felt his desire for her as his lips found hers.

He pulled back and his eyes were awake, alive. "Can't sleep?" he asked.

She nodded, not trusting herself to speak.

He smiled and scraped his chin against her cheek, the prickly contact causing a shiver of delight to course through her.

"Let's see what we can do about, shall we?" he said, his words breathless against her ears. She shivered again and gave herself over to him, to the sensations of making love. Perhaps Jackson couldn't love her the way she loved him; in which case, her final thought was that she needed to take as much of him as she could get.

Chapter 45

"This will only take a moment," Lynn said as Jackson pulled the car up in front of Darby Callahan's house, a cute little Victorian on one of the main streets of the village. It was later in the day, the café would be closed and Darby said she'd be at home resting.

Lynn needed to drop some paperwork off to Darby, the contract for catering the fundraiser Caitlyn had urged her to set up. The plan was to use the money raised as the seed funds for the Healthy Kids Now foundation. Lynn had wanted to use her own money but when she had mapped out all she wanted to do, she realized that it would take more than she could give. A kickoff event was what was needed, Caitlyn had told her, and so she'd been planning one.

And now it was time to put everything in motion, and she wanted to give Darby all the details before she and Jackson headed out on their errands.

They, she and Jackson, were going furniture shopping. Well, TV shopping. He wanted a new one for his basement and he had asked Lynn to come with him. She had only hesitated a moment, thinking that this was what it was supposed to be like, right? This quiet way they had moved into being a couple. Shopping for electronics during the day and incredible sex at night. Still, they hadn't ever really touched on anything more than that talked-about some kind of future together. She tried not to mind it, not really, trying to remind herself that they had time, that there was no reason for her to rush him on anything, that she should just enjoy being with him.

"I'll come with you. Maybe she'll have some fresh cookies," he said, smiling.

He got out of the car, and his hand found the small of her back as he guided them up the tidy flagstone path towards the front porch steps. There were pots of mums sitting on the steps, in dusky oranges and maroons, reminders that autumn was fully upon them. It was a sunny day, but the weather had turned cold and there was a crispness to the air, overlaid with the smell of a wood fire.

Lynn breathed it in, her feet crunching on a few fallen leaves that hadn't been raked up. Behind her, she could see if she craned her neck the harbor, blue and bright, the light wind kicking up small waves. Jackson had pulled the boat in for the winter, but already she was looking forward to springtime and the chance to get back out on it.

She glanced up at him and he looked down, gave her a quick smile and a kiss before they stepped up the stairs that led to the wide wraparound porch. A wicker chair and couch were still out, their cushions pushed up. Potted plants swung from the porch, twisting and turning in the breeze. The house was freshly painted, a light cream color, with contrasting white woodwork and sharp green shutters. Everything about it looked inviting, and while Lynn was convinced her own style was more contemporary, the house, though compact, was more than charming.

Lynn raised the knocker and let it down once, then again. There was quiet and she knocked again, and finally she heard the sound of feet moving slowly toward them. The bright red door opened and Lynn was taken aback.

"Darby, are you ok?" she asked. Darby, even though she was eight months pregnant, had always looked glowing and strong. But today was a different story. Her face was pale and she was in a pair of sweats and an oversized t-shirt. Her reddish brown hair looked dull and lifeless, pulled back in a ponytail, and her hands were rubbing her giant belly.

"I don't know, I feel..." She took a deep breath and then she doubled over. Lynn saw her face contort in pain and immediately her instincts kicked in. She stepped forward, grabbed a hold of Darby, and guided her into the living room.

"Let's get you someplace where you can lie down."

"I'm having contractions," Darby said, through gritted teeth.

"It's going to be ok," Lynn said, feeling calm and collected. Her specialty wasn't delivering babies, but she had done a rotation in obstetrics and assisted in several births.

"How long have you had them?" Lynn asked, guiding her onto the couch. There was a fire already crackling and Darby must have been resting here, because there was a stack of magazines, a glass of water, and blanket.

"When's your due date?"

"It's supposed to be three weeks from now," Darby said, and Lynn could hear the worry and pain in her voice.

"It's going to be ok. Just tell me how long the contractions have been going on."

"I don't know, I mean, I was tired this morning, so I decided to rest, and I think I might have fallen asleep and then I woke up and there was something that almost felt like cramping. It's been going on for an hour. I've had them before, but they've always passed. But these are worse."

Darby bit her lip as another contraction hit her. Lynn did a mental calculation. The contractions were close together and obviously painful.

Lynn could feel Jackson hovering behind her.

"Where's Sean?" Lynn asked.

Darby shook her head. "At the restaurant. I told him I would be ok." There was worry and fear in her voice.

Lynn took her hand, knelt closer, and looked in Darby's eyes. "You are going to be ok. I'm a doctor, right?"

Darby nodded, then grimaced as another pain hit her.

"I just need to do a quick examination. Jackson," Lynn turned to see him standing there in the doorway, looking scared. "Will you go get my bag from the car—the black one. And call Sean."

"Should I call anyone else?"

Lynn shook her head. "Not just yet; it could be a false alarm." Calling someone or rushing to the hospital might not be a great thing. It all depended on whether or not Darby would rather have her baby at home or by the side of the road.

She could hear Jackson's rapid steps as he went to do as she asked.

"Darby, I am just going to take a look, to see if this is the real thing or another warmup, all right?"

Darby just nodded and Lynn went to work.

#

Jackson had made the phone call to Sean and gotten Lynn's bag from the car and then stood back, wanting to ask if he could help. Then he realized how silly an idea that was. Lynn was in complete control. Calmly, Lynn had told him to call 911 and Darby's doctor, but had also just as calmly told Darby that the baby was coming, sooner rather than later, and that in her best guess, they didn't have time to wait for the ambulance or drive like lunatics to the hospital.

"What do you need? Towels, boiling water?" he asked.

Lynn looked at him from where she was busy helping Darby.

"Towels, lots of them. And yes boil some water. And dump these in," she said, handing him scissors. "And a cup of ice chips," she added as Darby gave a grunt that turned into a scream.

"Go," Lynn said and turned her attention back to Darby.

It was over sooner than he would have thought, but judging by the sounds that Darby had made, it didn't hurt any less because things had been quick.

Sean had come bounding in the door, the ambulance right behind him, but by then Lynn had been coaxing Darby to push, towels spread all about.

Jackson held onto his friend's shoulder, but Sean went right in, going up to Darby, getting behind her and talking to her in a soothing voice.

The EMTs came crashing in and Jackson was jostled out of the way, but not before he heard Lynn's triumphant, "That's it," and one final loud exclamation from Darby, and then there was a moment of silence and then the wail of a baby.

Jackson fell back against the wall, realizing that he was sweaty and that his legs were shaking. He unclenched his palms and looked back in the room. The EMTs were standing around, with all their gear, looking disappointed that they didn't have more to do, and Lynn was handing the baby to Darby, who had tears streaking down her face.

"A beautiful baby girl," Lynn said. "Congratulations." She took a step back as the EMTs jumped in.

Sean was next to his wife, staring in awe at the wrapped bundle in her arms. There was another faint mewl and cry, and then Sean and Darby were laughing.

Lynn looked at Jackson, calmly wiping her hands with a towel. Her hair had escaped her hair clip and she looked flushed from the heat and the adrenaline, but she was smiling.

She came to him and he took her in his arms. "My God, that was amazing. You were amazing," he whispered.

"I didn't do anything. Darby and the baby did all the work."

"You just delivered a baby."

She looked at him, "Well, it's kind of my job."

"And it's amazing, you're amazing," Jackson said. The last of the setting sun came in through the windows, hitting her brown hair, and she stood there, as calm as if she did this every day. Something shifted in Jackson and his stomach dropped. He looked over at Sean and Darby and saw the way they looked at each other and their baby daughter. Then he looked at Lynn, who too, was absorbed the scene.

"I wonder who will have won the baby pool," she said, seemingly oblivious to the fact that she had just participated in a miracle.

Jackson swallowed, not sure how he was going to handle the fact that he was madly, deeply in love with Lynn Masters.

#

They never made it out to find a new TV, but Lynn was happy. The ambulance had taken Darby and the baby, whom they had named Emma, to the hospital, and they had gone too, to fill out some paperwork. A celebratory glass of champagne followed in Darby's hospital room and then they had left the happy family behind as more family and friends crowded in to visit them.

Lynn felt like she was walking on air. It had been pretty cool to deliver a baby, and not just anybody's. A friend's. And not in a hospital room. Not every day you got to do something like that. Yup, these were the days when she was glad of what she did. When all the hard work really and truly paid off.

She leaned back against Jackson, comfortable on the couch. He had been quiet since they had left the hospital, pensive almost.

The adrenaline of the day was slowly wearing off and she felt drowsy.

"Come, I'll carry you to bed," he said, and before she knew it, she had been scooped up and he was carrying her down the hallway towards the bedroom. Part of her wanted to protest that she could walk, but there didn't seem to be much point in it.

Slowly, carefully, he set her down on the bed. There was just one lamp on and she could see the way he looked at her. Suddenly she wasn't tired anymore and felt herself responding to the look, to the hunger, the desire in his eyes.

Their lips met at the same time, coming together, his kiss soft and sweet, which left her wanting more; but when she tried to push the pace, he kept things slow, his hands trailing over her body with a moving tenderness and a careful touch that made her insides coil with intensity.

Delicately, he undressed her, clothes peeling off until she was on the bed, and he looked at her, the hunger replaced by an almost reverent look as his gaze traveled over her. She felt the way his eyes burned into her and realized that something had changed between them. That her fight against her feelings for him was a losing battle. Somewhere along the way she had lost herself in him.

The thought scared her, and then as he kissed her, gentle at first, but then with passion, the heat, the electricity sparked between them. She rose up to meet him, bringing him down to her, giving her whole self to him, letting him give himself to her.

There were no more boundaries, she thought as his hands moved over her, his simple touches leaving her quivering with excitement, her climax building to the breaking point before he finally entered her and together they moved, the motion pushing them both up and over the crest until finally they both hit the edge and tumbled down the other side in an exquisite cascade of feeling.

They held each other in the dim light, not a word said between them, quietly wrapped together. Lynn felt Jackson's breathing deepen as he dropped off to sleep, still holding her tight. She didn't want to move, afraid to wake him, but at the same time her thoughts were racing, tumbling at what it all meant.

Tonight had been different, she could feel that with him. Perhaps it was only because he too had been affected by watching a miracle. Most people, men especially, never got that close to something that amazing. It wasn't her, she told herself, it had to be the situation; she needed to not read too much into it. Doing so would only get her hurt. In the morning, they would be back on familiar ground. And that's where she would try to keep it.

Chapter 46

They had just finished a run and were doing their cool-down walk along the boardwalk. It was cold, but they had dressed in layers. Jackson was trying to convince her that the first snow of the season couldn't be too far behind and she was asking him when they could go skiing. He laughed and mentioned that he knew a guy with a place in Vermont.

"How come you always know a guy?" she grumbled, but she wasn't displeased at the fact that they were making plans for the future, even if it was only for a weekend of skiing. She had visions of snowstorms, roaring fires with blankets and pillows piled high in front of them.

All, in all it was a totally normal day in the life of a perfectly normal couple as they made their way to The Golden Pear to check on the daily soup specials.

"It's just not the same without Darby here," Lynn said, looking over the menu board, inhaling the savory aroma of baked goods and hearty soups.

"Oh well. I guess a new baby means you don't have much time to cook the clams for the chowder."

Darby and Sean were in seventh heaven taking care of Emma, sleep deprived as they were. Darby was taking a much-deserved rest, with her dad and a few key employees picking up the slack at the café.

"She did say not to worry about the Harvest Ball fundraiser. She told me that between her, Sean, and her dad, they would have everything covered."

Jackson smiled. "I hear tickets are a hot commodity for the fundraiser."

Lynn laughed. "Perhaps, but I think people are afraid to say no to Caitlyn. Every day someone orders more tickets and they say Caitlyn told them it was a good cause."

The Harvest Ball was the event she and Caitlyn had planned as the fundraiser for the Healthy Kids Now foundation. It was a kids' costume party, to be held in the high school gym, with games and activities, plus a silent auction with lots of goodies for grownups too. Darby had worked out a healthy, Halloween-themed menu and had seemed to be excited to make hundreds of ghostly cupcakes that were secretly teeming with vitamin-packed pumpkin puree.

Lynn laughed and snuggled into Jackson's arm, which was slung across her shoulder, loving the feeling. They still hadn't talked about anything other than what they planned to do over the weekend. Still, there was the assumption that they would be spending it together. Slowly, Lynn had noticed she'd been spending more than a few weeknights at Jackson's house, where they chatted about their day while he cooked and they watched TV or read together and made love and then woke up to showers, breakfast, and rushing off to their separate workdays.

It was all perfectly perfect; but Lynn wondered how long she could go on with it before she would burst out and demand to know how he really felt, where he saw things going. But something always stopped her, that look in his eyes—the haunted, wounded look that told her he was still hurting and that she wouldn't like the answer if she asked the question. It was cowardice she supposed, because it would hurt too much to know, that after all, she wasn't enough.

#

They picked up their soup, and took it go, sitting on one of the benches overlooking the harbor to eat it.

"You have some pumpkin bisque on your nose," he said, looking down at her. She glanced up and went to reach for it.

"Here let me." He moved in closer with his napkin and paused. She was looking up at him, her dark brown eyes liquid, full of life and laughter.

He ignored the soup and instead angled his head and went down for the kiss. She seemed surprised but pressed herself into it. He took his free hand and snaked it around her back, pulling her closer. She tasted sweet and spicy, like the season, and he couldn't get enough of her.

A small sigh of what he hoped was happiness escaped her. He angled down and brought up his hand to run it along the straight line of her jaw. Her skin was soft and smooth and he felt the small shiver that ran through her.

He broke the kiss and saw the look in her eyes. They were almost finished eating and he knew without asking that they would head back to his house tonight, together, that this had become routine. He liked it, wanted it, and was always disappointed if for some reason she couldn't come to him, if next to him the bed was empty.

He knew that she was starting to wonder, wonder where things were going. Still she never asked, but he could tell in the glances she sent him sometimes, in the brief, clouded looks that crossed her beautiful face when she thought he wasn't looking. He loved her, he knew that; he had admitted it to himself—but what did it mean? He had made a promise to himself never to lose himself again; but with Lynn it was desperately easy to do that.

It was the ghost of Ashley that saved him. Lynn would dance around the subject, but she never pushed it. He let it be that way, letting her think that there was only so much of him to give. He hoped that she would be happy with that but also dreaded the day when she asked for more. Because even though he loved her, he couldn't be in love with her, couldn't give himself to her. And he knew she would never accept less than that, not in the long term. Nor, he admitted, did she deserve it.

#

They walked together, Lynn quiet but unsettled. She knew she had almost said something to him, about what he was thinking back on the bench, but she had chickened out again. So they strolled on, and she almost didn't notice as Jackson slowed and she felt him stiffen beside her.

She looked up, surprised by his sudden stop. He was standing as if frozen, the look on his face as if he had seen a ghost. Lynn followed his gaze. A woman, an attractive middle-aged blond, dressed in black leggings and a brightly patterned top, stood there, almost blocking their way.

"Jackson." Her voice was high, pitched with shock, and Lynn decided that she too looked like she had seen a ghost.

"Mrs. Moran," he said, his voice hoarse. Lynn stood still, looking between the two of them. They were all standing by the water, caught in a chilly breeze. A nor'easter was coming, Tory had predicted earlier that day and Lynn, feeling the sudden heaviness in the air, believed it.

"I didn't expect to see you here," Mrs. Moran said, looking between the two of them.

"I'm back in town. I thought you had moved."

A bitter look came across her face. "So that's why you thought you could come back? What, have you just been waiting all this time for us to leave so you can come in and take over this town? That would be just like you."

"I just...I didn't think I'd meet you," Jackson said, and Lynn could tell he was stumbling to find the right words.

"Well, here we are," Mrs. Moran said, and she turned slightly to include Lynn in the conversation. There was a pause and Lynn realized that the woman was waiting for an introduction. And that Jackson seemed to be tongue tied.

"I'm Lynn Masters. I work at the clinic," she said. She held out her hand.

"Libby Moran." The woman stepped forward, took Lynn's hand, and shook it. Lynn could actually feel the discomfort and tension suspended between Jackson and Libby Moran. Lynn sucked in a deep breath. This was Ashley's mom; it had to be.

"You must be new to town, right?" There was a nasty edge to the woman's voice.

"Relatively," Lynn answered, feeling as if the woman's eyes were searching for answers, and then as if finding one, swiveled and turned to Jackson.

"I can't believe you would dare to come back here, to where she walked and lived, and flaunt your life in my face. You lived, she died," Libby hissed.

Jackson said nothing, his face pale, his eyes sunken. Lynn swallowed, wondering just what to do. She took a step forward, but Jackson's arm held her back.

"I'm sorry, Mrs. Moran. You're right…"

"Libby!" There was a short, bark of a voice and a man, also in his fifties, with thinning light brown hair and watery blue eyes, wearing khakis, boat shoes and a windbreaker, came hurrying up.

Behind him trailed a teenaged girl, gawky all long legs, blond hair and with an endearing bit of awkwardness about her.

"Libby," the man repeated, grabbing the woman by the arm and holding her as she took a step toward Jackson.

He didn't make a move to defend himself, though and the slap took his cheek hard and fast.

"Jackson," the man said, pulling his wife back, "I'm sorry. Libby, you can't do this."

"I can!" she yelled, her voice a wail. "I can and I will. Bill, he lived and she died. How is that fair? It was his fault." Her face dissolved into tears and the man, Mr. Moran, Lynn had to assume, pulled his wife to him and rocked her as her body shook with sobs.

"I'm sorry," he said quietly over his wife's cries. "We had to come back and settle a few things with the house sale. It's hitting her hard."

The girl behind them, whom Lynn thought must be the little sister, Lindsay, stayed still, watching, her eyes darting between her parents and Jackson.

"Come, dear. Come," Bill Moran said soothingly, and Jackson took Lynn's hand and all but pulled them past on the boardwalk, his face set, his shoulders rigid.

Lindsay reached out a hand to touch Jackson's arm and he looked down at it and then her.

"I'm sorry," Jackson said tonelessly.

"Jackson, please, let me…" she said.

He gave a quick shake of head and said, "No, Lindsay. No."

Her father called to her, and she followed, shooting Jackson one last look.

Lynn stood frozen, watching the retreating figures of the Morans. In a moment, they were alone, the only sound the flag flapping and snapping in the wind, the single shriek of a gull as it wheeled above them, catching the currents of the air.

Lynn looked at Jackson, concern flooding her. "Are you ok? You don't look so great."

With a visible shake, he moved, starting to walk and saying, "I'm fine. Sorry, just a friend of my mom's. Haven't seen her in a while. Shall we get home? You said you have to work tomorrow?"

As if nothing had happened, Jackson continued walking. Lynn stopped, wondering if he thought she was stupid. But still she said nothing, thinking that he really did look like he had seen a ghost. It was all the answer she needed—all the answers to her questions about the future. How could she have been so stupid, to think that maybe, just maybe there could have been something permanent with her and Jackson? She saw it now. No, he hadn't built a shrine in his house to his dead fiancée but he had kept one in his heart.

With a sudden wrench, Lynn knew that Jackson could never, ever be hers the way she wanted to be his.

They went back to his car, ready to head home. Like a sleepwalker he got into the driver seat and she slid into the passenger seat. Jackson reached to start the car but she put out a hand to stop him. "We need to talk."

Chapter 47

All men dreaded those words. Actually, Lynn thought, just about everyone dreaded those words. They were the words you said to a parent when you were about to tell them that their child was sick—very sick. Only bad news could follow. But she had said them and now she couldn't take them back. She saw the clench of Jackson's jaw.

"Must we?" he countered.

"That was her mother, wasn't it?" Lynn found her voice but barely. "That was Ashley's mother." It was the first time she had said that name to him aloud, and all of a sudden it felt like there was a presence in the car with them. Lynn knew it was just her imagination but she couldn't shake the feeling.

"Yes. I thought she had moved out of town."

"Is that why you thought you could come back? Because you wouldn't have to face her?"

"Something like that." Jackson ducked his head.

"She certainly looked surprised."

"She was like a second mother to me," Jackson said. "And she's angry with me."

"For what? Jackson you're still running. God," Lynn said and her voice gathered force, "how could I be so stupid? Everyone warned me, told me that you weren't ready to move on. But I thought I could fix you. They were right about that too, that I have a God complex. Comes with being a doctor, you see. We're trained to diagnose, treat, prevent things, and if something is wrong, find a way to fix it."

Lynn could feel the tears, the hot burning prick of them starting behind her eyelids. She couldn't, wouldn't cry. It was no more than she deserved, thinking she could replace the love of anyone's life.

"And I thought I could fix you, Jackson. I thought you were fixed. I was just giving you time."

"Lynn," Jackson said. His voice was low but his face was unreadable. He reached for her but she couldn't let him touch her or then she would be undone.

"But you aren't. You can't be fixed."

"You don't understand," he said, and his voice held a tinge of desperation.

"Because you haven't told me. You won't talk about her. You won't talk about it."

"It's complicated," he said.

She laughed. "Yeah, life is complicated. I know when we started we said there would be no strings, a grownup relationship." She saw him swallow, but didn't let him speak. "But I'm past that. I need strings, Jackson; but you don't seem to."

"We've been happy the way we were," he said.

"I know and I am, I was happy. But Jackson, I need more. And if you can't give it, then I need to get out."

"Out," he said, repeating the word, dully.

"I won't compete with a ghost, Jackson. No one can. And until you figure out if you're ready to let her go, then I don't think we have anything left to discuss."

She put a hand on the handle of the door. They were still in downtown Queensbay, near enough so she could walk to her own apartment. The fresh air would do her good, she knew, help fight back the tears that were more than threatening to form. A single one escaped and she knew she had to leave.

Opening the door, she felt Jackson reach for her, but she moved quickly, not wanting to risk his touch pulling her back in.

"Lynn, please don't go." His voice was rough.

She stood outside the car and willed herself to look at him. "Tell me you're over her, that you're ready to move on."

He shifted in his seat, ran his hand through his thick hair. "It's complicated. There's something. I can't...it's not mine to tell."

"You have a secret?" She laughed and knew it sounded as if she were on the edge of hysteria, "Don't worry, Jax," she tossed his hated nickname at him. "It's not a secret that you're just as messed up as everyone said."

She swallowed and didn't care that the tears were streaming down her face. "As a doctor, the hardest thing to learn is that you can't save everyone, no matter how hard you try. And that the only thing, the best thing you can do sometimes, is just to accept that. And this is me, doing that."

She slammed the door and walked a little unsteadily across the parking lot. She thought she heard him shout her name, but she didn't stop to see, just walked faster. Going to her apartment was her first thought but then she realized he would find her there. She needed to be alone, to be away from him. There was only one place to go. To her parents. It was a hike, up to the Heights, but she could do it. She began to move faster, almost running, until she was sure he wasn't behind her. She was soon up the twisting road to the thicket of streets above the harbor. She came to her parents' house. The lights were off, which meant that her parents probably weren't home. All the better, because she didn't think she could handle talking to them right now.

Chapter 48

If her mother was surprised to see her, she said nothing. Perhaps that was because Lynn was muffled under two blankets and a comforter in what had recently been her bedroom. Her mother had checked in, seen her crying but hadn't asked why. Lynn pulled the covers over her head and drifted back into a state, halfway between sleep and awake.

Eventually, Lynn wasn't sure after how long, there was a slight knock at the door and without waiting for an answer, her mother showed herself in, carrying a tray with a steaming cup of tea and toast. She set it down on the nightstand next to Lynn and then leaned in and pulled the covers back. Lynn blinked in the sudden light then tried to pull them back over her, but her mother wouldn't let her.

"Have some tea. Sugar and milk—just what the doctor ordered."

"What kind of doctor," Lynn said, still trying to burrow further into bed. She knew her eyes were swollen and her nose was red. She was in her t-shirt and underwear from the night before, the rest of her clothes dumped on the chair in the corner.

"Dr. Mom, of course," her mother answered tartly. The bed sank under her weight as she sat down on the edge of it. Lynn waited and so did her mother, who apparently wasn't going anywhere.

"I have all day, Lynn."

"So do I," Lynn muttered back. She wanted a good sulk and her mother was interrupting it.

"Good. So you can start it off by telling me what happened?"

"I don't want to," Lynn said.

Her mother reached down and stroked Lynn's hair. "You are in my house. You did come in here, crying. I think if you want me to keep putting Jackson off that you had better tell me what is going on."

At his name, fresh tears threatened and Lynn had to blink them back rapidly. Prepared, her mother handed her a box of tissues.

"What do you mean?"

"He's been calling, wanting to know if you were here. Wanted to know if you were safe. Apparently, you didn't go home to your apartment last night. Or with him," her mother said.

"What did you tell him?"

"That I knew where you were, that's all. He sounded worried."

"He's just being a nice guy, a gentleman," Lynn said.

Her mom looked at her and Lynn saw herself reflected in the chocolate brown eyes, the freckles and even in the dark hair, though Lynn knew her mother's color now came from the bottle. Her eyes were kind, concerned, and Lynn felt like she was a little girl with the flu being told it was all going to be ok.

"Oh, I think that it was more than that. He was very worried, and very relieved to know you were safe."

Lynn drew her knees up, and propped herself back up on the pillows. Her mother handed her the mug of hot tea. Lynn thought about asking for coffee, but knew what her mother would say to that. Tea was her mother's cure-all, from an upset stomach to an upset heart.

She took her first sip after blowing on it to be sure it was cool and it slid down her throat—milky, sweet, and hot—and she instantly felt comforted.

Her mother gave her a smile. "Never argue with Dr. Mom."

"Thank you," Lynn said.

She expected her mother would leave but she didn't. "I don't know exactly what happened. I mean besides some sort of disagreement with Jackson. And I'm guessing it doesn't have to do with the color he wants to paint the clinic walls."

"Oh, Mom. I was so stupid. Everyone warned me, told me that he wasn't ready, that he wasn't over her. And I thought I could fix him, make him whole. I wanted to be the one to show the world he was ready to move on." She knew her mother had heard the story of Jackson and Ashley Moran.

Her mother stroked Lynn's knee through the fabric of the comforter. "Occupational hazard of being a doctor, I guess. The need to mend people?"

"Broken bones, stuffy noses…they're all a lot easier than broken hearts."

Her mother nodded.

"I don't think he is over her, I mean, really over his fiancée. I thought that if I loved him enough, gave him enough love that he would forget about her. He was happy with me, Mom; he would laugh and be playful. We did things together, the little things, like make dinner together, go shopping, and big things like dates, hikes, and boat rides, and we even talked about going skiing together. I felt like he was different than when I first met him, that he had changed, that something in him was better. But I guess it, or I, wasn't enough."

"You don't know that, do you? Did he ever tell you that?"

Lynn shook her head. "I knew from the beginning that it was just casual relationship. He even said he couldn't offer anything more than..."

Lynn's mother held up her hand. "Please, I get the picture. And don't let your father or brother know. One of them will feel honor bound to punch Jackson's lights out."

"But I thought, I don't know, that things were changing between us. And they did up to a point, and then they just stopped. I didn't know why. But last night—God last night—I realized that it would never change. He's still in love with a dead woman. How do you compete with that?"

"I don't know, honey, I don't," her mom said and pulled her close for a hug.

Lynn let herself be surrounded by her mother's comforting arms. Through the hug, Lynn asked, "If dad died, would you get over him?"

Her mother broke the hug and looked at Lynn. "That's a morbid question."

"I know. I'm sorry."

"But I suppose it deserves an answer. I can't imagine a life without him, but I also can't imagine not wanting to live again. And I mean really live, in all ways. And I don't think he would want me to. And I wouldn't want that from him either. No. I expect that I might be able to move on, eventually. It wouldn't ever be the same, of course, but you do move on, even if things are different. That's life. You have to move on, Lynn. Either by yourself or not."

"I can't make that decision for him," she said.

"No, but have you really given him the chance to know what the choice really is?"

Chapter 49

The Harvest Ball was a resounding success. Lynn could see that and knew it was no thanks to her. She still felt as if she were moving through a layer of mud, everything clouded and fuzzy, her thoughts still on Jackson. But it was her friends and family who rallied to her cause. Darby and her staff had come through, providing veggie burgers designed to look like monsters, chicken hotdogs shaped like spiders, and cupcakes cleverly loaded with shredded carrots and pumpkin puree and decorated like ghosts.

The games and stations were being manned by the local high school service clubs, and the little kids were running to and fro, in their costumes, thrilled. Caitlyn was selling raffle tickets and Lynn's mother was quietly bidding up the silent auction items. Phoebe was doing face painting and Tory was showing a softer side at the jump rope station, thrilling the kids with her Double Dutch skills.

Lynn's dad came up and dropped an arm around Lynn's shoulder as he surveyed the controlled chaos. "Pretty impressive turnout."

"I guess it helped it's raining out. Nothing else for kids and parents to do."

"Lynn," her father rebuked, "it's not like you to be so glum. Come on, this is impressive. Everything you've done is impressive. I know I didn't give it much thought when you started the program at the clinic, but I can't believe what you're doing here. And I heard you've been asked to present your results at a conference in December?"

Lynn nodded. Tory's website and the new materials she had printed had gotten the notice of the local paper, which had written an article on the program, and from there she'd been asked to talk to a local moms club about it. And next up was a meeting of the regional medical association. Things were taking off faster than she could have imagined.

"Like I said, looks like you have the whole town here," her dad said. "And I better go stop your mother from outbidding everyone at the silent auction. If I've told her once, I've told her a hundred times that we don't need his and her massages."

Lynn almost laughed. "There's always a first time."

Her father kissed the top of her head and went off to find her mom. Lynn looked around. The turnout was better than she could have hoped, but her dad was wrong. The whole town wasn't here. Jackson was nowhere to be seen, but she hadn't expected him, of course. After all, what would a guy like Jackson do at a school full of kids? She had to remember that she had no right to expect him here.

He had tried calling her, and she had answered once. It had been an awkward, strained conversation, just a few ordinary questions about her day before she made her excuses and hung up. Since then, she had dodged his calls, managed to time things so she didn't run into him at the clinic. She had felt like such a fool, cried all her tears that she didn't think she could handle seeing him. Being told in person what she already knew would make it no better.

Phoebe came over. "Oh my. I've used up all my face painting materials, can you believe it?"

Lynn checked her watch. "We only have another twenty minutes, so I think it's ok. Maybe you can help Tory out at the jump rope station."

Phoebe shook her head, "Promise if I trip and fall you'll give me free medical advice. It's been a long time since I used a jump rope."

Lynn managed a smile, but Phoebe, her eyes filled with concern, pulled Lynn in for a hug.

"Usually you're the one giving out hugs, but this time you look like you need one," she said.

Lynn closed her eyes, fighting back the tears as her friend held her close.

"I'm sorry he's not here. I thought maybe he would but…"

"It's not your problem. I knew what I was getting into." Lynn took a deep breath and felt the tears subside for the moment. She needed to hold it together.

"Still, it doesn't mean we can't curse his name."

Lynn laughed bitterly. "You're going to be related to him."

"Doesn't matter. I'll still take your side." Phoebe broke the hug and looked at Lynn. "Have you talked to him, I mean really talked to him? He's…he's not himself."

"What good would it do, Phoebe? I mean, do I need to hear it out loud, that he's just not over her? I'm not sure I could take it."

"Are you sure that's what he said?" Phoebe asked softly.

Lynn shook her head. "He didn't have to."

Phoebe nodded, but kept her arm around Lynn and drew her toward the ticket booth. "Maybe you two just need a little more time to work things through."

Lynn didn't say anything else.

#

"You made nearly eight thousand dollars," Caitlyn said, looking at her calculator in satisfaction.

The Harvest Ball was over, and the gymnasium was mostly clean and quiet, with only one table and a few chairs left. Caitlyn, who had agreed to act as her temporary treasurer, had just finished counting all the proceeds from the day.

"Wow," Lynn said, gratified but also amazed. "I can't quite believe it. I mean, there were a lot of kids here, but we really made that much with the raffle tickets and the silent auction?"

Caitlyn looked up, glanced at Tory and Phoebe, and then said, "Not quite. There were a few straight up donations that added to the total."

"From who?" Lynn asked. "Besides you and Noah?"

"There was one anonymous donation for six thousand dollars."

"What?" Lynn said, her mouth dropping open in shock. "From whom?"

"Well, as I said, it's anonymous," Caitlyn answered, but her gray eyes slid away from Lynn's face.

"You mean you don't know or you won't tell me?" Lynn stood up. "All of a sudden was there a wad of cash dropped into your lap? Or did this 'anonymous' donor use a more traditional payment source like a check or a credit card."

"Look," Caitlyn glanced at Lynn, "he didn't even want me to tell you, but I think you should know."

"Jackson?" Lynn breathed the name.

"Yes. But really, he didn't want you to know, wanted me to tell you that you made it all from raffle tickets. But I can't be dishonest with you."

Lynn looked at the faces of her friends who were watching intently.

"It doesn't change anything," Lynn said. And knew that it didn't, shouldn't. Jackson couldn't buy her forgiveness. She could be thankful for his support, but it didn't make a difference. She wasn't going to forget that he was in a love with another woman and carry on their relationship.

Tory gave a short laugh. "You are stubborn. I think the man is trying to tell you something."

"I can't be bought, Tory. The money's great, because it's for a good cause. But Jackson can't make himself feel better by giving me money. I don't think he's a bad person. He doesn't have to prove that to me."

It was something else entirely. She knew Jackson could be generous, could be a gentleman. But he couldn't be hers. And she was just going to have to live with that.

Chapter 50

"I am not going to serve you another one." Paulie the bartender was implacable, wiping down a glass as he stood behind the bar of the Osprey Arms.

"You do know who I am, don't you?" Jackson said, trying to focus on Paulie. But there appeared to be more than one of him.

"Yup, you're the guy my boss told me to cut off," Paulie said, putting the dry glass down and picking up another one.

"I'll sleep in an empty room. Please, just give me another drink."

Paulie just shook his head. Jackson started to get up, figuring he would head to Quent's and grab a beer there. He would still find an empty room at the hotel to sleep in. He knew well enough that he was in no condition to drive, but still a man had a right to drown his sorrows.

"Just what do you think you're doing?" Jake appeared next to him and Jackson tried to push against his friend, but Jake still retained enough of his quarterback bulk to stop him.

"Paulie has cut me off," Jackson said, glaring at Paulie.

"Chase told me to," Paulie said in his defense. "Jackson's been here every night for a week eating French fries and drinking beer, and he's had enough."

"What happened? I haven't seen you in days. I thought you and I were supposed to be starting a business together." Jake's voice was annoyed as he plopped Jackson back onto the barstool that he had so recently tried to vacate.

"I've been busy," Jackson said, his own voice sounding thick in his ears.

"Paulie, will you get us coffee and water please?" Jake said, turning his barstool so that it faced Jackson.

"Sure thing," Paulie nodded, and in a moment there were two cups of steaming black coffee and two pints of water in front of them.

"Pick one and get started," Jake said.

"What are you trying to do?"

"Sober you up. Find out what the hell is going on, though judging by your condition I'm going to make a wild-ass guess that it's woman trouble."

"A whole heap," Jackson said, hearing the misery in his own voice.

"I thought you and Lynn were happy," Jake said carefully.

"We were. And then I ruined it." Jackson decided to start with the coffee. He had a sip, decided that it was mistake on a stomach full of beer and Scotch, and tried the water instead.

"What did you do? Ask her to play doctor? I hear real ones hate it when you do." Jake's voice was light, teasing.

Jackson said nothing, too sunk in his own gloom to know what to say. God he was miserable without her. But she wouldn't talk to him, let alone let him explain. She wouldn't return his phone calls. He had wanted to go to her fundraiser tonight, but he just couldn't bring himself to see her, not if he didn't know that she would want to see him. But he knew she wanted the one thing he couldn't give.

"What are you muttering about?"

"She thinks I'm still in love with Ashley. Says she won't compete with a ghost."

"Don't know any good woman who would," Jake said, adding cream to his coffee and taking a sip.

"How can I be in love with a ghost? It doesn't even make sense," Jackson said.

"What have you told her?"

"I haven't told her anything. It's what everyone else says. That it hit me hard, that I have baggage, that she was the love of my life. What is Lynn supposed to believe?"

"What you tell her," Jake said simply.

"But I can't."

"Why not?"

"Because it's even worse than that. I'm not still in love with Ashley. I haven't been, not since..." Jackson faltered. He'd made a promise that he still intended to keep.

"Ok, so if you're not still in love with Ashley, what's wrong with Lynn? If you just don't feel that way about her, let her down easy. It will be messy and it will make Chase and Phoebe's wedding complicated, but you'll get through it. Lynn's passionate but reasonable. She'll move on eventually."

"It's not that."

"Then what is it?"

"After Ashley died, I realized that I'd spent years of my life loving someone who didn't love me back, who used me to feed her ego, telling me how important I was to her, how she couldn't live without me. And I bought it hook, line, and sinker. Hell, she was even cheating on me, and I think I knew it, and I made excuses for her. What a sap I was."

"Ok," Jake said neutrally, "so you're not, or haven't been, in love with Ashley for a long time but..."

"But I told myself I would never make that mistake again. That I wouldn't ever love anyone again, you know, get so wrapped up in them that I lost myself."

Jake nodded sagely. "The self-preservation vow. I think we've all made it when we've gotten burned. But no man is an island, you know. What I don't get is why you left then, if you weren't all torn up about Ashley. I mean, when did you realize this?"

"About three months before she died."

They turned and swiveled at the same time, looking at the speaker. Libby Moran stood there, her blond hair pulled back in a twist, dressed in wool slacks and a blouse, clutching a purse in front of her like it was a shield. Her eyes were sad, but they were no longer accusing.

Mrs. Moran's eyes were wide and so bright that for a moment Jackson thought she was going to cry, but then she blinked rapidly and the moment was over.

"Jackson, I am so sorry."

"No, Mrs. Moran. You don't have to do this," Jackson said desperately.

"Lindsay told me everything, and then Bill spoke to the police captain. God, Jackson why did you do it?"

"I…"

Libby looked at Jake. "Did you know?"

Jake held up his hands in bewilderment and Jackson sagged against the barstool.

"Look, Mrs. Moran, you don't have to apologize."

She closed her eyes, blinked back what he thought were tears and then took a deep breath. "Lindsay told me everything. About the breakup, Ashley wanting to leave, Tucker Wolff, and how you told the police you'd been driving. But why?"

Jackson closed his eyes, memories of that night flooding back. Why had he done it? If he'd known how the Morans would blame him, how everyone would look and point and whisper, would he have the courage to do it again?

"I didn't want you to think of Ashley that way. I wanted you to remember her, well, the way she was."

Libby's head sank down and her eyes closed briefly. "Thank you. I don't know what to think. I mean, I knew something was different, was up with Ashley; but I wouldn't have thought all that. And I blamed you, all these years."

"It's ok," Jackson said. "Mrs. Moran, you don't have to do this."

"No, I do. I never would have let you do it if I knew what it would cost you. Why did you let me blame you?"

Mrs. Moran didn't wait for an answer but rushed on. "I know Ashley broke up with you months before she died.

And that she was running off with Tucker Wolff. That's why he was in the car with her, not you, right?"

Jackson couldn't say anything, just nodded.

"Lindsay told me how Ashley broke off the engagement and of her plans to go away with Tucker Wolff. But still, that night, you were there for her like you'd always been, covering for her, saving her from her mistakes, doing the right thing. I know she was drinking that night, driving wild with Tucker. And if people had known that you two weren't together or that Tucker was involved, they would have talked."

Jackson didn't know if he could say anything, could only feel the pounding in his chest, feel the relief rising in him. He had kept the secret for so long, kept silent about him and Ashley because he wanted to protect the Morans, because they were good people and had been like second parents to him. It had been a simple decision and had felt right at the time, to help a grieving family. But then they had turned on him. Hell, it had felt like the whole town had turned on him and they were all serving up the sentimental bullshit about how wonderful Ashley had been. It had been too much. He'd had to get out. He'd been wounded, and then he had gotten angry. Angry at them, angry at Ashley, angry at himself for letting himself love her.

Mrs. Moran reached out and took Jackson's hand in her both of hers. "So again, I want to say thank you. It did make it easier to blame someone else, not her. And you owe us nothing, Jackson. You deserve to come home, to find some happiness. You will find no judgment from us and if I hear even a whisper of it from anyone else, I will give them my two cents, even if it's from afar."

"Not everyone needs to know; it doesn't matter," Jackson said, but already he wanted to find a way to unburden himself.

Mrs. Moran smiled sadly and looked at Jake. "It does. You gave Ashley everything, more I think than she deserved. Ashley was driving the car, she had been drinking. I am trying to get around to accepting that, and I will. But I do know that you deserve to have a full and rich life, without her memory holding you back, here or wherever you go."

Jackson sagged. Loving Ashley had been a rollercoaster of highs and lows, and there had been that edge to it of neediness, as if Ashley had only been happy if she knew you were worrying about her. It had taken him a while to realize that it wasn't love. It had been selfishness.

There was a pause, and before the silence could become awkward, Libby Moran took a step back, clutched her bag, and smiled brightly. "I have to be going. Bill and Lindsay are waiting for me. We're just about wrapped up here in town, so I am not sure when we'll see each other again."

She nodded and slipped out as Jackson sat there stunned, not sure what this meant. For five years of his life he'd been keeping a secret and now he'd just been told that it was no longer important. That it was time to move on. But what did that mean? Did it even matter?

Jake, who had risen from his stool as Mrs. Moran left, sat back down and fixed Jackson with a stare.

"And what, my friend, was that about?"

Jackson looked up. The bar was comfortably crowded but they were tucked back along the far corner of the bar, private enough. Mrs. Moran had said she trusted him to know who could be told.

"Sit back and order another cup of coffee. This is going to take a while."

#

Jake took a sip of his lukewarm coffee, watching Jackson finish his story. It made sense and it explained a whole hell of a lot of things. He'd known something had been wrong with Jackson back then. Just as he had noticed that the ever-present Ashley was no longer so ever present. Still, to think she'd been running around with Tucker Wolff, behind Jackson's back. After the accident, Tucker had quietly slipped out of town too, joined the Navy. Jake had never given much thought to that. Now it all made sense.

"So you let the Morans think you were with Ashley when she crashed? And that everything was hunky-dory between the two of you?"

"I thought it would make it easier for them to grieve. I never thought they would blame me the way they did. And to tell them would have been to destroy the memory of their daughter."

"But Tucker Wolff?"

"I guess Ashley still had a thing for him, and when she came home from college, there he was, here—ready to fill her with promises to go off and see the world and take her with him. Turns out Ashley never quite bought into the whole living our life out here. Tucker Wolff was just her way out."

Jake almost winced but didn't. He thought it was a pretty fair assessment of Ashley's character, but it would do no good to say that now. He did, however, decide to ask the question that had been on his mind for five years. "So do you think if Ash had lived...that you would have gotten back together? That it was a temporary case of cold feet?"

Jackson took a sip of coffee and then said evenly, "No. Ashley and I wanted very different things. She thought living here was confining. She wanted to travel, to have adventures. She liked the thrill of the chase. That isn't me. Yes, I left; but because I felt I had to, not because I wanted to. Ashley wouldn't have been happy living here. And as it turns out, I wasn't happy not living here."

"So what are you going to do about her?"

"About Lynn?" Jackson ran a hand through his hair.

"Yeah, her. How do you feel about her? Do you love her?" It was a simple question and it deserved a simple answer.

"Yes, I love her. I told her that I couldn't be anything more than a..."

"Friends with benefits," Jake finished for him.

"Something like that. And now..."

"And now you two are in love. I don't understand what the problem is. It's not rocket science. You two are crazy about each other, you want to spend time with each other, you love each other."

"The last time I loved someone I lost myself. In more ways than one. You said it yourself, remember. She consumed me."

"Is that what you're afraid of? It's not that you still love someone else, is it? You're afraid you'll love Lynn too much, that she'll use you the way Ashley did?"

Jackson looked at his friend, not surprised that he had guessed the truth.

"So that's it. You're not all caught up in Ashley, you're just too afraid to love again. Well let me ask you, do you feel that way with Lynn?"

"No," Jackson said quietly, and realized that the water and the coffee were beginning to have their effect. "It feels different. Steady, constant. I mean, don't get me wrong, it's exciting too but I don't feel like I'm dancing on the edge of a flame. I don't know if that's love or companionship. I've only experienced moods and passions so fierce they engulf you or well, not that this makes me a standup guy, but you know, just simple physical attraction. This is something different. But it doesn't matter because..." he muttered.

How could he go back and tell Lynn about Ashley? She had said she didn't want to compete with a dead woman. Well she had, but not the way she thought. Would she think that his lying to her was worse than the truth, that he didn't think he could ever love that way again? Would she think it meant he wasn't capable of it?

"I think it does. And it should. Look, like Mrs. Moran said, you did your duty. You stood by them when they needed it most. They moved forward, moved on. If, God forbid, the situation had been reversed, I don't think Ashley would be down here swearing off men."

"I am not swearing off women...It's just with Lynn, it's..."

"Different," Jake said. "Face it. With Lynn you're a better man. Happier, chiller, you know, all around less broody and all that. Why? I don't know. Maybe she smiles and you see rainbows and unicorns. Or maybe she tells really funny jokes. Or really dirty ones. Or she can cook, or maybe she just gets you. I don't know how, but whatever it is it works. And maybe you've lived so long working on not caring that you're afraid of what it feels like. But this time, it might just be the real deal."

"When did this become the Tao of Jake?"

Jake shrugged. "Look, man. It's one thing to want to run around and sample all the fish in the sea when you're seventeen. But add in a few years and you realize that there's more to life than sitting in a dark bar listening to crap music and drinking beer with other guys. If you feel something for Lynn, something real, well then you should go for it. Tell her the truth and let her decide. You owe her that much."

"Yeah," Jackson said.

Jake picked up his glass of water. Listening was thirsty work. "The truth will set you free, man. It will set you free."

Chapter 51

The truth did set him free. He told Chase the next morning, making him take a walk out along the docks so that he could move around. Somehow it seemed easier to talk about if he didn't have to sit in a chair and feel like he had been called into the principal's office.

Chase said nothing at first, and then, "Wow. That is some heavy baggage you've been carrying around."

Jackson looked up as a gull circled the sky. He found himself glancing up toward the Osprey Arms annex and what would be Lynn's apartment. The blinds were closed, he couldn't see anything. But it didn't matter, she was sure to be at work. After all, that is what he had done—lose himself in work when he didn't want to deal.

"It feels good to be free. I mean, I don't intend to shout it to the whole world, but I know when I left that I let you down too, left you with the family business to run. Not that, as it turned out, you needed me."

Chase smiled, an eyebrow quirked up. "I'm just glad to have you back. It's been fun, but it will be more fun with you around. You're staying right?"

Jackson smiled and shook his head. "I never want to leave again."

"Good," Chase said, and leaned over the railing so he could peer into the depths of the water lapping at the dock below. "Now we just have to fix your love life."

"What?" Jackson sputtered. Really, he was glad to be honest with his brother but this was pushing it.

"Don't try to deny it." Chase waggled a finger at Jackson. "You're crazy about her. And miserable without her."

Jackson shoved his hands in the pocket of the coat he had put on against the autumn chill. "It's too late there. I screwed it up. She thinks I'm…"

"An emotionless hard-hearted bastard in love with somebody else."

"Something like that."

"But she's pretty miserable too; I have that on good authority."

"She's just mad," Jackson said, shaking his head. He couldn't let himself get his hopes up.

"I like Lynn, I really do. And not just because she's friends with my bride to be. Did I ever tell you about the time she saved my life?" Chase laughed at the expression on Jackson's face. "Ok, so it was just a paper cut. But seriously, I think when two people are in, how shall we say, in sync with one other, then just about anything can be fixed."

Jackson sighed. He knew he wasn't going to escape the brotherly advice, solicited or not. "What's your idea, big brother?"

Chase smiled. "It's time for the grand gesture, my friend. Think big, think wow, and then prepare tell the truth and grovel. That should do it."

"What should I get, a skywriter to say I'm sorry? What do you mean by a grand gesture?"

Chase shrugged. "How the hell should I know what Lynn wants? She's not my girl. Though it seems like money isn't the way to her heart. Apparently, she was unmoved by your donation."

Jackson sighed. "It was supposed to be anonymous. I didn't want her to think I was trying to buy her forgiveness."

"Classic guy move, thinking you can throw money at a problem. I think this time you need to figure it out. She's your girl after all. For Phoebe it would probably be a new set of drawing pencils or fancy new sheets. Seriously. But you have to figure out what's going to melt Lynn's heart, if you know what I mean, long enough for you to get down on your knees and beg. Got it?"

Jackson nodded. He thought he might just be finally getting it.

Chapter 52

"Next." Lynn barely looked up as the next patient entered the small exam area. If she thought that she had managed to put Jackson out of mind, she realized she had been mistaken.

"You." Lynn couldn't keep the surprise out of her voice.

"Doctor." Lindsay Moran stepped into the exam room and hesitated, as if waiting for Lynn to say something.

The nurse, as if she could feel the tension, looked at Lynn. Lynn swallowed, then waved her away, taking the proffered chart. She was a professional and she was pretty sure that anything Lindsay had couldn't fluster her. She just needed to remain detached, above it all, and she would do just fine.

Lindsay smiled shyly as the nurse left them alone and took a seat on the examining table, as if she had all the time in the world.

"Do your parents know you're here?" Lynn asked.

"I'm eighteen so it doesn't matter, and this isn't because I'm sick. We're leaving today and this seemed like the fastest way to get to you. I tracked down Chase and he told me where to find you."

"Ok," Lynn said, not sure where this was going.

"You should give Jackson another chance, you know," Lindsay said, her legs swinging off the side of the table, her eyes, big, blue, round.

"Excuse me?"

"Look, I saw the way you looked at my mom. And the way you looked at Jax. I don't know what you heard about my sister's death, but whatever it was it wasn't Jackson's fault. I told my mom that, and she believes me I think, but I didn't want you holding what you thought you knew against him."

Lynn gave a bitter laugh. "What, that he's in love with a dead woman?" As soon it was out of her mouth, Lynn regretted it. Her hand flew to her mouth, covering it, and she wished with all her heart she could take her words back. "Sorry."

Libby shrugged with a world weariness that Lynn knew could only have come from having suffered a tragedy.

"See, that's what you think you know."

"So what don't I know?"

"Well, everyone thinks she was St. Ashley. But she wasn't."

"I have a brother and he's no saint either, but he's still a good person," Lynn said carefully.

Lindsay shook her head. "No. Ash had some serious issues. Deep down issues. Poor Jackson got suckered right into it. He adored her, worshipped her, and she treated him like a faithful puppy and he put up with it. But he was never happy. Ashley," and here her voice dropped just a bit, "liked drama. She liked to keep Jackson on his toes. It fed her ego, her self-confidence to know that he was always a bit more in love with her than she was with him."

"Did you think this was going to make me feel better?" Lynn asked. She balled her hand into a fist, aware that it was trembling. She took a deep breath, trying to get control of her emotions.

"No. But perhaps you need to give Jackson a chance to explain," Lindsay said.

Lynn closed her eyes, shook her head, wished she could make all of this go away. "I would like for him to, but he won't. Just said I wouldn't understand."

"Yeah, that sounds like Jackson, Mr. Goody-two-shoes. He has a serious knight in shining armor complex."

Lindsay said nothing more, just hopped off the exam table, the white paper crinkling as she did so. She landed neatly on her feet and looked down at Lynn.

"I think that Jackson needs to explain it himself. I knew of course. Can't keep things from a nosy little sister, but he swore me to secrecy, told me it would be better this way. I believed him; only I didn't realize how bad things would get for him."

Lynn shook her head in bewilderment. She had no idea what Lindsay could possibly be talking about.

Lindsay started toward the opening in the curtain that separated them from the rest of the clinic.

"You know, he's happy with you. I could see it, hear it."

"Hear it?"

"Yeah, he sends me emails, little presents sometimes. Nothing weird, don't worry. But he was kind of like a big brother to me when he was with Ashley, and just because my mom went all crazy on him, he never stopped being there for me."

"He talked about me?" Lynn said.

"Sort of. I mean, he hardly ever gave me any details about his personal life, but well, he did mention you, so I thought that was kind of, you know, significant. And I don't know, there was just something in what he did say. You know, like he was happy."

"Happy?" Lynn repeated.

"Yes. He's happy with you. Trust me." And with that she was gone.

Lynn sank slowly to the small rolling stool, needing a moment to calm and pull herself together as the clinic hummed around her.

Happy? Had she truly made Jackson happy? She remembered his smiles, his laughs, the way he teased her, looked out for her, his thoughtfulness, his loving hands. All so different from the stern, serious man she had accused of having ice in his heart and closing down the clinic. He was the man who had given the clinic a new lease on life, who fixed up the ball fields, who made an outrageous donation to something that was important to her.

But could being happy with someone compare to being crazy in love? Was happy a good enough substitute for passion? Lynn's own heart, its breaking, told her the answer. She was crazy in love with Jackson and miserable over it.

Chapter 53

She drove up the driveway, the pit in her stomach growing larger. It was dark early now, and there was a soft glow of a few lamps on in the house, as it sat low slung to the ground. Beyond, she could see shimmering lights on the far bluffs across the expanse of the harbor. The moon sat large and fat in the sky, a harvest moon.

She pulled up in front and just sat in her car, allowing the warmth of the heater to caress her bones, trying to do anything that would postpone the inevitable. Sure, she had thought about calling the items a loss, but then she had told herself to grow a pair. If Jackson wasn't planning on moving and if neither was she, then she was bound to run into him here and there. Better to be mature, to be grownups about it.

So she had to will herself to get out of the car, pulling her barn coat more tightly around her. She had her scrubs on and the thin fabric caught in the wind and it cut right through her. There might still be leaves on the trees and a warm spot of sun in the afternoon, but fall was giving up the ghost, no doubt about it. Winter would be upon them soon.

Shivering, she started up the crushed gravel walkway to the wide redwood planked steps. Maybe he wouldn't be here, she thought, then shook herself. She was not going to weenie out of this. And besides, what Lindsay Moran had said kept coming back to her.

Ringing the doorbell, she rocked on the ball of her heels, pulling on her ponytail. There was the sound of a click and then Jackson's voice over the intercom. "Lynn?"

"Yes," she said, trying to keep the irritation out of her voice. Was he expecting someone else? Maybe he had moved on to another woman he couldn't commit to. The thought stabbed at her heart and she waited for another moment before he answered.

"Come in." The disembodied voice was eerie over the loudspeaker. Behind, the tree branches moaned and scraped together in the wind.

She glanced back and saw only shadows and dark, so she scooted into the inviting warmth of the house.

The lamps were on dim, the fire was crackling in the fireplace, and there was music, something soft and low playing on the stereo.

She looked around for the box of her stuff, hoping that perhaps he had just left it for her up here on the main floor and she could grab it and go.

"Down here," he called, and seeing that there was no obvious pile of stuff, she took a breath and started down the staircase to the bottom floor.

The lights were on brighter here, and she saw that he had been doing some work. It smelled of fresh paint and new wood, but the main room seemed untouched, with its bar area and pool table.

"I'm back here," he called again. Feeling frustrated, wondering what sort of wild goose chase she was being led on, she followed his voice, past the pool table, to the corridor off to the side of the bar. This area had been unfinished, except for the laundry room. It had been a good-sized space, open, broken by only by steel columns and cold concrete.

She stopped, coming to a halt, her mouth not quite working.

"Surprise," he said, looking at her.

"What is this?"

"A rock-climbing wall. Well, a rock-climbing ceiling."

She looked around. It wasn't a tall wall of course, but the room's walls and ceiling had been lined with plywood, painted gray and studded with toe and handholds. One could climb up the walls and then across the ceiling. The floor, she noticed now, was squishy and well padded.

"A rock-climbing room?"

Unsure, she put her hand up and touched one of the toeholds, feeling the smooth plastic.

"Why," she whispered, feeling her throat close up.

He took a step toward her, his hands out. "I think you know why, Lynn. It's a peace offering, a gift, a way to show you that I messed up."

"But nothing has changed," she whispered. "You're still in love with her, and I won't come after a dead woman. I'm sorry, I don't mean to be harsh. But I need you—all of you."

"But you do have me," he said, his arm reaching out to her, stopping her so she wouldn't go. "There's something I need to tell you…"

He took a deep breath and Lynn waited.

"I haven't been in love with Ashley for a long time. Even before she died."

"What...? But..." Lynn took the step back and he didn't stop her.

"I told a lie. To you, to her parents, to my family, to my friends. And I think—I know—I would do it again. It was the right thing to do at the time."

"Why?" she asked, but suddenly the conversation with Lindsay was starting to make sense.

"I thought it was the right thing to do then to protect her memory. To protect her family. I just never thought the lie would overtake me the way it did. Somehow it became the defining point in my life. I was Jackson Sanders, poor Jax who lost his one true love in a car crash. And then, before I knew it, everyone blamed me for killing her. But I wasn't even with her."

Lynn's head was reeling. "I don't understand."

"Ashley broke up with me months before she died. Told me the wedding was off, that she never wanted to live in a small town, that she was made for better things. She even told me she was seeing someone else. At first, I thought it was just cold feet so I begged her, asked her to reconsider. We told nobody—she agreed to that—but she wouldn't see me. The only one who knew was her little sister.

"I was devastated but I also felt, like for the first time in a while, I could breathe. I could be myself. I could take a damn step without worrying what Ashley would think or do or how she would try to twist it into whether or not I really loved her. I realized that I had loved the idea of being in love with her more than actually loving her."

"I…" Lynn started to say but Jackson kept going on.

"I was getting over her, moving on, making plans with Jake for our business, planning on working another year or two to get the experience. I was happy."

"And then what happened?"

"Her parents knew something was wrong. Ashley was staying out late, partying a bit, blowing off work. They came to me. Ashley hadn't told them, so I lied to them, covering for her. But soon I was pissed. Until she came clean to her parents, I was trapped in a lie. I couldn't say hi to a girl or stay out late without half the town giving me looks like I was stepping out on her. But she didn't tell them because it kept them off of her back. And I couldn't do it. Too much of a gentleman, I guess," he said ruefully.

"And then…"

Jackson swallowed. "I got a call one night, from this guy I knew on the police force. There had been an accident and I might want to get there fast. He was doing me a favor, I think. I went to the scene. Ashley was there, in bad shape, still alive, and I thought she might make it. She'd been driving too fast, drinking probably, and there had been a passenger, Tucker Wolff—some guy we had gone to high school with. Of course, he was fine, not a scratch on him."

"Let me guess—that's who she was seeing."

"Exactly, and things were confusing. By then, EMTs and the other cops got there, people just assumed I was with her. It wasn't a cover-up, just not quite the truth. Wolff was able to walk away, and I even gave him my car keys, had him take my car. Everyone made assumptions and I played vague. Some people kept quiet and before I knew it, we had a story going."

"You let it happen?"

"I rode with Ashley to the hospital, and the doctors tried everything they could, but it was too late. Her mom leaned on me for support and it just seemed easier to play along with it, to not let the rumors and the scandals start."

"So you played the grief-stricken fiancé?"

"I was grief stricken, for a while. I did love her once. And for what it's worth, she was a vital, commanding person. But Ashley was selfish in life and in death. And then Mrs. Moran, well she went off the deep end, not that I can blame her. But she kind of took it out on me. So I went from the poor, grief-stricken fiancé to one step above a murderer. The fact that the cops did nothing to me only made her crazier."

"But you could have told the truth at any time, gotten it all to stop," Lynn said.

"And what? Let everyone know Ashley had been stepping out on me? Ruin her memory? There would have been plenty of people who would have liked to see her fall a bit from her pedestal. No way. Ashley was drunk, she was driving that car. Thank God she only hurt herself. I could take the blame if it meant protecting her parents from that kind of truth."

Lynn nodded. "I see."

"Do you? Do you know what this means?"

Lynn wrapped her arms around herself, hugging her close, suddenly cold, and said, "You lied to me as well. You let me believe that you were still in love with her. That we couldn't have a real relationship because you were broken. What's changed?"

Jackson looked at her, his eyes big, bright, intent on her.

"After Ashley died, I vowed I wasn't ever going to get caught up in a relationship like that again. I lost something of myself—when I was with her and even after she died, when I had to leave town. It took me a while to get myself back, to get back to here. To do that I had to stay detached. And it worked. Until you."

He took a step toward her and she almost moved away from him, but didn't, letting his words spill over her.

"Lynn, you broke through that feeling, made me realize that I'd been telling myself a lie to protect myself. I stayed away from relationships, real relationships, because I didn't ever want to be hurt again. But you showed me that things—love—can be different. It can be passionate, but constant, faithful and exciting, committed and true and real."

"But you never said anything," Lynn whispered, not quite believing it.

He took her by her arms and held her so she wouldn't go, his eyes looking down into her. "I thought I knew what love was. That it was crazy, passionate, ups and downs. And with you it is," he said, twining his fingers around her hand, "But it's also warm and even and sexy and full of surprises and joy and happiness and laughter. That's what you've given me. And I don't want to lose it, I don't want to lose you."

"But…"

"From the moment I saw you launch yourself into Petersen's office, to the way you beat me at the rock wall, to our first kiss, I knew I wanted you. On some level, I knew you made me whole. And then I realized I loved you. Slowly, deeply, always. You're the woman who can steer a boat, stitch up a hand, give out lollipops, make kids healthy, and deliver babies. You're an amazing, sexy, beautiful woman. And I want to be with you."

She could feel the electric pull of their connection, the need for him. She had missed him, been miserable at her core every day without seeing him, without knowing that he was waiting for her.

He touched his forehead down to hers but did no more. "I missed you, so much. Every night you weren't here, I would come home and this house would be empty and cold; there was no laughter, no fun, no you."

"Yes," she agreed, still not able to look at him.

"So you missed me too?" he asked, hope lighting his voice.

"From the moment you first kissed me and walked away," she said, knowing that she could finally admit it. "I love you too, all of you. And probably most of all, the knowledge that you will do what's right...even if it hurts you." She could forgive him for keeping his secret, respect what he had done. He was a good man. And he was hers.

He kissed her then, a deep, tender kiss that had her melting into him.

They broke finally, coming up for air.

"I don't want to ever lose you again," he said.

"I'm here. You built me a rock-climbing room."

He smiled. "Marry me."

"What?"

"Marry me. I want to be with you for the rest of my life, Lynn Masters. You're intelligent, compassionate, and beautiful. You make me happy. You make me remember what it's like to have fun. Marry me and we'll go rock climbing and skiing, and kayaking and skinny-dipping on a hot summer night. Whatever you want. But build a life with me, a family, and marry me."

She waited for a just a heartbeat, feeling, seeing all the possibilities, knowing that with Jackson there was everything she wanted: a home, love, adventure.

"Yes, I'll marry you," she said. And he swept her up into his arms.

THE END

About Drea Stein

Drea Stein is the author of contemporary romance. She writes the Queensbay series, set in the quaint New England town of Queensbay. In real life, she lives in rural New Jersey with her husband and children.

Read the other books in the Queensbay Series:

Book 1: Dinner for Two - Darby and Sean

Book 2: Rough Harbor - Caitlyn and Noah

Book 3: The Ivy House - Phoebe and Chase

Book 4 - Chasing A Chance - Lynn and Jackson

Book 5 - With You - Tory and Colby

Read an excerpt from **With You - Book 5 in the Queensbay Series**

With You

Chapter 1

Colby Reynolds woke up, feeling the warmth of the sunshine pouring in through the clerestory window that lighted his loft-like sleeping peace. He rolled over, chasing the last, elusive bit of sleep until he was reminded that he had a pretty lady in the bed next to him. The lady, his Princess, grunted, rolled over and flopped an ear as she opened one eye. Princess was not a morning dog, he thought as he got a whiff of doggy breath and wet kiss on his nose.

"You are not supposed to be in bed," he told her but she woofed and ignored him. He got up, pulled on his running pants and a t-shirt. Princess, sensing something interesting was about to happen, lifted her mix of black lab and retriever butt off the bed and headed downstairs, now ready to start the day.

They had the beach to themselves this morning, the sun rising over Long Island Sound, making the waves twinkle and sparkle. To their east stood the headland, where the old lighthouse speared up, guarding the bluff. To the west, around another rocky headland, was the entrance to harbor and the village that overlooked it.

They headed to the east and Princess wanted to play so he tossed the Frisbee more than ran, but she was happy and worn out by the time they were done. It meant he only had time enough for a quick shower before heading to work.

As he drove along the coast road he could see that it was a perfect day, the hint of spring firmly in the air, yet something was putting his mood off, a mounting sense of disquiet he'd been feeling lately. Wondering, if this indeed was it. It wasn't a bad it, he thought, as he drove through the impossibly charming New England town of Queensbay. It was just that it was it.

Problem was, there had been a whole string of good enough days for a while, almost a year now. Back then he had looked up from his spreadsheets and realized he didn't need to check them every hour. Business, if not booming, was predictable with a steady growth rate. That more and more clients were seeking him out instead of the other way around.

It should have been a good feeling. It was he assumed, what success felt like. Except it felt, day in and day out, just like regular life. He'd been pushing so hard, working so diligently toward this point he didn't quite know what to do with himself now that he was here. And while Princess was a swell mutt, she wasn't the most engaging of dinner companions. Still, she was better than Kayla, his ex. She'd only been interested in herself and in what Colby could do for her. And when he refused to play the game of fame and fortune, she'd made it clear that she was done with him.

It had hurt, to know he had been so clearly used. And for what? He'd been a second-rate race car driver, in a world of bright lights, fast cars and people with more money than sense. For a while, Colby had bought into it all - the scene, the adrenaline rush of winning, of being adored, the women who draped themselves over you while the press snapped pictures. At the end of the day, though, fame and fortune were fickle. It was hard to keep winning time and time out. It had been almost impossible to stay on top and Colby had never regretted his decision to take a step back to evaluate what really mattered.

It had been money. He had seen that clearly. Money drove everything and there were clearly better and more reliable ways to make it than to chance it driving a car around a track against a dozen other guys who wanted the same thing. So that's when he had changed course - pivoted - those fancy MBAs called it. He'd taken what he was really good at - fixing cars - and his natural charm - and become a used car salesman. And made more money in a three months than he'd made in three years chasing trophies.

It had been the right decision, he knew it. His business was successful and though he didn't miss the bright lights and cheering crowds - the lows of losing - he was missing something. Colby pushed these unsettling thoughts away as he pulled into the driveway of his shop. Classic Autosports. Stopped a moment to take it all in. Large plate glass windows gave a view to a showroom where gleaming concoctions of metal, leather, and chrome rested under the bright lights.

This was his, all his, the result of hard work, a little bit of luck and some of his God-given charm. He parked precisely in his reserved spot and steeled himself for another day of perfectly good enough. And that's when things started to go south.

He walked into the office and discovered his top of the line, Italian made coffee maker, one of his most prized possessions, had shorted out, leaving him caffeine-less. Shandy, his office manager, blithely informed him that a repair man couldn't be out for a week, and if he tried to fix it himself he would most likely void the warranty.

Oh, and on top of that she was quitting. Effective immediately. Something about getting a job as a stand-in on a movie set. Her big break, she called it, as she packed her bag, leaving a tornado-like mess behind. He peeled off as much cash as he had handy, wished her good luck and waved her off with more relief than regret. Shandy had been easy on the eyes but couldn't seem to wrap her head around the proper order of the alphabet, how to transfer a phone call or when not to hit reply all to an email.

Now of course, he'd have to answer the phones himself until he found a replacement. Maybe nice and easy hadn't been so bad after all.

He'd resigned himself to a cup of coffee from the break room machine, one of those one cup at a time things, with all the different flavors lined up in a rack. He hated it, but the customers and the guys who worked for him seemed addicted to it. It wasn't a smooth cup of Italian espresso but it did the trick and he felt mildly less peeved as he made his way to his desk and contemplated the stack of papers on it.

He looked at the message Shandy had left on top, weighted down with a die-cast model of a 1976 Ford Thunderbird that he'd built himself. He swore, running a hand through his close-cropped light brown hair as he read what she'd written there, in all caps: ALFIE LANDAU NEEDS TO SPEAK WITH YOU RIGHT AWAY.

Colby crumpled the slip of paper with Alfie's number on it and threw it in the waste basket. He knew the number by heart, just as he knew why Alfie was calling. He had recently agreed to purchase a beautiful 1964 Jaguar convertible, in veritable mint condition and Colby knew Alfie usually second-guessed himself. That was until Colby praised his brilliance and good taste over an expensive steak and an even more expensive bottle of wine. At which point, Alfie would write Colby a check on the spot and all was well.

Alfie was one of his best clients, high maintenance but reliable. And since Colby had paid for the Jaguar upfront, snagging it before another avid collector swooped in, this quarter's profit margin relied heavily on Alfie writing that check. There was no getting out of giving Alfie the VIP treatment.

He was going to tell Shandy to call Alfie back, tell him he was traveling but would love to take him to dinner at the Osprey Arms real soon. Then he remembered he'd have to do it himself and swore again.

Colby leaned back in his chair. It was leather and dark wood, like most of the office, a décor meant to conjure up an image of taste and sophistication. He would have preferred something a little more modern and streamlined but he had to admit, most of the clients seemed perfectly happy here, especially after he produced a bottle of single malt from a specially built bar cabinet and offered a toast to their good taste. Selling classic cars was selling a fantasy, no doubt about it and most who came here were ready to buy into the whole thing. It was a far cry from how he'd grown up but he couldn't say he didn't enjoy it.

He leaned forward, took a sip of his coffee and decided that the stack of paperwork would have to wait. He glanced over the calendar on his computer, assessing the work schedule for today. They were backed up, no way could they get it all done, not even if they hustled into overtime. Nope they'd need an extra hand in there. Colby couldn't quite keep the smile off his face as he realized what it meant.

He stepped out onto the floor of the showroom and breathed deep. It smelled of oiled leather, rubber tires and motor oil, a combination that never failed to please him.

The real magic happened in the garage space behind the showroom. More thick glass separated the show room from the garage, so there was a full view of the work stations. Colby had wanted all the guys - and truth be told, it was almost always men - who came in to get a glimpse at the alchemy and skill that went into turning these old hunks of metal into the gleaming chrome and enamel beauties they coveted.

Colby entered the locker room, a decent sized space where the mechanics could keep a change of clothes, shower and throw their dirty clothes into a laundry basket. He popped open his locker and saw his grease stained Carhartt coverall hanging there. Washing never quite got it clean, but it didn't matter. He stripped off his dress slacks, boots, blazer and button down and stepped into the work clothes, pulling a beat up pair of boots out of the bottom of the locker and shoving his feet into them.

Perhaps the day was starting to look up, he thought, as he headed over to a 1974 Corvette with its hood up and engine half out. This one was a total rebuild, a messy, dirty job, just the kind he liked.

#

Colby was knee-deep in refurbishing the grimy carburetor for the 'Vette. It was a complicated, tedious task but he was enjoying himself. He didn't often get to work on the cars he bought anymore, since he now had to spend his time hunting them down, dealing with buyers and sellers, doing all the things it took to run a business rather than actually doing the work the business was known for.

When one of the guys pushed the swinging glass door of the garage open and called his name—twice—with a loud, insistent voice pitched to rise above the blaring noise of the one and only local country station, he was so involved in what he was doing he hit his head on the shelf above the counter where he was working.

"You got a call," Joe told him with his usual verbal precision.

"Who is it?" he asked, rubbing his head where he had hit, forgetting he had oil-streaked hands. He'd neglected to wear gloves and knew it would be hell to scrub off the grime, but it had felt good to get his hands dirty.

"Mrs. Eleanor DeWitt," Joe said. His disapproval was silent but deadly.

"Tell her I'm traveling." It had worked on Alfie Landau; he could only hope it would work on Eleanor, too.

"She said she's tried your cell phone and that you're not picking up."

"Tell her I'm traveling," Colby repeated. His phone, face down on the countertop next to him, had vibrated with calls on and off throughout the day, but he had ignored them.

Joe just glared at him. Joe had worked for him the longest, maybe knew him the best. Also knew that Eleanor had been calling persistently for the last few weeks and that Colby was just as persistently dodging her.

"She wants to have dinner with you on Thursday," Joe said.

Colby sighed and this time, resisted the urge to rub his grease-covered hands through his hair in frustration.

"Fine. Tell her I can make lunch," he said. Eleanor wasn't going to let this go. He'd have to deal with her head on, as much as he hated the idea.

"Ok," Joe said and disappeared for a moment before coming back into the garage. *Things would have been fine then*, Colby thought. He'd dodged two major crises and was having fun working, getting his hands dirty, making the guys listen to his country music station. Of course just before closing time it had to happen. There was a grinding of metal against metal, a sound that registered dimly in the back of Colby's mind and then more acutely when there was a loud crash followed by an agonizing howl of pain.

Colby turned quickly and ran over to where Joe was curled up on the floor, his hand clutched tightly to him. It had to be one of those days.

Made in the USA
Columbia, SC
03 June 2017